HUGH MacLACHLAN was born in the West Highlands of Scotland. He took up writing following a career in HM Customs & Excise. *The Great Melnikov* is his first full length novel. He has had short stories published and broadcast on radio, and was enormously encouraged by having stories shortlisted twice (1995 & 1996) in the prestigious Macallan/Scotland on Sunday Short Story Competition.

The Great Melnikov

HUGH MacLACHLAN

Luath Press Limited

EDINBURGH

www.luath.co.uk

First Edition 1998

The paper used in this book is recyclable. It is produced in a low energy,
low emission manner from renewable forests.

The publisher acknowledges subsidy from

THE SCOTTISH ARTS COUNCIL

towards the publication of this volume.

Printed and bound by Interprint Ltd., Malta

Typeset in 10.5 point Sabon by
S. Fairgrieve, Edinburgh, 0131 658 1763

For Ashley, who fills my world with love

Chapter One

SIR, I SAT ALONE IN London's Trafalgar Square in my twenty-ninth year. Seventeen years trailed behind me with the self-obliterating quality of a steamer's wake since I shipped out of St Petersburg as a stowaway on a German cargo boat. What I had been and done was washed away and forgotten. My life was reduced to the raw ache of hunger dragging one minute into the next – for I had eaten nothing but bin-scavenged crusts for two days.

A human rat in a long brown coat edged his way round the Square, watchful and furtive. When he saw me he coiled back on his haunches and looked at me with bright, estimating eyes. Unblinking, he defied my hostility and crept a step nearer. Apprehension tightened its grip on my shrunken stomach for he was the sort that lives off pestilence and refuse. Did his sharp, twitching nose catch the taint of decay in me?

I know what he saw for I myself had seen human derelicts putrefying in public squares throughout the world. He saw a blotched, unshaven face; a buttonless greatcoat with the neck of a gin bottle sticking out from a torn pocket; mouldering trousers; matted socks; unlaced, ill-fitting shoes with flapping soles. I could smell my own rankness.

The rat in the brown coat was not repelled. He moved closer. I tried to banish his presence by pulling a salvaged newspaper from my pocket, hoping that its printed words would smother my fears. *On Western Front a ceaseless bombardment continues in Flanders. French advance south of the Somme. London searchlights prevent the escape of a German zeppelin. Residents in Potters Bar witness it crash in flames. They will long remember Sunday, 1st October 1916.* But the words on the page quelled neither my apprehension nor lessened the gnawing ache in my stomach.

The brown rat turned and darted away. I watched his scurrying progress through the soldiers, the ladies and the promenading, stiff old men. He stopped and looked back over his shoulder to check I had not gone away.

Men looked at me with disgust. Women averted their eyes. Children made long detours round where I sat. How different it once had been! I let my eyelids fall and hugged the suffering of enforced sobriety.

A light tap on my shoulder caused me to turn and look up. Terror squirted through me, right to my toes. The rat in the brown coat was almost on my back. His lips parted over yellow teeth.

' 'Ello sir! Mind if I sit 'ere? P'raps you'd like to share me luncheon?'

He pulled a steaming mutton pie from a brown paper bag and held it ten inches upwind from my nose. I knew that it was poisoned bait but, although my nose smelt the spores, my eyes watched my fingers close over the warm succulent pastry. With the cunning of one who has lived his life in sewers, he was trying to get close enough to sink his teeth into my neck.

'Had an interestin' life I'd say, guv. Been all over the world, shouldn't be surprised.'

I wolfed the pie and ignored the words which came with it. He put a grimy paw on my hand which was again on its way to my mouth.

'Ain't English, are you?' The whine and the smile were laced with treachery.

'Russian.' I stopped up my mouth with pie.

'Russian! Now that I didn't expect.'

His eagerness was waning and his eyes drifted with regret to what was left of the mutton pie. I crammed the last of it into my mouth.

He sniffled. 'Speak any other languages, guv?'

'German.' The word puffed precious flakey pastry on to the thankless paving stones.

He half-closed one eye and twitched his nose to one side. The garbage raker was estimating the value of his find. 'And p'raps you don't speak German so well neither, mite!'

He was sniffing for any scraps he could claw from my carcase.

I licked the juice of the pie from my fingers. It was perilous wriggling out of his claws. Slowly the words came together in my mind. I spoke in German, softly so that passers-by did not overhear. I said, 'I am not a German, so you cannot extract a penny from me on that score. If you wish we will go and discuss the matter with that policeman over there.' I gathered my threadbare coat about me.

Knowing no German, he understood only that I wished to go

to the policeman. He was uneasy. In that slimy wrestling I was slipping from his clutches. He sidled closer and half-turned his back on the policeman. 'No offence, mite! Wot was it you just said there, then?'

I repeated it in English.

His face contorted with hurt, with disappointment and with anger. 'Gives you food! Speaks to you! Is a good Samaritan to you! You eats me pie, don't yer? Look 'ere mite, if I wanted somefing it wouldn't be from you! Policeman? God bless me soul! Wot we want wif a policeman? I only got yer own good in me heart! The kindest geezer you ever met in yer life! Tell you wot, to prove it I'll take you to a dear old gent as will give you a decent dinner and a clean bed, or me name's not - well never mind wot me name's not. Can't say fairer than that now, can I? Wot you say? Mean it guv. Or maybe yer don't fancy a plate heaped wif hot bacon an' eggs an' sausages an' bread an' butter an' lashings of tea. I arsked you, wot you say guv?'

Saliva trickled through the stubble on my chin. I ceased to wriggle. I was paralysed by his poison.

'Come on mite! Make up yer mind! Do I or don't I go and tell me friend 'e's got a guest for dinner, – eh?'

Unable to reason any more, I shrugged my shoulders.

'Grateful, ain't yer, I don't think! Right then, back in a tick!' He slipped and glided smoothly through the strollers and out of my sight.

Could I have escaped then? Escaped! I could perhaps have crawled behind a block of stone and rotted there like a sodden leaf. No, I decided to let the rodent pull me into his nest. At all events, whatever he might gain or whatever I might lose would not amount to much – and I was not defenceless.

My chin sank to my chest; the air oozed from my lungs; meditation congealed to a torpid numbness of mind.

Grinning and prancing he was back before me. I knew what he wanted me to do, so I compelled my cramped muscles to wrestle my six foot body into a form of standing up. Then, as if an invisible halter stretched from my neck to his hand, I shuffled along behind the swaggering runt.

He stopped at the edge of the pavement. I shambled to a standstill at his side and waited mindlessly. He stood there grinning and winking and jerking his head.

Beside us, one wheel in the gutter, was a smart, black, horse-drawn cab. He wanted me to get in. I was mystified. This was not our style. Our sort slunk head-down in the shadows. My value - rag, bone and tallow - did not equal that of one brass lamp on that vehicle. Even passers-by saw something amiss and stopped to stare at the soiled scarecrow clambering over the soft upholstery. They guessed a prank, a bet, a masquerade.

While my dull mind tried to find the link between the mean scallywag at my side and the expensive odours of leather and cigar smoke I was breathing, a brown sleeve reached across and closed the window curtains.

The cab set off at a smart trot. It swayed and swung gently on its springs and I knew we were constantly changing direction. If that was to confuse me it was unnecessary, for I did not know the streets of London.

After ten, or perhaps thirty minutes – time had no meaning for me – we were rolling along a gravel driveway. The cab stopped close to the side of a large house. I knew the house was large because a precipice of brick hung above me as I was hustled through a side door by a small, pock-faced manservant in dark blue livery.

A muttering of voices at my back and the unmistakeable rustle of paper money told me that I was being paid for. I felt no resentment. Perhaps I should have felt conceit but, standing in that well-appointed pantry, was I going to be better or worse off than if I had been disembowelled and looted in a dark alley?

The manservant circled round so that no part of him touched me. He snapped his fingers for me to follow. I searched the dregs of my being for some scrap of dignity and stood still. He turned a face which was crabbed with annoyance. Ignoring the insolence, I made a courtly bow and held out my hand, 'Sergei Melnikov!'

He dismissed the civility with a snort and two more finger-snaps.

The loose soles on my shoes mocked me with their slow clap-clap as I shuffled after him along a mahogany-panelled corridor, past brass door handles which shone like gold, and through air which was warm and thick like a syrup of beeswax and port. When I looked up, the corridor ahead of me was empty.

The flunkey could have gone through any one of half a dozen doors so I stopped, let my legs fold stiffly under me, and squatted against the wall. Staring at the floor between my feet, I groped for the gin bottle.

The flunkey returned and without notice or apology set about kicking flames of agony into my ribs. Each searing kick pumped a little strength – the strength of vengeance – into my hollow carcase; enough to get me to my feet. Through eyes stinging with outrage I looked into his flushed and pock-marked face. He was very near to death, the vicious little weasel; but my hands tangled in my overcoat and I watched him turn away.

He led me down a flight of stairs into a chill, shadowy, white-tiled room. As we entered, a serving girl clutching a half-plucked duck bolted through a second door. The flunkey stretched a pointing arm and, snapping his fingers like the crack of a whip, said, 'Sit!'

Behind the door through which we had entered was a scrubbed deal table and beyond it against the wall, a wooden bench. Scorning his churlish arrogance, I walked with my tallest dignity to the bench, swept up my coat-tails and, with an off-hand wave, dismissed him. His flint-hard eyes tried to stare me down, but unable to overcome my disdainful smile he finally tossed his head, wheeled about and was gone.

Chapter Two

IT WAS NOT THE first time in my life that I had exchanged a portion of pride for a mutton pie. I knew, however, that the rat in the brown coat was no philanthropist. His trespass on my existence had not been for my welfare.

Tales were sometimes told in the many refuges I had shared of guttering bodies being bought for strange and macabre purposes. I checked the sighing of my breath and listened for cries of fear or pain or protest.

Far away and indistinct as in a dream, a ship's horn groaned. Through the wall on my right I heard the stone-deadened murmur of voices and a clatter of pans and dishes. On my left, a brass tap dripped, plip... plip... plop, into a white porcelain sink.

I looked around for anything which might disclose the reason for my presence. Outside the barred window above the sink, sunlight slanted into a basement well. Facing me, between a meat safe and a rack of brooms, were crates of vegetables, chests of flour and meal, and a giant drum of salt. Above them, a shelf was laden with bars of soap, cans of polish, jars of pickles and canisters of cleaning materials.

I pulled the gin bottle from my coat pocket and held it up. Not so much as a moist haze dampened the glass inside so, lifting the lid off the garbage can at my side, I disposed of the bottle.

For days I had lived on scraps filched from garbage cans. Once I had salvaged a whole apple tart. So I leaned sideways and rummaged in the can by my side. Underneath a layer of feathers, my fingers sifted cold potato peelings and the entrails of animals. My hand came up wet, pink and empty. As I wiped the slime from my fingers on to my coat tails, the flunkey strutted in. He turned about in the middle of the floor and stood motionless as a little blue statue.

'Got a fag to spare, Buddy?' I asked.

He listened only to the even tread of footfalls coming down the steps from the panelled corridor. The door opened and through it stalked a tall, withered old gentleman buttoned up to his throat in a black frockcoat. With measured pace the spare figure advanced to behind the servant and then, turning, came forward and placed himself before me on the other side of the table.

The face which I looked up at was bony and pale like weathered marble and the eyes which systematically examined me held neither welcome nor compassion. His thin lips tightened. I responded by pulling myself upright. He took a pace back, tilted his chin and regarded me down the length of his long nose for a moment longer.

'You speak German I understand?'

'Sure I do, but I'm not a –,'

He had already turned away and now went to stand with his back to the room looking out of the window. The prospect of enlightenment or even of polite discourse being thus extinguished, I slumped down on to the table again.

The flunkey all this time stood tense as an overwound spring and when the head above the frockcoat swivelled and nodded to the kitchen door, the lackey jumped and rapped on its panels. The serving girl must have been awaiting this summons, for she opened the door instantly and entered with a tray upon which rested a tin mug, a jug of coffee and a large platter heaped with sandwiches.

That the girl now wore a spotless apron mattered not at all, only that she came forward and placed the tray on the table in front of me. I was scarcely aware of her backing out with frightened glances towards the figure at the window because the aroma of fresh coffee overpowered my other senses.

Half-turning, and with a flip of his hand, the old man dismissed the flunkey and indicated the sandwiches were for me.

Both my hands snatched up a sandwich and thrust them as one into my salivating mouth. Ah! that soft white bread, that creamy butter, that savoury roast beef, that tang of salt and mustard, ah!

I pushed the first six sandwiches into my mouth and not taking time to chew, swilled them down my gullet with sweet, scalding coffee. A noisy slurp drew no more than a half-glance over the black shoulder.

I had devoured most of the sandwiches and half of the coffee when a billowing, tweed Inverness cape topped by a grey felt hat flurried into the room. Instinctively I hugged the platter. The cape was thrown back and the hat doffed to expose a rotund little man who wheezed through an enormous red moustache. He stood just inside the door with his hat clutched to his chest.

Without turning, the old man said, 'You are four minutes late. Now shut the door.'

The plump little man shut the door. Still clutching his hat to his chest, he picked his way across the floor as if it were a minefield and sidled up alongside the black frockcoat.

Above the frockcoat, the stern face lifted and spoke to the topmost pane in the window. Lit by the evening sun, its marble features were briefly changed to brass.

Unable to hear what was said, I applied myself to devouring what remained of the sandwiches.

Eventually the old man fell silent. He folded one hand into the other at the back of his frockcoat and turning his head just enough to take in the perspiring face at his shoulder, said dryly, 'Proceed then.'

His head still nodding compliance, the fawning, fat nincompoop turned to me. Making little attempt to conceal his distaste for my presence he moistened his lips and croaked, 'Would it —,' He cleared his throat, 'Would it be convenient for you to answer questions as you eat?'

I proffered the plate with its last sandwich. 'Sure, Bud! Let's both answer questions as we eat.'

His nose wrinkled at the sight of my unwashed hand with its blackedged fingernails and he shrank back, shaking his head.

'We wish to find out how well you speak German. I am therefore going to ask you questions in German and you will attempt to reply in German. Do you understand?'

I spread my hands in friendly invitation.

Meticulously spacing his feet, he pulled out a notepad and uncapped his fountain pen. Now the stern inquisitor, he asked in German, 'What is your name?'

Pretending that his words were affably intended, I scrambled to my feet. 'My name is Sergei Melnikov.' I too spoke in German. Offering my hand, I asked in turn, 'And yours sir? May I compliment you on this generous reception.'

He squirmed under his cape and, scratching pen on paper, pedalled from one foot to the other. 'Ser-gei Mel-nik-ov. Where were you born?'

I looked down on him with steadily darkening countenance, pretending to await his reply to my request for his name. His face suffused with pink but he remained silent. I flopped to the bench,

8

pushed the tray away and spoke with all the truculence I could muster. 'Have I mistaken charity and bad manners for welcome and hospitality?' This question too, I let twitch the tic in his cheek before going on, 'However, not to answer your question would merely double the rudeness. If you think it is of your concern sir, I was born in St Petersburg in 1887.'

The old man by the window turned and, although his face was in shadow, I saw it harden with displeasure. Fine! I meant them to know that I had been a man of consequence and would be so again. Whatever their game, it clearly was not robbery. Did the frockcoat indicate a lawyer and the scratching pen his clerk? Using derision, I might provoke a revealing outburst.

Fearful now of my threat to his petty authority, the dumpling stabbed the end of his pen at me. 'Be careful my man, and truthful. We shall check your statements.'

I let my head roll back and laughed, 'Ah, you already know that you have the Great Melnikov as your guest?' I turned to the old man and pointed to his companion, 'Is this roly-poly here to entertain us?'

Merciless, unblinking eyes stared relentlessly into mine until I was obliged to break away and fumble with the mug. As I gulped tepid coffee I heard the bleak command, 'Continue!'

'What was your father's occupation?'

Intent on gaining information if not respect, I let another mocking silence destroy the fat man's act before I put my forefinger on the handle of the mug and set it spinning on the table like a top. When it rattled to a standstill, I looked up with smiling good humour. 'My father, sir, did not have an occupation. He was by profession a dancer – although rarely employed as such.'

'Do you mean a ballet —?'

'More than that; an imaginative and creative aristocrat.'

He covered his mystification by mouthing the words, 'A dancer.' Then he continued, 'Did you ever go to school?'

'School? Don't you suppose from what I have said, that I had my own tutors?'

A dry voice thrust in, 'If your father was rarely employed, must we assume that you went to a charity school?'

I turned and let soft words deliver my dart. 'Charity? I thought we had done with charity.' The quick lift of his head marked my hit but I got no apology. I went on, 'What common men dissipate in idleness, those with talent cherish as opportunity. My father diverted himself and supported his family by re-distributing envy and avarice. He did so by taking trinkets from the ladies of St Peterburg, and permitting those in Moscow to display them.'

Bewildered, the little man glanced sideways at the old man who was now looking at me thoughtfully and stroking his chin. The unexpected silence caused him to look up.

'His father was a thief and his education is of small importance.'

If not my education, what? I fished for their interest in the stream of their questions: why did I leave Russia? how old was I? what was the name of the ship in which I stowed away? what date did she dock in Hamburg? where did I find accommodation?

Where did I find accommodation? I looked down into the empty mug and in the dregs of coffee saw a little boy unable to speak German running through the cold wet streets of Hamburg and hiding from every shadow. Starved near to death, he was picked from the gutter by old man Rott, the accordian mender – good man Rott playing his accordians and laughing at the child's grateful, acrobatic dances and capers.

The little man prodded my shoulder with a broom handle, 'I have asked you three times, how did you pay for food and lodgings?'

'Oh, Old Man... an old man got me work in a circus.'

'What sort of work?'

'As a performer – what else?'

'You could have fed the animals or swept sawdust.'

Only the English, I thought, could be so insolent. In any event I was not likely to gain much by going on with the interrogation. I gathered my coat about me and stood up. I was every inch as tall as the old man. Walking from behind the table I said, 'Give me your card, sir. In due course I shall repay you for the fare I have received. The insults I leave on your doorstep, for I bear no grudge against the unenlightened.'

My action produced a distress bordering on panic in the little fat man. Beads of perspiration stood on his bald head as he bounced the broom handle on the stone floor. 'You are not permitted to stand up! You are not permitted to go! You are not permitted to speak without permission! Sit down!'

The old man waved a hand to pacify him but none of the hardness went from his face. 'We accept you were a performer, Mr Melnikov. Now return to your seat. You may not leave.' He made no move to detain me but he spoke with absolute certainty that he would be obeyed.

'Am I a prisoner then?'

'You are not free to leave.'

The little man had calmed down. I heard him say, 'You have been told to resume your seat; please do so.'

The austere face into which I was looking expected compliance. Even the moment of my hesitation produced a menacing impatience in his eyes. Although I pretended indifference as I shuffled back to the bench jauntily swinging my coat-tails, in truth I felt like a scolded schoolboy. For the thousandth time I had tried and failed to recover the regard due, if not to my person, to my talent. Nothing, however, would be gained by defying him, even were he no more than a tyrannical schoolmaster. The little man waited until I was seated again.

'How long were you with the circus?'

'Eight years.'

'Why did you leave?'

Anyone with the least perception would have seen the answer in my condition; would have known that such matters require a delicate and sensitive touch. Yet he blinked, waiting for my answer. I spoke with smiling sarcasm, 'I possessed aptitudes the other performers found it difficult to match or to live with.'

'Aptitudes? I do not understand —,'

'In that at least we agree. I must therefore discard propriety. I was the star performer of that famous circus. I am indeed the Great Melnikov! Every night I, the Great Melnikov, had to face a thousand savage, sullen Germans. Every night I tore out little bits of my Russian soul and fed it to these boorish Huns until they were amused, made hilarious and finally satisfied. And how did the Great Melnikov nurture his ravished Russian soul? From a bottle – a bottle of Russian vodka. Oh just a little to start with. Yes, yes, just enough to melt the frozen terror in my chest. But that icicle of dread grew larger every night until just before the start of a performance in a town not far from Berlin I tripped over an empty bottle, fell on my face and slept where I lay. The rising sun found me on a mound of straw, alone in an empty park. A sack containing my belongings lay beside me. The circus had moved on.'

The little man raised his pen to stop me. 'Please speak slowly.'
The old man took out and frowned at his watch. 'And be brief.'
he said, 'You were abandoned by the circus as a drunkard.'

'No sir!' The circus abandoned its chief claim to fame! Indeed
I celebrated my release in every tavern I came upon until, unac-
countably, I found myself steeping in bilgewater at the bottom of
a Norwegian tramp ship on its way to the United States.'

The old man interrupted again. 'You were carried to the
U.S.A. A little about your time there, if you please.'

Fatigue was again overcoming me. I heaved a weary breath,
'Swept snow, shovelled sand, carried bags, washed plates and yes,
sure, I made a buck or two from my father's profession.'

'Stealing or dancing?'

'A little of both I guess. For a year or thereabouts I worked in
the gambling backroom of Mistress Pettyleg's saloon in Kansas
City. Sometimes I performed for her customers but mostly I took
their money at the tables.'

Now walking round the room, the old man examined everything he came to as if my history was of little interest or consequence. If I could not inspire respect, I must settle for dismay.
Pausing for silence to lend impact to my words, I said, 'And it was
there that I murdered a man. A Spaniard who accused me of
cheating. I shot him dead.'

The stooping man in black folded over the top of the sack he
had been looking into, straightened, and half-turning, asked with
mild interest, 'And had you been cheating?'

I felt as David might had the stone he slung at Goliath missed.
The now awesome figure moved menacingly in my direction until,
like a black colossus, he towered over me.

'Do you usually react viciously when you are frightened?'

My tired mind groped for words with which to parry his
thrusts. 'I ... everyone who was in the room swore that I acted only
to protect my life. I was in prison for three years.'

The old man turned away and walked towards the window.
His voice was without compassion and almost without interest.
'What then?'

My tiny portion of vitality was spent. Self-pity gushed from
my emotional wounds. 'I found it hard to live. I owed money to a
Pole for liquor and he threatened to... my life was in danger. I had
to get away. I stole a bracelet – I admit that – and I gave it to a

Dutch stoker to share his berth. His ship docked here in London five days ago. I possess nothing of value; so may I now depart?'

The old man dusted his fingertips together as he walked over and laid a hand on the little man's forearm. He spoke in English. 'Unless you have something you specially want to ask about, I think we have heard enough.'

'We have indeed, sir! He is useless for our purpose.'

'Not as unsuitable as you may think. Speaks tolerable German. English of a sort too. Not basically unintelligent. A capacity for self-preservation. Russia is an ally of England, remember, and America neutral. We may indeed have found something we can use.'

Some*thing*, not some*one*! O Melnikov! They moved side by side through the shadows now filling the room. The little man glanced back at me and shook his head. 'But not reliable, surely sir? And his, um, weakness – dreadfully dangerous.'

'It may be, however, that his reliability and loyalty are best secured through that weakness... for the short term. We have so little time. I very much doubt if we shall get anything better. Yes, let me have a transcript of your notes. I shall come to a decision before dinner.'

The little man fingered the brim of his hat. 'I trust my interrogation was satisfactory, sir?'

'Adequate.'

He stood aside to let the black figure precede him from the room.

No one said, 'Goodbye,' or 'Thank you,' to me.

Chapter Three

FOOD AND SHELTER WERE PRIZES I did not often win in the contest of life and the idea that my loyalty was to be secured through my weakness denied any kind of benevolence. The old man's presence indeed radiated a ruthlessness which I had never before encountered. I would be wise, I thought, to take myself out of their lives.

A heavy door led out to the basement-well but it was secured by two locks. The bottom sash of the window, however, went up easily enough. Leaning over the sink, I was tugging and thrusting on one of the iron bars, endeavouring to dislodge it, when a shadow fell on my hands. I glanced up. A brutish man in a long black coat stood looking down from the top of the basement-well. His arms cradled a club and his eyes smouldered with hostility.

I shut the window and backed off. If I were not a prisoner, what was I? Like a city sparrow, I had been lured with crumbs, netted and caged. But for what purpose? I returned to the bench.

The room was now deep in shadow and quiet. When in prison I had learned how to pass long, purposeless hours. Resting my chin in cupped hands I closed my eyes and turned the inside of my skull into a bright and crowded amphitheatre. Centrestage, under a spotlight, I bowed and bowed again to rapturous applause – deserved applause. Had I not, with lithesome panache and inspired creative mime, filled drab lives with wonder and laughter for the space of an hour? 'Encore! Encore!'... Oh Sergei – when? The curtains of sleep dropped gently.

A brightness wakened me. The white tiles intensified light from a gas lamp hissing under the ceiling. Over by the sink the kitchenmaid stood on a stool closing wooden shutters on the window.

My face had slipped down in my hands as I slept and I watched her through the spaces between my fingers with half-closed eyes. She stepped down and picked up the stool. I guessed her age to be not more than seventeen years. Her large brown eyes made up for a face which otherwise gave the impression of having been carelessly put together. She was humming a tune as she came over and pushed the stool under the table. The hand she stretched for the tray was red and chapped with rough work.

I held my head motionless. When her wrist came within reach I meant to snatch it and pull her bodily across the table. Surprise and fear would ensure honest answers to my questions about the house and its occupants. There was also a chance she knew of a way to get me out.

As her finger touched the tray I must have twitched in readiness for she sprang back with a yelp. 'Lumme, you didn't 'alf give me a fright! Thought you was sleeping.'

I spread my fingers across my face and winked through the lattice. 'The beast didn't wish to scare away someone of such beauty.'

'Ow, you ain't no beast. You startled me, that's all. But flattery 'elps – cos I know I ain't no beauty.'

I hauled my trunk up and leaned back against the wall with folded arms. 'Not true, my goddess, not true at all! Have you no mirror? You're the prettiest thing round here or, come to that, any other place I've been.'

'Need a white stick, you do. Or maybe you ain't been far. Anyhow, wot they brought you 'ere for then?'

'Ah, my dear, I hoped you would know the answer to that. English snobbery, I'd guess. Want a Russian prince to grace their dinner table.'

She laughed. 'You ain't no Russian prince, you ain't!' Then, lest she had offended me, 'Are you?'

'Cursed by a wicked witch. Give me a kiss, princess, and I'll turn into a frog.'

'Ow, don't like frogs. An' if you is a Russian anything, I'd keep quiet about it round 'ere.'

'Why so, my lovely?'

'Why? Cos of the Sultan, of course! 'E hates Russians more'n 'e hates good English pork - an' that's sayin' somefing!'

'The Sultan? That the tall old gent or the suet dumpling with whiskers?'

'Ow, you're a right card, you are! The Sultan's the little clothes peg in blue togs wot met you when you come.'

'A Turk, is he?'

'I ain't sayin' nothin' more 'cept I'll tell you wot he'll do if he catches me talking to you. He'll send a complaint upstairs so he can beat me; that's wot he'll do. Goodbye, Mr Russian Prince. I don't like it when I gets beaten.' Holding the tray in one hand and plucking her skirt with the other she dipped a playful curtsy. 'And don't go calling him the Sultan where 'e can hear you, cos that ain't his name, or you'll never eat another supper neither. I promise you that!' She pushed herself backwards through the kitchen door.

I reached a hand under my coat and caressed my bruised ribs. If the flunkey was indeed a Turk then I as a Russian had been fortunate not to have had a knife blade thrust between them. That was the style of the Turk. The whole world knew the treacherous infidels crawled in the shadow of the Kaiser's army like beetles hoping to feed off Russia's carcase. By pressing hard on my bruised ribs and thus intensifying the pain, I spiced a resolve to crush the blue insect.

While I nursed vengeance, the kitchen door opened and the maid came back noisily dragging a long metal bath behind her. She trailed it over to the sink and there let her end fall to the stone floor with a deafening clatter. When there was silence enough, I said, 'Grace, beauty and such musical talent! You must be famous, ma'm. I'm sure I shall recognise your name the instant you say it.'

'Me name?'

'Yes, my exquisite child, your name if you please.'

'Wot you want to know me name for? Ow, all right. No harm I suppose. Rosalind.'

I spoke with resonant passion. 'Rosalind, gentle and beautiful Rosalind! Your very presence warms my life like the sun; it really does! Give me a smile Rosalind, a keepsake for my heart. What a lovely name! What a charming presence!'

Her cheeks glowed with embarrassed pleasure and she busied herself wiping her hands on her apron. Then the door opened. Her blushes vanished to be replaced by a guilty pallor as the blue flunkey entered carrying a bundle of clothes under his arm. He looked with suspicion from Rosalind to me and back again. 'Why is there no water in the bath, drudge? And you have been told not to talk with this tramp.'

'Gentleman,' I said, correcting him, 'Not to talk with this Russian gentleman.'

His lips curled with contempt. 'Russian gentleman? Yes, you stinking gutterdrunk, you are indeed the typical Russian gentleman! Take off your rags. They are to be burned in the furnace. Bath yourself, shave, and then dress in these.'

As he spoke, he laid out on the draining board a cake of carbolic soap, an open razor, a comb and a bundle of clothes. He watched Rosalind struggle in from the kitchen with two pails of hot water. When she had emptied them into the bathtub, he said, 'Leave the buckets, fool, for him to add cold water!'

I thought he meant to follow her into the kitchen but he went only as far as the table and pulled out the stool. Standing on it, he took a bottle from the shelf, stepped down and removed the stopper. He poured the contents of the bottle into the hot water, saturating the air with the smell of lysol disinfectant.

'Have I not told you to remove your clothes?' he snarled.

He was a detestable runt but I wanted those clothes on the draining board. Here was a better chance than I was likely to get again to exorcise the curse which corrupted my genius. The rotting garments I had on damned me even to myself. I did not, however, want the Turk to be around while I changed. I rose from the bench, spread my arms wide and with my open coat wafting the stench of my unwashed body before me, bore down on him like a bedraggled vulture.

'You dear, dear little rodent! Am I the first to warm to your verminous charm? Come, let me embrace and kiss you.'

He jumped back. 'You disgust me!'

I made to follow, flapping my arms. He ran to the door and turned. 'Make sure you wash the lice out of your hair!' and, slipping out, slammed the door shut behind him.

Knowing that I was safely alone, I spent the next few minutes going through the clothes which he had left. They were slightly worn but of the very best quality and, I was sure, had once belonged to the old gentleman. Eager to exchange them for the garments I was wearing, I pulled off my shoes and socks. I listened. No one was about. From my overcoat pockets I took the only articles of value I possessed: a brass watch I had stolen from the Dutch stoker but had been unable to sell and my little protector – a lady's pistol I had acquired in the States. I wrapped both articles in a sock and stuffed it up behind the sink.

Not having bathed since I left prison six months earlier, I wallowed in the hot water, letting it coddle my aching, undernourished body. When done and dried, I opened one of the shutters. Using the black glass in the window as a mirror, I shaved the stubble off my face. The razor had been stropped to a fine edge and was still keen. So, before getting dressed, I used it to shorten and style my hair.

The old man's clothes fitted me well. I knotted the tie, put on the jacket, drew myself up and postured in front of the window - a man of distinction again. I had only to get out of the house, stand firm against my addiction and, surely, acclaim was assured.

None too soon I remembered the sock behind the sink. Having recovered it, I was in the act of dropping the watch and the pistol into a pocket of my new jacket when the flunkey returned. He sensed something amiss in my urgent movement and looked with distrust at the sock in my hand and then all round the room. Before he could utter a word I made a ball of the old matted sock and threw it at him.

'For you, my pet rodent. I knew you would want a keepsake for under your pillow.'

He took a half step back and let the sock fall to the floor. 'Empty the bath into the sink and put your rags into it. The drudge will remove them to the boiler furnace.'

The bath and fresh clothing had revived my conceit. I crossed my feet at the ankles and, leaning elegantly on the draining board, said, 'Now, now, you mustn't play upon my good nature. Remember you're the flunkey round here; you do it. Or do you wish me to box your ears?' I pushed myself away from the sink.

His face flushed but after a brief pause he turned on his heel, 'Follow me!'

'If you please, sir!'

He half turned, 'What did you say?'

'When you speak to a superior you should add, 'sir'. And remember, my little blue bully, the seat of your pants is only a swift kick in front of my shoe.'

We went out and up and turned back half the length of the panelled corridor then through a door on the opposite side. A splendid entrance hall opened on our left but the flunkey turned to the wide carpeted staircase rising on our right. Glancing over his shoulder to make sure I was still with him, he went up to the first landing. He paused before a mahogany door, knocked, opened it hesitantly, and entering, beckoned me to follow.

Chapter Four

ONCE AGAIN DRESSED LIKE A gentleman, I composed my features to a grave thoughtfulness, hooked my thumb in my vest pocket and advanced into the room with what I hoped was an air of learned dignity. I did right. The deep carpet soaked up the sound of our footsteps like russet moss and a hush of scholarly affluence enveloped me. Venerable books buttressed the wall on my right, mulberry velvet drapes hung on the wall facing me and all around were deep, leather armchairs.

At the end of the room the old man was seated, stiff-backed, behind a leather-topped table and in front of a blazing coal fire. At his back, on the right-hand side of a white marble fireplace, hung a six-foot map of the world. On the left-hand side hung a six-foot map of Europe.

I inclined my head to the stern figure and proceeded to one of the armchairs. Before I reached it I was intercepted by the Turk swinging round a plain wooden chair which he placed directly in front of the table.

The old man looked up briefly. 'Thank you, Ismet. Please sit, Mr Melnikov.' He returned to his papers.

The flunkey waited until I sat on the wooden chair, then he left. To demonstrate that I was perfectly at ease in such surroundings, I rested my right ankle on my left knee and looked about me. Of the articles on the leather-topped table, the gold writing set, the silver cigar case and a matching cigarette box were worth stealing. Of course I marked the crystal brandy decanter on a side table but, just then, I might possibly have declined a share of its contents.

I had binged for four days on the proceeds of what I had stolen from the ship and traded for booze. For one, two or even three days, while my head throbbed and the fiery ache in my guts prevailed, I would convince myself that I could solve my problem with alcohol any time I wished. It was in this recurring stage in my addiction that I made resolutions – sincere if short-lived – to abstain for ever.

The old man was dressed for dinner. His white shirt front had been starched and ironed to a shining flat surface. Was it possible, I wondered, to patent a wipe-clean shirt front made of porcelain.

The coals settled in the fire. The old man slid aside the document he had been reading and rose from his chair. He stood with his back to the fire looking down on me. Perhaps I filled his garments with an elegance he resented or perhaps the smell of lysol displeased him because his lips were pressed together as if bile had just risen to his mouth.

'I may be able to offer you a form of employment – please do not interrupt when I am speaking – an offer which you will either accept or reject now. If you do accept, you may never change your mind in any circumstance. Well?'

I rested my hands on my right ankle and smiled encouragement. 'Sure! Let's have the details and we'll see.'

'I can give you the details only after you have accepted.'

I wagged a finger for I was not to be so easily caught. 'Suppose I accept the job and change my mind when I hear what it's about?'

Drawing a slow breath through his nose, he pulled his head back and looked steadily into my face. 'Society does not miss your sort, Mr Melnikov. As you yourself have implied, there are no records of your existence. You will be disposed of.'

My foot slipped to the floor with a thump. Fragments of questions fluttered and collided inside my head like one-winged butterflies and it took several seconds for me to grasp his meaning. I steadied one hand with the other and, because my breathing was uneven, spoke falteringly, 'You mean you will kill me? Why? I have done you no harm! You give me no choice then.' I swallowed again and again as I searched the face above me. It was as passionless as a mask of steel.

'You have the choice of undertaking the commission I am offering or of not undertaking it.'

Struggling to make sense of my predicament, I feared to ask the penalty of a refusal. My life it seemed was suspended by a frayed thread and I must do nothing which would imperil it further. Refusing his offer outright would be reckless. Every minute I could extend my existence held the chance of escape. On the other hand, I must not sacrifice myself for only a brief reprieve. My brain fumbled the best case it could.

'I suppose you want me to kill someone for you or something of that sort.'

'Kill someone? Kill someone? If you are to execute this business you will put that aspect of your life entirely behind you. Understand clearly, we want no violence of any sort!'

I tried to see myself as he had first seen me downstairs. What possible use could I be to him? 'Then I am to do something which is dirty or dangerous or unhealthy.'

He pulled out and looked impatiently at his watch. 'What you will be required to do is neither dangerous, dirty, diseased, nor for that matter, difficult. And you will receive appropriate recompense. May I have your decision now?'

I had swilled around the plughole of life since I was born and I had learned to go no nearer the slippery edge than I must; but appropriate recompense could mean many unpleasant things. I asked him to be specific and held my breath.

He clasped his hands at his back and took two thoughtful paces to his left, 'Not money. No, not money.'

He turned and measured four paces to his right, studying me as he crossed in front of the fireplace. 'Adequate good food. New clothes too.'

He turned and took four paces to his left. 'Do you smoke cigarettes? Very well, let me see... one hundred and fifty cigarettes each week.'

Two paces to his right took him back in front of the fire. 'And,' he turned and looked down on me, 'And two bottles of whisky each week.'

Two bottles of whisky a week! That solemn, long, miserable face told me that was the exact price of my soul... neat whisky stinging my tongue; neat whisky exploding warmth in my chest; neat whisky dissolving the hard edges of the world. Two bottles a week: enough to put away without too-obvious signs of drunkenness yet not quite enough to start up the shakes. Enough in prospect to hold me in bonds of expectation for ever. A merciless, callous wage! A diabolic bribe! An unforgivable insult! My lips curled up from my gums with disdain. Rage puffed me full of courage. My nostrils flared with derision. Here was the moment to show my quality. I spoke softly. 'Sure, I'll take your commission, mister. I'll take it whatever it may be... but without the bribe of whisky.' My quivering lips could say no more.

With cool detachment he waited until my pathetic moment of bombast fizzled out. 'Good, but it would not be prudent to test you to that extent.' He leaned forward and placed his hands flat on the table, and said, 'You have now committed yourself so I am free to describe the background of your employment.' He turned about, lifted a walking cane from beside the fireplace and faced the wallmap of Europe.

I buried my face in my upturned palms. Oh, what had become of me? Even were distinction lost, where was common dignity? Had I been religious I would have cursed the god who had thus forsaken me. Were I but one tenth the man I imagined myself to be, I would have struck that pitiless Englishman to the ground. Tears wetted my hands.

Groping in my pocket for a bottle which was no longer there, my fingers touched then curled round the solid butt of my little gun. Its cold potency transformed self-pity into a spiteful urge to retaliate. At that moment I felt I could recover my self-respect only by hurting – no, by annihilating – the compassionless tyrant who was humiliating me.

My first impulse was to confront his contempt with the lethal power of my gun – to make him grovel. I breathed deeply to still the clamour in my head. If I were to get the better of this dessicated monster I must act with coolness, plan each move, and then carry it out swiftly.

I would rise quietly; hold my stance to gain the poise needed for accuracy; fire the gun once; pocket the writing set and silver boxes; run down the wide stair, out through the front door and into the dark city streets. Primed to act, I eased the pistol up, raised my face and opened my eyes.

Turning, he glared down on me. Then his arm arced above his shoulder. The cane whooped through the air, struck the flat surface of the table in front of me with a petrifying report and whooped up again. Instinctively I raised my empty palms to protect my head. He was pressing his knuckles into the leather table top and driving words into my face.

'You dreamer! You imbecile! Give me every scrap of your attention! You are not privileged to sit cow-faced day-dreaming. Six days is all we have! Six days!'

His mouth shut like a trap. He straightened his back stiffly and let his arms drop to his sides. Fury gave way to spaced, intense words. 'This is not one of your squalid adventures. If you do not give me your full co-operation I shall make the worst miseries of your past life seem like paradise. Can you conceive of that? I shall break you to the point where you would gratefully seek shelter in the vilest torture chamber of the Spanish Inquisition.'

He sucked in a long breath through his teeth, 'You have no discretion left.' Extending an upturned, open hand, he stressed each word, 'Your life is entirely in my palm.' His fingers curled upwards into a white-knuckled, crushing fist. He looked at me down his long, bony nose. Almost reluctantly he turned away.

Only as the distance between us widened did my fugitive wits begin to flutter back. He picked up the cane again and stood in front of the map of Europe, facing me. He spoke like a weary schoolmaster, 'What is your attitude to the war?'

My thoughts were still in disarray and the question did not make sense. 'My attitude?'

'Do you want England and Russia to win the war?'

His question still had little meaning for me unless the man was gleaning fodder for the guns in Flanders – and I had no intention of standing in line to be a muddy, dead hero. But I was polite. 'I have no particular preference, sir.'

'Hmf! And no loyalty either!' He turned about, 'Attend and I shall repeat the salient points.'

The point of his cane rapped on the map, 'Here is London where we are now.' The cane swept upwards, 'And here, roughly seven hundred miles to the north, is the North Atlantic.' The pointer dropped to London again. 'The government is here, so it is in London that strategic information – naval information – is gathered: information which is needed almost instantly by our ships in the North Atlantic.' He turned and thrust the end of the cane at my face. 'How can we get such information from London to the North Atlantic?'

He was gripping the cane like a cutlass. Suddenly it came to me: this grey-faced martinet was no schoolmaster, he was a sailor – a high-ranking naval officer. Brass buttons and some gold braid on his black dress coat and there stood a captain or an admiral. The cane was twitching and I delayed answering no longer.

'Ships. Use ships!'

'Much too slow.'

'Flags! Signal lamps! Aeroplanes!'

'Visual signals at six hundred miles? Don't be a fool! And beyond the range of aeroplanes too, even if any were available.'

It seemed enough that I was trying. He hitched a leg over the corner of the table, 'You might have suggested radio signalling. However, even with the best equipment, radio signals cannot for the present be relied on to carry beyond a hundred miles. Moreover, radio signals can be picked up by anyone with the means to do so – and our information is secret. No, the solution is much simpler. Look at the map. You will see that two thirds of the distance between London and the North Atlantic is overland. So from London to the north-west coast of Scotland we can swiftly and privately send our information by telephone. The rest involves a trifling risk – something you will easily manage.'

'If you will pardon me sir,' I said, for I was confused, 'I cannot see my part in this at all.'

He lifted himself off the desk and pointed to the west coast of Scotland. 'Your part is here. You will be the link that keeps in touch with London by telephone.'

I had need of yet more information because I still did not see why he had chosen me, a down-and-out-bum. He was expecting me to say something. I said, 'I have been led to believe, sir, that this island has many citizens eager to do their patriotic duty; or surely just one smart sailor could be spared from the Royal Navy to sit up there and speak into a telephone.'

My utterance dumbfounded him. His lips moved wordlessly and purple suffused his pale face. He stepped towards me and crashed both fists on to the table top. 'Royal Navy! Royal Navy!' he shouted, 'You inattentive fool, you will do this for the Imperial German Navy!'

He collapsed into a chair behind the desk and sat there wheezing and glaring at me. 'Do you think I would use ... would use material like you if ... if ... ,' he ran out of breath.

I did not feel any better for his disclosure. Navies of any nationality meant warfare. My situation, however, was delicate, so I spoke respectfully. 'You're right sir, I don't think I am at all suitable. Thank you for the food, the shave and the clothes. I'll see myself out.' I pushed the chair back.

Leaning forward, thin-lipped and with the tips of his fingers pressed hard together, he almost hissed, 'It was made clear to you that having accepted, you may not resign.'

'But surely sir, you need a loyal German for this job?'

He was breathing easier, 'Indeed that is what we first thought but, on balance, we now think there are pragmatic advantages in using you. All Germans who were living in this country have now either gone back to Germany or they are interned and under surveillance. A stranger in a rural community will be the object of close enquiry so his background must withstand investigation. We have no time to find someone in Germany, bring him here and create such a background for him. Our best hope was that a suitable, English speaking, colonial German seaman would drift into our net. However, you must see that your Russian origin and your time in America aptly suit our requirements. And we have the means of securing your loyalty. You may therefore assume that within the week you will be in post. The location is already selected.'

'A week! Sir, I know nothing about what's been going on over here. Is there any particular need for this haste?'

'There is certainly no particular need for you to know what has been going on. However, I shall tell you a little of the background. Some four months ago, although vastly outnumbered, our Grand Fleet defeated the British navy off Jutland. The victory, however, served only to convince us that such dramatic confrontations will not win us the war. Our best course is to starve this island of food and raw materials. And that we can do effectively and speedily if we are able to give our U-boats prompt and accurate information. There is, as you may know, little secrecy here or in the U.S.A. about the movement of shipping. Our principal and immediate problem is to deliver the intelligence we gather to our U-boat captains. You are now part of a makeshift solution to that vitally urgent problem and will remain so until other means are developed.'

'Are you saying that all you want me to do is to lie up somewhere in Scotland and answer the telephone?'

'Yes. Precisely.'

Up to that point in my life any cookies I got for free always had stones for currants, so I bit cautiously. 'I should make something clear, sir, I have no stake in this war. If anyone starts shooting I shall have gone some place else.'

'If you look at the map, Mr Melnikov, you will see you will be far from any shooting. Rural inquisitiveness is likely to be your most dangerous enemy.'

I reckoned I could deal with rural inquisitiveness. I supposed also that the folks up there would not much care whether I stayed or left any time I chose. But free liquor and idleness made a drunk-ard's Garden of Eden, so I must find some way to fortify my resolve to overcome my addiction if I hoped to rebuild my profes-sional reputation. I lifted my ankle back on to my knee and sat back. 'Fine. I'll take your job.'

'That was decided some time ago.' He leaned forward and rested his chin on the tips of his long fingers. 'I wish to make one or two points and then you may go. Firstly, Mr ... Mr Smith, whom you have already met, will instruct you in your duties. Secondly, I understand you may require a degree of physical fit-ness so Ismet, my man, will exercise you twice each day, starting at six o'clock tomorrow morning. You will be representing your-self as an American citizen and it would perhaps be best if you assumed a more English-American name. Do you agree? Good. Then let me see ... I have a directory here. Let's turn to the back ... Yetstone? Sounds English. Now from the front ... Abraham?'

'Abe Yetstone. Sure! Fine!'

'You will be shown to your room now. I think you said that you smoked cigarettes. You may take two from the box on the table and I shall arrange for you to have your first supply tomor-row.'

He rose, pulled on a brass lever beside the fireplace and then turned and faced me again, his hands clasped at his back. 'I pun-ish indiscipline and indiscretion by flogging. Ah Ismet, show Mr Abe Yetstone to his attic bedroom. When you have done that, I wish to speak with you.'

Chapter Five

THE TURK DID NOT take me directly to my bedroom. Instead, without any explanation, he led me down to the white-tiled room adjoining the kitchen. When we got there a paraffin lamp, already lit, was on the table. For a fleeting moment he toyed with ordering me to carry it, then he picked it up himself. 'Follow me,' he said curtly.

This time we went through a green painted door at the near-end of the panelled corridor and up three flights of bare wooden stairs, the flights getting meaner and narrower at each level. On the second landing, he pointed to a brown varnished door, 'The lavatory.'

At the very top of the house I was shown into a room not much larger than a closet which had a sloping ceiling and was furnished with a bed, a wooden chair and a table. A tin basin and a jug sat on the table and above it on the wall hung a wooden-framed mirror. A skylight in the roof served as the only window.

My legs ached from the climb, I was weary and I longed to ponder the turn my life had taken. I loosened my collar and simply collapsed on to the bed.

The Turk remained standing just inside the door. He searched for some ill-tempered comment. 'You will use only the backstairs – the servants stairs – and you will not attempt to visit any part of the house except the kitchen stockroom and this, your bedroom. Does your drink-befuddled brain grasp that? If you are discovered anywhere else without authority, you will be punished. Now, so that you cannot pretend that you lost your way, take the lamp and go ahead of me back to the kitchen stockroom.'

' This time, my mangy little mongrel, find your own way back to your kennel.'

His lips shaped a smug rosebud, 'Very well, I shall tell the kitchen staff that you do not require supper.'

I rolled off the bed, seized the lamp and pushed past him.

Rosalind kept her gaze downcast as she brought in my supper: a flagon of milk, a chunk of bread and a pound of cold salmon. She made to return to the kitchen but the Turk snapped, 'One minute, Miss!'

She stood perfectly still, neither turning nor raising her eyes.

He went on, 'Firstly, you will witness that Yetstone has been told that he may go only from here to his room using the back-stairs and to nowhere else in the house. Secondly, let me remind you in his presence that you must neither speak to this man nor answer any of his questions. Now go.'

Rosalind moved on without a word.

'You now know the way to your room, Yetstone. Leave the tray on the table when you have eaten. The drudge will remove it.' He could not resist making one last jibe. 'I understand you are to benefit from my instruction in the morning. Doubtless you are conscious of the privilege.' He chuckled, turned on his heel and went out to the stairs.

The door to the stairs had scarcely closed when the one from the kitchen opened and Rosalind pushed her head into the room.

'Coo, he ain't 'alf a nark!' She leaned in a friendly way against the doorpost. 'Supper all right then? Captain says you got to be well fed to make you fit. Lumme, that's a natty outfit you got on now and no mistake! 'Ere, you always eat like that? At least you oughter cut up the bread. Want me to do it for you?'

I moved along the bench and she came round and sat beside me. 'You really a Russian prince? Course you ain't – you just think I'm a stupid skivvy.'

I let her take the knife and while she cut the bread into small slices and buttered them I sat back and studied her. Her lustreless brown hair was roughly cut and held back by a strip of calico. Her cheeks were powderless and lacked the glow which only fresh air and sunshine can bestow. Although her brown eyes were rimmed with tiredness, they yet held a spark of laughter. It was that spark which lit her face with what beauty it possessed. Below an apron made of sackcloth she wore a faded cotton dress. Rosalind, how-ever, was the nearest to a friend I had in all the world. Suddenly I wanted to do or to say something which would give this rag-a-muffin child a moment of happiness. 'You looking for a prince, then?' I asked.

'Fat chance! Got a lot to offer a prince I 'ave!'

'You got lovely eyes.'

'Then pity me eyes need the rest of me.'

'And a kind heart. The only heart in this house I'd guess.'

'Wot you mean? The Sultan's got a heart. Reckon his is small, an' black, an' bitter like a sloe.'

'Why then, the man is all heart!'

She threw back her head and laughter rippled from her throat. Oh for an audience made up of Rosalinds!

I took her hand in mine. She made no attempt to withdraw it. It was warm and rough and had ragged fingernails. An open hack gaped on the side of her thumb. 'To me, my dear, you are a princess. My Princess Rosalind.'

She laid her other hand on the table and looked at it gravely. 'Bet me hands ain't like any princess's neither!'

I leaned forward and gently caressed her hands. 'Princesses and their hands come in all conditions. Your hands, my angel, are helping hands; kind hands; hands one can trust. I behold only a beautiful lady with beautiful hands – the hands of the daughter of Venus.'

'No they ain't,' she said with a small frown. 'Me ma's dead and me pa's the coachman as brought you 'ere.' She took her hands from me with a sigh and laid them on her lap. 'Used to 'ave a leather shop up town, we did. Then the war started an' people came wiv bricks an' stones an' smashed our windows. Coo, it wasn't 'alf awful. An' not cos we'd done 'em harm; just cos we're Germans. Then we came 'ere.' She turned to me, now pert and grinning. 'Ain't no daughter of no one else.'

I rested my cheek on an upturned hand and tilted my face to look into her eyes. 'Your past, my child, was the dark night of your life; your present is the chill grey of dawn; come now and walk with your prince into the warm sunshine of your future.' Dreams, I knew, could nurture the most desolate spirit. I spoke mystically.

'One day you will fly from this place to a white marble palace in a sunny forest. There you will be a fairy queen with hands which are white and soft and sparkling with rings. You will wear gorgeous, frilly dresses of the finest silk; white ermine furs and satin slippers. Diamonds will glitter in your hair. Page boys will serve you champagne in crystal glasses. Dappled horses will draw your golden coach. All around you handsome nobles will pine for your smile.'

Her eyes were large and misty but her voice was saucy as she tossed me a sidelong glance. 'Got nothin' much to look forward to then, 'ave I?'

'Sure you have! You will recline on a velvet sofa eating cream cakes and sherbet. All this rich food and idleness will make you enormously fat, so that you'll waddle like a goose and constantly suffer indigestion.'

She gurgled with delight. 'You ain't fit to 'ave your bread cut up, you ain't! An' I can't sit 'ere all night neither.' She got up and went to the kitchen door.

'Rosalind,' I called after her, 'How far to the shops?'

'Shops? Ain't no shops round 'ere. Wot you want wiv shops then?'

'Diamond rings, silk gowns, indigestion powders ... and a box of matches.' I did not add that shops meant public streets.

'Matches? Lumme, plenty of them around. 'Ere's a box to start wiv.' She took a box from her apron pocket and tossed it to me.

'Not only gorgeous, but generous too. Will you permit your prince to escort you to the theatre some evening?'

'I'd permit you all right – never been to the theatre – but the Sultan won't, and he issues the passes. No one gets in or out of this 'ouse without a pass. An' I've never 'ad a pass in me life.'

'You never get out?'

'Me dad takes me an' cook an' Karl - 'e's the boy - round the park in the cab one Sunday each month, but I never gets a pass.'

'Then we'll have to outsmart the Sultan, won't we?'

'Not me! I gets beaten enough without askin' for it.'

'Rosalind ... oh, my enchanting Rosalind, if you just put your sweet mind to it you could find a way to get us out of this house - and back again, of course - without the Sultan ever knowing. I'd bet on that.'

'Maybe I could an' maybe I couldn't, but I ain't going to try.' She looked at me kindly but wearily, 'Now get on wiv your supper so I can get to me bed.'

'Where does the Sultan keep the passes?'

Her eyes widened with alarm, 'Keeps 'em in the closet in the pantry where he keeps the spirits.' She shook her head vigorously, 'I ain't going in there I ain't! He'll kill anyone as goes in there.' And she closed the door on me.

I lit one of the cigarettes the old man had given me. How many times had I vowed that food and tobacco were the whole of paradise? What sort of conjuring trick was it which now turned that paradise into a dungeon, a cold white-tiled dungeon? Scotland? My optimism was gone. Europe was a coop of riled polecats and

I was to be staked like a chicken in their midst. My ultimate death was certain. When I had served the old man's purpose he would never let me go free. The risk that I would tell of his presence in London condemned me. I tried to believe that I was living through a delirious dream, that my senses were being cheated by the delusions of an alcohol poisoned brain. I had indeed suffered horrendous hallucinations in my time, hallucinations which were terrifying. I held out my hand before my eyes. My hand was steady and my vision sharp and clear.

The house was silent. As I watched threads of blue smoke winding upwards from my cigarette, I knew the course I had to take. I had to tear myself free from the web of the black German spider before he destroyed me. I might well not find fame and fortune outside these walls but I would still be in the game and who could tell how the cards would fall?

I stubbed out the cigarette and got up. Yes, escape which embraced settling my score with the Turk would be an inspiring accomplishment on which to base my future career.

Chapter Six

FOR THE FIRST TIME IN six months I wakened feeling neither cold nor hungry but inside my head a leaden ball of anxiety rolled round and round in a tiresome rut. An urchin with a guttering candle stood beside my bed.

'Mr Yetstone, sir! Mr Yetstone, sir!' His voice faltered as weakly as the candle flame. 'Mr Ismet says you are to be down in the kitchen stockroom in five minutes.'

Like a sickening hangover, I remembered the wily Turk and his sapless master. 'Your name Karl?'

'Yes sir. Mr Ismet says—,'

'Fine, fine. You've done your job, Karl.'

'I'll leave the candle for you, sir.'

'Thanks.'

Cocooned in warm blankets I looked up at rain splashing on to the skylight above my bed. Was there safe shelter anywhere in the world for me? I pulled the blankets over my head and in the darkness tried in vain to dream heroic dreams. The plain fact was, I had been sucked into the turmoil of the European war, into a madhouse of killing where lice had a greater right to life than men. And the Turk was waiting downstairs.

I swung my feet on to the floor and pulled on my socks. Having slept in my long johns, I was then well enough dressed for doing exercises. I took my last cigarette and the candle and went down to the stockroom.

The Turk, his shirt cuffs turned back, stood in the middle of the stockroom drumming a broom handle on the floor. We exchanged no word of greeting as I went to the bench, sat, and after a jaw-stretching yawn, put the cigarette between my lips and lit it from the candle flame.

Savouring the delicious harmony of nicotine and silence, I reclined against the wall and closed my eyes. Had I not thus moved my head back, the flying broom handle would have struck the side of my face. Instead, amid a shower of sparks, it swept the cigarette from my lips.

'Get to your feet, or do you need to be flogged by the guards to wake you?' The Turk's voice grated and his eyes were spiteful.

I could easily have seized the broom handle and beat respect into him but, with restraint learned in prison, I picked up the cigarette, nipped out what was left of the glowing end and obediently rose to my feet.

He walked round me as a horsedealer might round a broken hack then nudged my shoulder with the broom handle. 'Start running on the spot and let's see how fit you are.'

I looked at the ceiling with forebearance and shuffled my feet in a slow rhythm. He strutted in front of me. Suddenly, gripping the broom handle like a bayonette, he lunged forward and rammed its end into my stomach. I doubled over in pain. He struck me across my shoulders. 'Get your knees up, you scrounging, lazy lout!'

Fury blazed in me but I curbed my eager fists with the promise they would one day pulp that malicious little savage.

Now striking my ankles with the broom handle, he sang, 'Faster! Faster! Higher! Higher! You Russian oaf!'

His voice grew shrill and, with heightening frenzy, he rained blows, first about my legs but soon blindly wherever the flailing shaft happened to strike. 'Dance!' he chanted breathlessly, 'Dance, Yetstone, dance! Jump, you drunken, thieving loafer! Jump! Jump! Jump!'

The Great Melnikov, whose capers had enthralled millions, was being whipped and teased by a pock-faced, talentless bluebottle. I shut my mind as best I could to the pain and pranced to his tune like an organ grinder's monkey, suffering every thrust, taunt and jibe until the whirling pole happened to strike a glancing blow to the side of my head. Seizing the opportunity, I collapsed to the floor with a groan and fluttering eyelids and lay still.

'Get up!' he screamed, whacking my thigh. I lay limp and motionless. 'Get up at once!' There was a trace of concern in his voice. 'At once! At once! Do you hear? Get up or I shall call the guards!' But with every word there was less conviction in his voice.

Cautiously he prodded my shoulder with the end of the broom handle. I made my body flop lifelessly over. He came nearer then and I could hear his breathing close above me. I lay slack as a sack of wet peas. He touched my hand. It slithered to the floor. I heard him run to the sink. Water gushed from the tap. That was enough.

I was not going to let myself be deluged with cold water. Groaning and with rolling eyes, I sat up. Relief spread over his features but all he said was, 'That will do for this morning. Go to your room. Wash, shave, dress and be down again in twenty minutes for breakfast.'

The jug in my room had been filled with hot water. A razor and a towel were placed beside it. As I bathed my shins where the skin was broken, I swore I would repay every stinging touch, and with interest.

I dressed quickly because I wanted to find a landmark by which I could later locate that house. Uncovering a spy-ring would in itself give me a place in British society and surely merit reward. However, I must first know where in the thicket of London buildings the old crow had built his nest.

Every door leading off from the backstairs was locked. The lavatory had no window, only a cast iron ventilator through which I could see nothing. I moved quietly, so quietly that on turning into the corridor at the bottom of the stairs I surprised Karl. He was standing perfectly still with his back close to the wall. He leaped a yard with fright when I appeared and then dived through a door on the opposite side of the corridor which, I guessed, led down to the kitchen. Had the boy been set to spy on me, I wondered.

In the stockroom Rosalind was laying out breakfast. She touched a finger to her lips, so I went silently to the bench. She came round to my side of the table and, stooping to place a platter before me, spoke softly from the side of her mouth, ' 'Ere an' I got a present for you.' She dropped a small package into my jacket pocket. 'Don't open it till you're safe in your room.'

Her body was between me and the door so I raised her hand and pressed it to my lips. It was no teasing act. Whatever Rosalind had given was given despite the risk and without hope of any return. I was touched almost to choking. She snatched her hand away and almost falling over her feet, dashed back to the kitchen.

A succulent smell rose from the three fried eggs nestling in a tangled wreath of bacon. I snatched up my fork, thrust a bursting yolk into my mouth and wiped the spillage from my chin with a wad of bread. While I chewed, I trimmed fatty rind from the bacon and deposited it on the table beside my plate. Twenty-four hours earlier I would have fought a lion just for a share of that rind!

The Turk's blue jacket lay on the draining board. I would not have time to destroy it so I decided to conceal it under the trash in the garbage can. When I lifted the lid off the can, however, I found that the feathers and garbage of yesterday were gone. In their place the lifeless, misty eyes in a sheep's head looked up at me.

I wrenched a cold moist eye from the skull, intending to put it in a pocket of the Turk's jacket before depositing the jacket in the can. Footsteps approached from the kitchen. I laid the sheep's eye on the bench at my side as Rosalind came in with a bowl of hash. She placed the bowl on the other side of the table and walked briskly out with her head high. Ismet entered carrying a mug of coffee.

The Turk swaggered up to the table with smirking insolence. A taunt was on his lips but as he set the mug down, I nudged the table with my knee, splashing hot coffee over his hand.

Not much put out, he shook the liquid off. 'Thank you for reminding me. We must try to beat some manners into you this evening. A challenge, certainly, but something which we can both look forward to all day.' He skipped across the room and picked up his little jacket.

The instant his back was to me, I plucked the sheep's eye from the bench and lowered it gently into his coffee. It had scarcely submerged from sight when he returned, wriggling into his coat.

He pulled out the stool and sat facing me. Still smirking, he dipped his fingers in the hash and plucked out a piece of meat which, with a merry little flourish, he popped into his mouth.

I scowled, pretending resentment.

Delighted, he lifted the mug and without taking his eyes from mine, chirped, 'I understand that you played the part of a dancing bear - or was it a clown - in the circus? Wonderful! Knowing how eager you are to please and entertain me, I'll make sure that you get an opportunity tonight. No, no, don't be modest. I shall insist.' He sucked in a happy draught of coffee.

Encouraging his conceit, I puckered my face with vexation. How happy that made him! He twitched a bowl of hash and slipped it into his mouth. A blithe little smile was playing round his lips as he lifted the mug again. His head went back but he never took his eyes from my face until the sheep's eye touched his lips.

Puzzled, he lowered the mug and peered into it. His nose wrinkled and his lips curled with disgust.

Clutching his mouth in one hand and the mug in the other, he kicked the stool back and ran to the sink.

His face moist and white, he bent over the sink and looked down on the sheep's eye. A long strand of saliva hung from his mouth.

With bland interest, I asked, 'Pig's eye in coffee a Turkish delight, then? Learn something every day. No need to be ashamed, flunkey, you may eat it at my table.' As I spoke, and while he washed out his mouth with water from the running tap, I lifted the heap of bacon rind from beside my plate and pushed it with my fork to the bottom of his bowl of hash.

Pale and breathing hard, he flounced back to the table. I spoke with concern. 'Say, you don't look well, old son! Sure it ain't the trash you eat?' I stretched my hand for his bowl. 'Better I tip it into the garbage can.'

His eyes glowed with suppressed rage as he snatched the bowl out of my reach.

'You could say, 'Thank you for your concern, Mr Yetstone, sir'. But then, since you ain't had much of an upbringing, it's best I tell you what to eat and how to eat it. Let's start by ditching that swill you got there.'

He stood glowering, his mouth working and desperate to find words which would crush me.

I shook my head, 'Don't you even have the wit to heed good Russian counsel? I got to make it an order then. Now, you listenin' good? Eat no more of that hash! Got that?' Again I reached for the bowl.

He crashed a fist to smash my hand.

I moved my hand clear. 'Hey there! That don't mean you plannin' to disobey me, does it? Maybe you find it a mite uncomfortable sittin' with your betters. Sure, I understand and you got my permission to return to the kitchen and eat with the other servants. I'll holler if I want something.'

For a moment I thought he would indeed go, then his mean lips pressed together and defying my mocking laugh, he sat down.

'You so proud to be in my company you don't want to leave? Fine! Just have the humbleness not to eat any more of that hash.'

Perversity twisted his features. He yearned to overpower me.

'No shame in doin' what a Russian tells you. And boy, I'm tellin' you not to eat that hash.'

His eyes now incandescent with hatred, he plunged a hand into the bowl like a child in a tantrum and crammed a fistful of the hash into his mouth.

I affected puzzled annoyance. 'Never had a servant with such a defiant spirit! All right, I see fit to overlook just one disobedient act, but don't you go repeatin' it.'

Frustration and spite drove him to defy me again. He thrust his hand into the bowl and dredged a second fistful which he would have crammed into his mouth had he not first spotted the fronds of greasy, egg-stained rind hanging from his fingers. His adam's apple jumped in his throat as waves of nausea heaved up into his gullet. He let the mess slide off his palm back into the bowl. His chin trembled and he dragged a quivering, long sigh. Half gasping, half sobbing, he picked up the bowl and turned again towards the sink.

Almost every day of the three years I was in prison I had been taught a lesson in provocation. I knew that game. 'Glad you came round to obeying me, boy. Now you goin' to entertain me, right? Goin' to dance maybe? And jump a bit too, eh? Good! Dance then, flunkey. Dance!'

His hands were squeezed into little fists and his body trembled from head to toe. He was as packed with malice as a rotten egg with gas and it needed but a word to detonate him.

'Dance flunkey, dance! Jump! Jump! Jump!' I used the voice he had used during my morning exercises.

Releasing pent-up hatred, he swung round and with all his strength, hurled the bowl at my head. It missed by a foot and smashed on the wall behind me.

'That was amusin', but it ain't dancin'. Want me to get a broom handle?'

Like a cornered animal being teased, he watched me intently with bright, vindictive eyes. Had I put out a hand to touch him, he would have bitten it off.

I placed my feet apart and gripped the edge of the table. Then I let my head roll back and laughed derisively. 'Not much of a dancer, are you boy? Seen grandma skunks do better.'

His neck dropped between hunched shoulders. For a second he was still. Then he sprang. A long knife was clenched in his fist as he rose to clear the table which was between us.

I half rose, lifted my side of the table so that everything on it spilled to the floor, and then I rammed its sharp corner into his oncoming stomach. Letting the table drop to the floor, I watched his trunk and arms sprawl across it until his chin hit the boards.

The knife flew from his grasp, slithered to the floor and spun round and round at the feet of the little man in the Inverness cape who had just entered.

I flopped back on to the bench and threw up my hands. 'You see what I've got to put up with, Smith? Ought to be kept in a cage.'

Smith did not even glance in my direction. 'Goodness, Mr Ismet! What on earth is going on? Are you all right?'

I emphasised each word, 'I am all right too!'

The Turk hauled himself off the table and still hugging his stomach, groaned through his teeth, 'I'm going to kill you for this, Russian, and your end will be terrible! Oh yes, you are not going to live!' Doubled over, he stumbled out through the door to the kitchen.

I had not made an enemy of the Turk. We had been enemies before either of us was born.

Smith stood huffing and puffing and flapping his arms. He was frightened, too, and I wanted to use that fear. I stood up, towering over him. Though my arms hung at my sides, my fists were tight and hard.

'Yes of course I hope you're all right, Yetstone.' he stammered.

'Yetstone? Yetstone? Mister Yetstone!'

I moved forward and he backed away. 'Mister Yetstone.'

'Sit, Smith!' Although I knew I was too emotionally high after the fracas with the Turk to think clearly, I also knew I must seize the opportunity to get away from that house.

He backed round the fallen stool, glancing right and left, but he did not sit.

Menacing him, I followed. 'You're scared yellow of me and you're scared yellow of Old Rottenguts upstairs, ain't ya Smith? My guess is the old wolf has his blackmailer's fangs in your neck and you don't know what to do about it. Right?'

I had him cornered beside the meat safe. I leered down into the pink jelly that was his face and put an arm round his shoulders. He shrank from my touch but I pulled him to me. 'You little fat fool, don't you realise that whatever you've done, it can be as nothing to what he is doing here in London? Fifty yards from this house and the information you possess will cancel out every sin you ever committed in your life. Fifty yards, and he dare not follow you – no, not by just one step. So you and I, Smith, are going to take that little stroll. You and I are going to walk out through the front door like the best of buddies. You know the way so, move!'

I had no more than a vague idea that somehow I was going to use Smith to get me out of the house and past the guards, either as a hostage or a body shield.

'Get walking!' I hacked at his ankles and at the same time made sure with my free hand that the butt of my pistol was accessible. I did not intend to draw it until I had to because its existence must come as a surprise. Smith cringed – a sly ruse for, with a wriggle of his plump shoulders, he left me holding his empty cape.

He stood in the doorway, not crowing, just mightily relieved. 'No, Mr Yetstone, I am not the fool you take me for. It is impossible to leave this house without authority and you will be most unwise to try. Now, if you have had breakfast, follow me. We are going to the room in which you are to receive instruction. Please remember that there are guards within call everywhere.'

I was sick with fury at having let him slip so carelessly from my grasp and for disclosing my intention to escape. With a faked laugh, I tossed the cape into his arms. 'A piece of playful clowning, that's all. Not worthy of the Great Melnikov.' Even the laugh was badly done.

Chapter Seven

THE ROOM ON THE SECOND floor was furnished with an old school desk just inside the door and a blackboard and chair close to the opposite wall. The bottom panes of glass in the window had been covered over with brown paper so that nothing could be seen of the buildings which surrounded the house. A servile old man in a shabby black suit with a measuring tape hanging from his neck stood beside the desk. He clutched a swatch of cloth samples in his hand.

'Ah good,' Smith said, 'the outfitter is here to measure you.'

When he had taken my measurements, the outfitter handed Smith the swatch of cloth samples. 'Would you care to select for the gentleman, sir?'

Smith flicked through the squares of cloth, tweaked a coarse brown tweed and said, 'This will do. Shirt and socks to go with the suit and a pair of stout brogue shoes.'

I plucked the samples from his hand. 'On that we disagree, Smith!' I found a fine cloth of a light grey shade, 'This,' I told the outfitter, 'with a white shirt, a pale blue tie, pale blue socks and the very best in city shoes.' I was looking ahead and wanted something which would represent me as a slick performer, not as a clod-footed yokel.

Smith's headshake told me that he did not approve my choice but, because he still felt threatened by my presence, he did not dispute it. He dismissed the outfitter and said to me, 'Please sit at the desk, Mr Yetstone. A slate has been provided should you wish to take notes.'

Pleased at having got my way in the matter of the suit, I fitted my oversize frame into the desk without protest.

Smith then went forward and stood beside the blackboard. With a safe distance between us, he spoke brusquely, 'From this moment you are, and always have been, Abe Yetstone. Melnikov is but some half-forgotten acquaintance. From time to time I shall test you on this – perhaps by addressing you as Melnikov. If you respond when I do, we must be concerned. Slips of that nature may put your life and our operation in jeopardy.'

'Oh dear, oh my goodness!' Meaningless words, but I was set-tling my disposition following the episode with the Turk.

'In making the necessary arrangements in Scotland, we are implying that you come from a wealthy American family; that you are addicted to alcohol and that you were involved in an unsavoury gambling scandal. Your family think it is in your best interest that you remain abroad until the affair has blown over. We shall do little more than hint at these aspects of your past, thus giving you scope to cover any slips and to fill out the part as cir-cumstances demand.'

I now stared intently at Smith's nose until he became uncom-fortable and transferred his gaze from my face to a corner of the room above my head.

Thus freed of his direct attention, I looked out at the sky. My revenge on the Turk was a joy marred only by the botch I had made of my attempt to get away. I supposed Smith would inform Old Rottenguts and I wondered if I would suffer punishment.

It was not long before Smith's voice faded to an an irrelevant drone. His words swam round my head like motes of dust in the sunlight. Beyond the window thin white clouds drifted across a blue sky like wisps of gossamer on a summer's day. Heedless of time I let my thoughts float with them. One day ... one day when I was rich and famous again I would own a luxuriously appoint-ed zepplin in which I would travel all round the world; greeted wherever I went by enthuiastic audiences. Oh yes, what a glorious luxury it was to be warm and fed and free to dream!

For I know not how long, I sailed far, far away from that stuffy classroom in London. Eventually the numbing hardness of my seat compelled my return.

Smith was removing a map of Great Britain which he must at some time have hung over the blackboard. He replaced the map with a large, hand-drawn sketch depicting a green spit of land poking into a blue sea from between two blue inlets. Bit by bit, as my dream world faded, his words came together and made sense.

'Geologically, Dunmallach peninsula is a mountain ridge left when ice-age glaciers gouged out the sea lochs on either side of it. Loch Dunmallach is on the south side of the peninsula and Loch Dorch on the north. The white line running close to the shore on the south represents the only road on the peninsula. Although I have shown the road as ending at Dunmallach Post Office, there is a rutted track which leads on to a small farm half a mile beyond.'

I wrote on the slate, I must not pave that road to Hell with hangovers!

The screech of pencil on slate made Smith grimace. 'Your cottage – which, by the way, is named the Ghillies' Croft – does not have a telephone so you will take our calls at the Post Office. You will also collect what provisions you need there. Everything will be prepaid.'

'I take it the Ghillies' Croft is somewhere near the Post Office. So why ain't it marked on your map?'

'Ah, but the Ghillies' Croft is very far from the Post Office! To get to the Ghillies' Croft from the Post Office, you will follow a rough moorland path over the mountain to the other side of the peninsula. Your cottage is on the shore of Loch Dorch. It is indeed the only habitation on the north side of the peninsula. Limit your presence in Dunmallach to taking our telephone calls and to collecting your stores and your very existence may soon be overlooked.'

I tried again to banish the classroom from my thoughts but the sky was now overcast and Smith's words persistently penetrated my reverie.

'We have told the postmistress that the telephone calls you receive are from your sister in London. Listen attentively to everything you are told and memorise the intelligence you are to pass on to calling U-boats. If there is a possibility of being overheard, speak as you would to a beloved sister. You need not explain the abrupt change of topic.'

My lungs yearned for nicotine. I yawned.

Smith scowled, pulled in his chin and then almost barked, 'Have you any questions, Mr Melnikov?'

I noted the Mr Melnikov, but assumed it to be his way of getting back at me for the yawn. 'Sure,' I said to irk him further, 'When do I get the cigarettes I was promised?'

Words, cold as icicles, dropped on the back of my neck. 'Not only was your reply insolent, you should not have responded to the name, Melnikov.'

I knew without turning that the old martinet stood close to my back looking down on me with thin-lipped malice.

'Only when you apply yourself will you receive a ration of cigarettes. Another such insubordinate reply will, however, earn you six strokes of the rope. Inform me, Mr Smith, if you find Yetstone negligent in attitude. I will not dissipate valuable time on useless material.' He stalked off.

Smith mopped his bald head. 'You will be tested, Mr Yetstone, and only if you prove yourself competent will you go on to take up your post.'

Smith was as fearsome as an inflated pig's bladder. The danger lay in letting him get the upper hand. The old Captain, on the other hand, was lethal as a bare high-voltage cable and I would be wise to keep well clear of him. 'All right, Smith,' I said, 'give me your notes. I'll have nothing better to do in Scotland than study them.'

He was near to weeping. 'I told you ... I explained to you at the very beginning, you will take neither written notes nor anything else with you. And you will be searched before you leave this house. You may use the slate while you are here but—' He clapped his hands on top of his head and closed his eyes. 'This is awful ... terrible!' He opened his eyes and gripping the lapels of his jacket, spaced his words, 'Do ... you ... not ... realise ... the danger ... in which you stand? Are you incapable of making the least effort to save yourself? I do not want you to be harmed. Within the limits of my duty I shall help you, but ... but you must co-operate!'

He began to walk to and fro in front of the blackboard, flapping his arms like a hen flapping her wings. After about four turns he spoke in a voice drained of vitality. 'Go. Go now and have lunch. The doors are unlocked. Come back in thirty minutes.'

I went directly to the kitchen stockroom, hoping for an opportunity to speak with Rosalind. When I got there, however, my lunch was already on the table and the door to the kitchen firmly shut.

I ate quickly, and having twenty minutes before I was due back in the classroom, then went up to my attic bedroom. I had a feeling as I went that I was being followed – the creak of a stair-tread, the whisper of cloth brushing on cloth. Once inside my room I wedged the chairback under the door handle so that no one could enter without giving me warning. The Turk had been humiliated by a Russian and his revenge was certain.

I took Rosalind's present from my jacket pocket and threw myself down on the bed. When I removed the newspaper wrapping, I found myself holding a small, chipped china pepperpot. An old wine cork had been inserted where the pepperpot had originally been capped by a sprinkler top.

Never in my life had I received a present from anyone. But that was not the only reason the tawdry article held a value beyond price for me. For months – perhaps for years – the child had been denied a visit to the shops. Had she then given to me the only ornament she possessed? I hugged the pepperpot to my chest. Then I kissed it again and again because her hand – her dear, rough, red hand – had touched it. The darling child knew nothing of the Great Melnikov. What she gave, she gave to comfort a penniless tramp. My heart ached. Oh Rosalind!

How I now regretted the arrogance which had underlain my teasing adoration! The girl's simplicity was but a veil masking a saintly princess! She chanced a beating even in speaking to me. What then the possible cost of her gift? Humility cramped my chest – and compassion too. The lonely child had no one with whom to share the terrors of that corner of hell in which she lived. She had no one to console her when she was beaten without cause; no one to put an arm around her when she was fatigued; and certainly no one to bless her goodness with a kiss. How did such a rare and delicate flower survive that human slagheap? Never before had I felt for anyone as I felt for Rosalind at that moment.

I removed the stopper. Fumes of cheap brandy rose about my head. Dear, darling Rosalind! She had been told of my addiction and was trying to ease my pain. Sobs choked me. Half a gill of spirits! Oh my child, my child, when once I start on that medicine it takes not half a gill to satisfy my craving but as much as would pickle an ox! How could I ever repay such splendid, splendid love and courage? I closed my eyes but, try as I might, I could not even weave a fiction to cover my inadequacy.

It took until my half hour was up for me to regain composure but I regretted not one rapturous second. I replaced the cork in the pepperpot, hid it under the pillow on the bed and went down to the classroom.

Smith was standing beside the blackboard flicking over the pages of his notes. A half-glance and a little frown registered my arrival.

I despised him more than I resented the Turk. The Turk was at least frank in his enmity, yet Smith would as gladly have seen me dead. Sure, he would help me if I would co-operate. That was the sugar on his poison. But, however compliant I made myself, there was only one end for me: death. And he knew that. Yes, and for a mere nod of approval from his superiors Smith would prepare the deadly cup and hand it to me, smugly commending himself to the world for his sense of duty. My co-operation would simply make the business more agreeable.

My detestation of the man had deeper roots. I was ashamed of myself and part of that shame was that I could not now live without men like Smith. When I had stood in the spotlight of fame, I knew such boot-lickers were a natural part of humanity. Sometimes I satirised them in my comic sketches. Now, however, with all the evidence of my talent lying at the bottom of a lake of vodka, I found myself scratching in the very dross of humanity for failings in others with which to justify my own worthless existence. Although I despised Smith, my own self-loathing was sometimes much, much greater. What was the purpose of my life now? Only memories of what I once had been and a tiny flicker of hope kept me from ending it all.

Smith took out and looked at his watch, then beamed on me. 'I hope you had a good lunch, Mr Yetstone.'

'No you don't, Smith. You wish my lunch had choked me!'

He shook his head with uncomprehending sadness and looked down at his notes. Then, with a brave smile, the incident was put behind us and he began to speak briskly.

'About the telephone calls you will take at the Post Office, we would like these to be more frequent than twice a week but more on a regular basis might test the credibility of sisterly love. The calls are scheduled for five o'clock every Wednesday and Saturday - unless you are instructed otherwise.'

He turned a page. 'We shall make the calls from ... public call boxes ... so that they cannot easily be traced.'

This time I knew what lay behind the hesitation in his delivery. 'On the telephone we shall give you the information you are to pass on, in plain English. Or do you think it would be safer if we used a code ... Mr Melnikov?'

Knowing that the old captain stood at my back, I made no reply and began to draw a dagger on the slate.

Smith spoke sharply, 'Did you hear my question, Mr Melnikov?'

I wetted my finger and erased a line.

Smith drew a long breath of satisfaction and looked above me for applause. 'We do not wish to burden you with more code-learning than is necessary, that is why we shall speak in plain English. Be at Dunmallach Post Office five minutes before a call is due. We have no wish to hold prolonged conversations with the postmistress.' Each phrase was separated from the next by a pause because he expected an interruption – but not from me.

'Suppose I should want to get in touch with you urgently?'

'You cannot. You will possess neither a postal address nor a telephone number with which to do so. Further, the people of Dunmallach have been directed not to give nor to lend you money in any circumstance.'

'So, however desperately I may need help, I can reach no one. I shall be more or less isolated.'

The old man's frockcoat brushed my shoulder as he went forward to stand beside Smith. 'Utterly isolated. It is my intention, Yetstone, that you shall be as segregated from this organisation as a goldfish in a bowl on the planet Mars. If you allow your activities to be discovered, you alone shall bear the consequences. You shall lack the information with which to implicate us, to corroborate any tale you may care to tell or to trade for pardon. No one but you will be involved in your predicament. Further, if it serves our purpose, we shall assist any British investigation by anonymously providing evidence that you are a traitor to Russia and an enemy spy in Great Britain. Keep in mind at all times that your survival depends on your being both effective and discreet. If you listen attentively to the instruction you are being given, you will be in no danger whatsoever. Give particular attention to the next part for it concerns the purpose of your employment. Carry on, Mr Smith.'

Without dropping a glance in my direction, he strode out of the room.

Smith fluffed up the ends of his moustache as if God had just patted his head. 'Your function is to pass information on the movement of shipping to the commanders of German U-boats. These U-boats will enter Loch Dorch submerged and come to the surface near to the Ghillies' Croft after dark. You will be told when to expect one. But they will surface only if you tell them that it is safe to do so.'

'Look, Smith, why don't you give me the wink every time

Softshoe Sourpuss shows up? Then we could both be stars of the classroom.'

'Please don't be disrespectful. Now, where was I? Oh yes, you are being given signalling apparatus. When a U-boat is expected it is vital that you are the only person on the north side of the peninsula after dark. There is no reason why anyone else should be there, unless you have encouraged them. It may be, however, that a U-boat entering the loch in daytime will raise its periscope to check its position in relation to the Ghillies' Croft, and a shepherd on the hill spot its movement through the water. If you hear of such sitings, pass them off as the antics of seals playing on the loch. Have you any questions ... Mr Yetstone?'

'What if an expected U-boat doesn't turn up?'

He beamed, 'A good question, a very good question! If a U-boat has not arrived by three nights after it is due, you may abandon your vigil and report the matter in our next telephone conversation. Yes, a good point!' How that man yearned for me to be his eager student!

'The information on shipping will be given to you in a set form and order. This will make it easier to recall. Now, to make you familiar with the method, we shall devote the remainder of today to practising with simulated telephone calls.'

Late in the day, Karl came into the room. He stood beside me clutching a small box. Smith beckoned him forward, took the box and dismissed the boy. He then came forward to where I sat. 'You see, progress rewarded,' he said, as he placed the box on the desk. 'The work of a German craftsman and absolutely reliable.'

Inside the box I found a gunmetal pocket watch. Engraved on its face were the words, 'Stolen from the war wounded'. I looked to Smith for an explanation.

'A precaution. Being a civilian and a foreigner, you must not attempt to sell it. That would be suicidal. You must, however, have a reliable time piece. Just be discreet in how you use it.'

'And that is reward for progress?'

'A beginning.'

He went back to the blackboard and put on his hat and cape. 'Yes, we are making headway. You may go to the stockroom now for your evening session of physical exercises.' He raised a playful eyebrow. 'Can we trust you to carry them out unsupervised? I think so, I think so.'

I knew that the breakfast-time episode was what had decided them to withdraw the Turk's supervision. Whether this was for my protection or for the Turk's, I could not say.

I ran quietly down the stairs to the panelled corridor but instead of crossing it and going on down to the stockroom, I slipped sideways and stood with my back close to the wall, exactly as I had discovered Karl in the morning. If I were being followed, someone else was going to get a surprise.

Several minutes passed and no one appeared. I was on the point of moving on when, through the wood panelling at the back of my head, I heard a female voice – not Rosalind's – say, 'We don't make sauce like that in my kitchen and we never shall!'

I knew then that Karl had not been spying on me, he had been eavesdropping. The shaft of the service hoist from the kitchen to the dining-room ascended behind the panel, and when both hatch doors were open, the sound of voices from each would be carried up and down through it.

I was delighted with my find. Not only had I discovered a source of information, I had found an escape route. When I received my new suit, I would come down to the kitchen in the dead of night, climb into the hoist and pull myself up past all the locked doors to the captain's diningroom. From there I would gain access to unguarded parts of the house and so to freedom. Now I had only to find out when and where the guards patrolled.

In the stockroom, Karl was rubbing iron cooking pots with coarse sand. He flicked me a shy glance but did not speak. I tossed my jacket on to the bench beside him. 'Care for some entertainment while you work, kid?'

A half-hearted shrug was all he risked by way of reply.

I picked up one of his pots and, arching backwards, balanced it with the end of its handle resting on my forehead. A grin, slow as dawn breaking, brightened his face. I turned in front of a sack of potatoes and, still balancing the pot on my forehead, arched further back until my fingers found the top of the sack. I picked out three potatoes, tossed them up and juggled them over the pot. I half rose, and letting each potato drop to my foot, flicked it over my shoulder and into the open sack. His eyes were shining when I took the pot back to the table.

I sat down beside him, dabbed a piece of wet rag in the sand and started rubbing a pot with it. 'Ever been to a circus?'

He shook his head without looking up.

'Eight pots. How many does that feed, regular?'

'Seventeen, sir.' His voice flickered between treble and bass.

'Seventeen! And they all live in this house?'

'No sir. The six guards sleep in the gatehouse, but they eat here.'

'What about the night shift?'

'Cook leaves a pot on the stove, sir.'

'And what time do they have that?'

Before he could reply, Rosalind opened the kitchen door, pulled a comical face and said, 'Karl, Mr Ismet says you got to come 'ere this very instant!' She returned to the kitchen.

Karl gathered an armfull of pots and ran. He came running back, snatched up the rest and the box of sand and carried them off.

Hoping that the Turk was listening, I shouted, 'Next time bring two rotten eggs and the flunkey for me to juggle!'

I stuck the butt of my morning cigarette between my lips and reclined on the bench with my heels on the table. Supper would be along soon. Now I needed only to glimpse the guards duty roster then, my pockets stuffed with silver ornaments, I'd be on my way.

Chapter Eight

WHEN I WENT TO THE instruction room next morning, a freckle-faced young man stood beside my desk. His hand rested on a black metal box about the size of a small suitcase.

'You Yetstone? Good! Call me Jack. Not my name, but Jack to you mate, all right?'

He tapped the box, 'Signalling equipment. Going to learn to assemble it, charge it, polish it, use it, take it apart and repair it. Got that? Have a go at using it this afternoon. Know morse? No? Don't matter; printed on inside of the lid.'

He undid the catches and lifted bits and pieces out of the box as he talked. 'Signalling lamp. No electricity where you're going, so carbide and water. Bright, white flame – acetylene gas – seen even in bright daylight. But hot, bloody hot! Touch the top, fry your fingers. Likewise dirt in chamber. Turned to smoke and ash. Coats reflector with soot. So no debris in flame chamber, right? And keep it dry, mate, like it was your last lucifer. Watch now. Put together like this: that goes in there and this on that, see. Now turn that tight.'

His long, agile fingers lifted, fitted and screwed one piece into another until he had the lamp assembled on a small tripod.

'There you are. Easy trick!' He stroked the lamp affectionately. 'Now you got to know it better'n a mammy knows her baby's bum. Water control here. Lens here. Shutter lever here. Works like this.'

His hand fluttered the lever and the lamp produced a rhythmic clatter. 'Nice easy touch, see. Light and nimble like a fiddler's fingers. Comes with practice, Abe. So you got to practise, practise, practise. Likewise morse code. Got to know that too. Get so you see words with your eyes or hear 'em with your ears. Forget dots and dashes, right? Old man says you to know six set signals and numbers zero to nine by Saturday. First signal reads: DANGER, DO NOT SURFACE. Now watch, listen!'

The lamp shutter chattered. 'There, you could do that, couldn't you mate? 'Course you could – easy! Here's our roster of duties. This morning, get to know the apparatus. Afternoon, code learning and try a bit o' signalling. Friday, codes and signalling, codes and signalling. Saturday, your big day. Everything smart and shining. Assemble lamp; light it; all six signals and numerals – clickety-click. Pack up lamp and good-bye Jack! That's our programme, Abe. Now let's start.'

Jack was droll, friendly and forgiving. When I asked him in German if he was a British or a German sailor he replied in English, 'Not a question on signalling, is it mate? Not for me then. And don't thump that handle like you was crackin' nuts!'

When he was not talking, he made da-de-da sounds with his lips which I took to be morse signals. I wondered if he was trying to tell me something which I lacked the skill to grasp.

Suddenly, just before lunch, Jack fell silent. When I looked up I thought he had been seized by a fit, for he was rigid from head to foot. Then, from behind me came the now familiar cold voice.

'Is he making satisfactory progress?'

'Very good progress. Sir!'

'Very well, carry on.'

When the old man went off, Jack dropped to a squatting position and looked into my face. 'You heard me, mate. Making good progress I said, right? Wouldn't say that if you wasn't! Right? Have a fag then.' And he tossed me a cigarette.

When the session ended, he said, 'Take the box of tricks with you Abe. If such is your fancy, play around with the lamp this evening and bring it back tomorrow.'

In my room I found a pack of cigarettes on the table. The delight which surged through my body, right to my finger-tips, was cut short by suspicion and doubt. Consumed by covetous greed and furtive guilt, I stalked that pack of fags as if it were a sovereign I had spotted lying on the sidewalk. Oh, I knew what troubled me. Those cigarettes were not just a bribe to make me work, they were my first payment; payment for betraying myself, my country and those who would take me for an honourable man. They were the price of a defiled conscience and for doing something the meanest convict in my American prison would have despised. Alas, whatever scruples I had, they did not restrain my fingers from almost spontaneously tearing the pack open and sticking a cigarette in my mouth.

Confounded, I paced the room. With one inhalation of smoke I cursed the old man for his satanic guile, with the next I was pleading an entitlement to whatever comfort I could procure.

Going in one direction, I knew every act of conformity was a step towards my own extermination; going in the other, I longed for the comfort – yes, and the liquor – I knew that ruthless fox would provide. Indeed ... oh yes indeed, no binding could be stronger than the cords of my own weakness!

Time had always deceived me. My future constantly promised abstinence, inspiration and acclaim; a promise my present unfailingly mocked with self-indulgence. No, not self-indulgence. I truly loathed alcohol and had suffered the torments of Hell because of it - yes, almost to death when I had drunk a crude concoction in prison. But I could no more resist or explain its compulsion than a tin tack could the pull of a powerful magnet.

I put a gloss of reason on my submission – as I always did – by resolving I would co-operate only in order to better my chance of escape.

I smoked three cigarettes. Not being accustomed to such an abundance of nicotine, I then felt sick and dizzy. I lay down on my bed, nauseated in mind and body.

My humour was dark. I could not recall the look of admiration in Karl's eyes; I saw only his puny face. I could not recapture those delicious moments when I unwrapped Rosalind's gift; I felt only the appalling weight of gratitude which was her due. In prison, a kindness was a debt and every debt a bond which must sometime be redeemed. Had I not felt as I did for Rosalind, I might argue that only by a fluke of evolving fate had her life and mine converged; that they would soon swing far apart, and if cruelty finally extinguished that last spark of laughter in her eyes, surely it was her destiny. But I also knew that my debt to Rosalind was greater by far than a gill of spirits and a cheerful smile. If it went unpaid, I would go my way – yes, to my death – burdened with remorse and guilt.

I had but one possession to give: my stolen watch. In giving it, I told myself, I was giving Rosalind all my disposable wealth. That, of course, did not match her gift to me. Sure, she might sell it and buy some girlish trinket, but I prayed that she would treasure it for what it signified.

Somehow I had to assuage the pain in my heart. In the silence of the darkened room, I made a vision of Rosalind in drab old age, her moon face wizened and wrinkled, taking out the watch for consolation and fondling its palpable reality as evidence that once upon a time she had been lovely in someone's eyes; nay, adored by the very prince of performers.

It was a touching scene. I rehearsed it again. This time the frail and aged Rosalind fondled my watch as she read a newspaper obituary to the celebrated Great Melnikov, world-renowned and much-loved master of dance and mime, whose passing was mourned by millions. A tear rolled down her cheek. I was myself obliged to sit up and dry my eyes. Yes, the gift would do – but it would do only if it were the gift of that prince and not just something discarded by a pitiable sot. I pledged myself then that her pepperpot would be my talisman against alcoholism. I would take it to my grave unopened. Metaphorically kissed by his princess, the prince was at last roused from his drunken stupor. I turned the watch over in my hand. The sweet goodness of that plain child had made priceless a trifle which I might anyhow have had to discard before I was searched.

Recollection of that threat of search reminded me I should also make certain that my little pistol was not discovered.

There was only one place from which I might reasonably hope to recover it after I had been searched and before I was taken away: the lavatory. They could not surely deny a request to visit that place before I set out on my journey.

I got up from my bed. The room and the stairs outside were almost in total darkness and it took ten fumbling minutes for me to conceal the gun behind the cistern in the lavatory to my satisfaction.

Again, as I went down the stairs I sensed I was being watched but, although I stopped and turned quickly, I could see nothing in the darkness above. When the Turk struck, I had to be ready.

Properly nourished, my body thrived on physical exercise, but it was a determination to fulfil my pledge to enhance with fame my gift to Rosalind which spurred me to regain professional suppleness. I took off my jacket, went into the middle of the stock-room and there stretched muscles which had become shrunken and stiff with disuse. My condition was wretched. Soon what little vigour I possessed was exhausted and I was concluding my activity with a simple little dance when the door from the kitchen opened. A stocky young man wearing coarse black trousers and a collarless shirt stood in the opening.

I interrupted my jig and bowed. 'Do enter, pray! Admittance

to dress rehearsals half price. Dancing lessons a dollar an hour but worth double.'

He gave no sign that he understood my words but, blinking like a doltish bull, backed out again, shutting the door behind him. I guessed the dumb oaf was one of the guards. Doubtless he possessed the unimaginative stupidity of a trained animal. Nothing – not reason nor compassion nor bribery – would influence him into disobeying his master's command. And of one thing I was certain, he had been well trained.

The kitchen door opened again and Rosalind entered with my supper. As she crossed the threshhold she gave her head a tiny shake – no more than a twitch – but enough to warn me to be silent. Expressionless, she set the tray on the table and walked quickly and purposefully back into the kitchen, shutting the door without a backward glance. I guessed that the guard I had seen was in the kitchen or still within earshot.

As I gnawed the flesh of a goose, I pondered how I might present Rosalind with the brass watch. The child herself supplied the answer for, when I lifted one of the four chunks of bread which were on the tray, two cigarettes dropped from its hollowed-out underside. Clearly she had not been told that my ration of cigarettes had been restored.

That hollow in the bread was the perfect wrapping for my gift. I pressed the watch into the recess where the cigarettes had been and replaced the bread exactly as it had been on the tray, reasoning that if Rosalind supposed I had not touched that particular piece, she would be most discreet when she came to remove it lest the cigarettes were still there and fell out.

I smoked one of the cigarettes after I had eaten, hoping to discover the nightly routine of the guards from Rosalind if she looked in. The cigarette done, I could still hear muffled voices in the kitchen so I decided to wait no longer.

I made my way up to the corridor intending to listen at the panel which concealed the service hatch. If I heard nothing of profit from the dining-room, I could at least eavesdrop on the servant's gossip.

I had scarcely taken up position when I heard the Turk's voice, muffled but distinct, in the hoist shaft. A moment's silence then he spoke again, his voice loud and angry. Rosalind cried out in pain. Here was an opportunity to protect my princess and to teach the Turk another, and long overdue, lesson. I moved swiftly across the corridor and pushed open the door through which I had once seen Karl disappear.

Eight steps below where I stood, the Turk with his back to me gripped Rosalind's hair in his left fist. He was forcing her head back to make her look up at my brass watch which dangled from the fingers of his right hand. 'Oh yes, you are going to tell me! What did you give or tell him for this?' His words hissed viciously through his teeth.

A frightened squawk escaped Rosalind's parted lips as he wrenched her head still further back.

Had I been truly fit I would have leapt from the top of the stairs to the bottom. As it was, the sound of my descending strides gave him warning and he swung himself behind the girl to face me. Recognition transformed his face. Ferocious insistence gave way to spiteful triumph. He drew the girl close. A rapid movement of his free hand and he held the point of his long-bladed knife against her neck. I regretted then having hidden my pistol in the lavatory.

'Ah-ha! The skulking Russian sniffing around, polluting the world like a rat with bubonic plague. Oh yes, you infect everyone and everything with death! You made this stupid girl your accomplice and now she must die. You know, of course, that you too will be destroyed – flogged to death, if I have my way. Now, try any of your jailbird tricks and then watch the girl suffer!' He pressed on the knife and a bead of bright red blood swelled on the white skin of my darling and innocent Rosalind's neck.

I checked my stride, forced myself to appear relaxed and shrugged. 'The girl means less to me than you do – why should she? When you've finished with her, join me in the stockroom. We can then go up and hear what the old Captain has to say about this business of my being killed off. Flogged to death, didn't you say? Not what he told to me.'

I sauntered with simulated indifference towards the stockroom door, put my hand on its handle and made as if to pass through. Instead, and scarcely checking my stride, I swung round and smashed my fist into his face. I meant to hit his mouth, for he was about to call out, but he ducked and I flattened his nose like a ripe strawberry. Surprise and pain made him release the girl but he still held the knife. Before he grasped what I was about, I seized his right forearm in both my hands and crashed it down like a rotten stick over my knee. The sound of splintering bone was distinct. As the knife fell to the floor I kicked it beyond the reach of his left hand.

Ismet looked down disbelievingly at his abnormally angled forearm. His brain was plainly trying to reject what his eyes were trying to convey. He swayed as if about to faint then, wide-eyed and wordless, he slow-waltzed through the stockroom door and collapsed onto the bench.

Rosalind, too, was in an open-mouthed stupor. I went to her and gripped her shoulders. 'Listen to me Rosalind!' I shook her until her teeth chattered, 'Listen to me! I gave you the watch to give to one of the guards to buy me liquor. Tell them that. Do you hear me? Tell them I said I'd disfigure you – I'd carve up your face – if you didn't procure alcohol for me. Are you listening? I was compelling you to get me drink!'

Her eyes were wild. I knew not if she even recognised me. But she did. 'He says they're going to kill you! Oh, they can't do that!' She dragged for breath.

I put my arm round her shoulders and spoke gently. 'No one can kill a fairy tale prince, my dear, no one can ever do that!' My voice earnest, I went on, 'Just tell them that I was going to mark you for life if you didn't persuade one of the guards to get me spirits in exchange for the watch. Remember that and we'll both be all right. Oh yes, we shall!'

I ran into the stockroom because I did not want to be found coaching Rosalind in her lines. The Turk looked up and when he saw me his face blanched. Turning his head away as if I threatened to strike it, he screamed, 'Guards! Guards! Guards!'

I went to the other side of the room, sat on a meal chest and casually rested my right ankle on my left knee. That was how the guard, who appeared almost instantly, found us.

Chapter Nine

THE YOUNG OX WITH the collarless shirt came in from the corridor. Since Ismet was slumped on the bench behind the door the guard did not at first see him and so he stood, bovine-faced, scowling at me.

'Matinee's over, old son. Missed a good show. Just got time now for a dollar dancing lesson.' The Turk moaned.

The guard stared, speechless, at Ismet's misshapen arm, striving to fathom its connection with me. Then another guard appeared. This fellow was taller, older and muffled in a long black coat. His quick survey of the room was that of someone accustomed to taking charge. He did not waste time seeking an explanation.

He pulled out a heavy gun. 'Search the Russian for weapons. I'll cover you.'

With my own gun safely hidden and having no wish to be manhandled, I rose and obligingly held my arms above my shoulders. The younger guard carried out a brisk but thorough search.

'You're not properly dressed to make a report, so I'll do it myself,' the older guard said to the young ox. 'Stay here and kill him if he attempts to move off that chest. They say he's tricky with a smart mouth, so don't talk, shoot. Now Mr Ismet, you must come and have your injuries attended to.'

The older guard helped the Turk to his feet and supported him as they went out. The younger one stood, feet apart, in front of me pointing the weapon at my chest. Having no brain to speak of, I knew he would indeed press the trigger if I tried to discuss the matter with him or even if I twitched a muscle.

I breathed deeply to concentrate my thoughts.

Once before, when I had sat in court waiting for a verdict on my life, I had experienced that aching knot of tension in my chest. Then, like an amateur actor in a play who had never read the script, I had been bewildered by what was happening. Now, in telling Rosalind what to say, I had not only written the script, I had cast myself in a part which might well not survive the last act.

One self-willed old man held the key to everything that happened in that house. Without his presence, the others served no purpose. Remove him and they must disperse – quickly, if they had regard for their own safety. I saw what I had to do. I had to get my little pistol and remove his malignant existence from the world. Sure, no one need tell me that every step on the path to that objective was fraught with danger!

I dared not ask the young oaf in front of me even for permission to go to the lavatory he was preset only to kill. I must wait until the senior guard returned. Having been searched, I would not be searched again. Killing the old man with the guard there would not be impossible if I acted swiftly and shot them both, but it posed an added risk. Somehow, then, I must contrive to get a private interview.

Even when the old spy was dead, I would not be free to leave the house immediately. Until the fact of his death became known, his security measures would remain intact. If, however, the guards could not find me quickly, they would have to assume that I had escaped and then they too must get away or risk capture. My best course was to conceal myself in the hoist shaft for half an hour before pulling myself up to the dining-room and making my bid for freedom from there.

The older guard returned and took his gun back. 'Tidy yourself,' he said to the younger man, 'We're taking him upstairs. Go ahead and keep your wits about you. I'll be at his back.'

I faked a relaxed smile. 'I take it we're going up to visit my old friend, the Captain. Good! Before we do, old son – if you have sufficient authority – give me a couple of minutes to go to the lavatory.'

'I have but I shall not. And remember this, Russian, if you wet yourself, I'll take it as an act of insubordination and have you flogged.'

'Hey now, surely—,'

'Be quiet! Get to your feet and clasp your hands at the back of your head. Keep two paces behind the guard in front and do exactly as you're told.'

When we reached the first-floor landing of the wide staircase, I knew I could safely take my hands from behind my head. Although now far from certain I would be able to preserve my life, I nonetheless meant to stand trial with the bearing of a great performer. I walked tall and with measured pace – pointless, as it happened, because again, the old man did not look up until I was standing in front of his table.

Ismet was sitting on an upright chair at the old man's side. His arm was in a white sling, whiskers of cottonwool sprouted from his inflamed nostrils and his upper lip had a lump as big as a gooseberry. He watched me as intently as a hungry, puffy-eyed viper might watch a vole. I gave him a big, comradely wink.

The captain put down his pen and looked up. His voice was unemotional. 'Yetstone, you are charged with obtaining forbidden information and with maliciously injuring a member of my staff. Do you admit the charges?'

I would not be allowed to leave that house alive if the old man believed I knew its location. My best line, I decided, was to convince him that I had tried only to obtain spirits and anything else was a fabrication of lies founded on the Turk's antagonism. Pretending an ease I did not feel, I rested a hand in my trouser pocket and although it was instantly removed by the guard, I spoke with a chuckle as if the old man and I were fellows of equal standing.

'I think we've both received disturbing – and I hope, maliciously false – information which neither of us would wish to be true – and from the same source. I've been told by your servant that it's your intention to have me – as he put it – flogged to death when I've completed our operation. Makes going on with the business rather pointless from my angle, wouldn't you say?'

His face darkened. 'You have been told what?'

I nodded our shared concern. 'Yep. Reckon we both need reassurance—'

A punch to my ribs cut my words short.

'Answer the charges and say nothing more!' the senior guard barked.

'Thank you,' the captain said. His eyes were bleak and his lips moved with the friendliness of a talking machine. 'We are not play-acting, Yetstone. Did you attempt to extract information from the scullery-maid?'

'Of course I didn't! The girl—'

'He's lying!' the Turk spluttered through swollen lips.

'Be silent! You appear to have questions to answer on your own conduct.' The captain spoke with pent-up fury. Turning back to me, he said, 'If a single statement you make is proved false, you shall answer for it with your life. Do you deny giving this to the girl?' He held up the watch.

'Of course not!'

'Then for what purpose did you give it if not for information?'

'Information?' I laughed. 'Don't you know the girl's stupid even to knowing her name? She can scarcely speak. In fact—,'

'Answer the question!' the guard ordered.

I glared at the guard with resentment. 'I imagine this ... this lout knows perfectly well that the girl got the watch so that she could exchange it for spirits in the nearest liquor store.'

'What made you suppose she would be able to obtain liquor?'

I dropped my voice to a sulky mutter. 'Because I made the wretch get me some when I first came here.'

That was too much for the Turk. 'He's a liar!' he slobbered, triumphantly, 'The girl has never been out of the house!'

The old spy turned a cruel face on Ismet. 'You were told to be silent. I am the one conducting this investigation. Your punishment for disobedience is that you will lose three days' pay and live on bread and water for three days. If you speak again without permission, you will be flogged – despite your injuries. Log that punishment, guard.' His mouth shut like a steel trap. Then to me, 'You are alleging that the girl obtained alcohol for you?'

'If not the girl, then someone else on your staff surely did.'

The sibilant hissing of the gas lamp was the only sound in the room. The captain's face was gaunt as if he suffered a griping of the guts. 'Someone else in my household? What influence have you with members of my staff?'

'The girl because I threatened to carve the map of Europe on her face. Others presumably because they think I can reward them.' I pointed to the brass watch.

He looked into my face with fierce eyes, assessing the possibility that anyone on his staff was disloyal or could be bribed. 'Can you prove any of this?'

'Might do.'

'Then you shall, if it takes breaking every bone in your body. Proceed.'

'Will you give me your word, sir, that the simple girl will not be punished for any part she has been compelled to play?'

'I shall not!'

'The child is innocent. I cannot leave her to be bullied and beaten. If you do not give me your word that she will – at the very least – be protected from the vicious brutality of that animal,' I pointed to Ismet, 'then I take no further part in this inquiry and you may do as you wish.'

For a full ten seconds, the old spy estimated the strength of my resolve. 'If you prove your allegations,' he said evenly, 'I give you my word the girl shall have my protection in future.'

That he was a man of his word, I was certain. 'Well then, there is evidence in my room; under the pillow on my bed. If you'll allow me, I'll get it for you. And, since I'm in some discomfort, sir, may I also go to the lavatory?'

'You will remain where you are.' He said to the senior guard, 'Search his room.' He then addressed me again. 'If this is a time-wasting exercise, be assured it will serve you nothing.'

He glanced down at the papers on his desk then addressed the younger guard. 'You were on surveillance duty today. Has he had any opportunity whatsoever to concoct this story with the girl?'

'None whatsoever, sir. I observed him go from the instruction room to his attic bedroom. He remained there until twenty minutes after six o'clock. When he came out he went down to the lavatory. From the lavatory he came directly to the kitchen stockroom.'

'Was he alone in the stockroom?'

'Yes sir.'

'Can you be sure?'

'No one entered the room or left it, sir. Rosalind was in the kitchen with me all of the time. Hearing noises, I myself went in to check that he was not trying to escape. He was jumping about in the middle of the floor doing his exercises.'

'Doing his physical exercises?' The captain frowned but there was a trace of gratification in his expression.

'I think so, sir. He was stretching and leaping about all over the place. But, as instructed, I did not speak to ask him. I returned to the kitchen and waited until the maid served his supper. She put the tray on the table and returned directly to the kitchen. They did not speak at all. I left the kitchen and went to the corridor observation point. Sir!'

'Are you certain the girl did not return to the stockroom?'

'Mr Ismet had arrived by then. He said that he'd remain in the kitchen until Yetstone went to bed. At two minutes to eight, Yetstone came out. He stood in the corridor for about seven seconds then he crossed it and went through the door to the kitchen. I knew that Mr Ismet was there so I remained where I was. Three minutes later I heard Mr Ismet call out. I went in and, and found ...,'

'You had no authority to enter the kitchen, Yetstone. Why did you do so?'

'Any humane and civilised man would have done so. I heard the girl screaming in distress and went to investigate. The Turk was tearing hair from her—'

The senior guard returned and the captain waved me silent.

'Did you discover anything?'

'This, sir. It was in our messroom until a few days ago.' He placed the pepperpot on the table.

The old man picked it up and turned it over in his hands. He removed the cork and a little of the spirit it contained splashed on to the table. With meticulous care he replaced the cork and set the pepperpot down. 'Somehow you have obtained this receptacle of alcohol. In the absence of any other explanation I must accept that you obtained it by threatening the girl. Whatever the threat, she disobeyed my orders and for that she must be punished. However, not only shall the mitigating circumstances of her disobedience be taken into account, I shall also see to it that she suffers no persecution from anyone else, now or in the future.'

He sat back in his chair. 'Your own wilful misconduct is quite another matter. The most favourable interpretation I can put on your actions is to regard them as inspired by prejudice, personal weakness and a proneness to buffoonery. You have committed a number of offences, the cumulative punishment for which would disable you for some considerable time, if not for life. However, we have now made a considerable investment in you and our arrangements in Scotland are well advanced. It is not, therefore, in our interest to render you unfit to travel.'

Although plainly relieved that I had obtained nothing but a phial of alcohol, the cunning old fox meant to use the incident to his advantage. 'I understand that you have taken the signal lamp to your room. Very well. You will be taken there now and locked inside. Your sentence is suspended until the morning when an assessment will be made of your attainment in code learning and in operating the lamp.' He turned to the older guard. 'Have you searched his room? I want no more watches or trinkets turning up.'

Partially from a craving for alcohol with which to fortify my courage, but mostly to further convince him that Rosalind had been intimidated into giving me the brandy, I pleaded, 'A ration of spirits now would assist me to concentrate on what you request.' Even that boldness, I knew, did not repay my debt to the girl.

'I did not request anything. Let the fact that you are still alive and that you will receive ample spirits when you are in post be your incentives.'

From that moment a guard accompanied me wherever I went. Even when I was locked in my room, I heard them moving about outside my door. Except for mealbreaks and between the hours of midnight and six in the morning, I was made to work continuously. And I worked diligently, even for Smith, because that was the only way I was going to get out of that house alive. No one spoke to me except for instruction and for testing my progress. That, however, was no hardship because I was so utterly fatigued I could not compose even the simplest greeting. My one lasting regret was that I never saw Rosalind again and so I could neither apologise for my part in making her life more difficult than it already was, nor declare my true feelings towards her.

On Sunday evening after supper I was taken, not to the instruction room, but to the library on the first floor.

The old man, venerably elegant in his evening clothes, stood behind the table in front of the magnificent marble fireplace. He pointed to a comfortable leather armchair, and said, 'Please be seated, Yetstone.' To my guard he said, 'Wait outside until you are called.'

Such an encouraging start led me to hope that I would be offered a cigar or a glass of brandy. I was not. The old man clasped his hands at his back and looked down on me quite without expression.

'You may have some notion, Yetstone, of absconding when you leave here. I must warn you against any such attempt. From the moment you go from this house you will not only be under surveillance, you will be, as I have already told you, compromised with the authorities of this country. I have taken steps to ensure they will not only capture you but that they will have whatever evidence is needed to hang you as a traitor. Your performance, too, will be monitored. If it fails to serve my purpose and I have to abandon this project, you will not escape condemnation.'

I neither acknowledged nor made comment on those uncivil remarks.

'I am satisfied,' the old man went on dryly, 'that you are competent to perform your function, and if you do fulfil your assignment successfully, I shall endeavour to get you safely by submarine to a neutral country. With regard to your more immediate safety, much depends upon your ability both to fulfil your role and to allay suspicion. I cannot protect you from yourself. Mr Smith has touched upon most aspects but there are one or two points I should perhaps underline. You may smoke if you wish; an ashtray is beside you.'

I took a pack of cigarettes from my pocket and stood to offer him one.

'Remain seated. You have not received permission to move. Your use of English is irregular and at variance with anything spoken in this country. Your accent, grammar and syntax have elements of several languages. If questioned, admit to a Russian mother. Indeed, do not hesitate to use your Russian and American origins to excuse odd behaviour and to gain acceptance. Do your drinking in solitude and with circumspection so that you are always in command of your thoughts, words and actions when in the company of others. Do not make close friends with anyone but do not hide yourself away. Remember, you will remain an alien mystery until people have met you. Above all, do not in your conceit mistake rustic simplicity for stupidity. Finally, the crew of a U-boat may attempt to persuade you to supply them with fresh meat. Under no circumstance allow them to steal sheep. It may not seem so, but farm livestock are counted and mysterious losses will inevitably lead to day and night vigils. You may go now.'

He turned away, pulled the bell lever and left me to find my own way from the room.

Chapter Ten

ON MONDAY EVENING AT FIVE minutes to eight o'clock, I was in Kings Cross Station sitting in a third-class compartment on a train to Edinburgh. A third-class compartment! I recognised Smith's petty mind at work. The Great Melnokiv, dressed like a duke in a fine grey suit and a white shirt travelling third class!

I glared through the soot-encrusted window at the back of the fat charlatan's Inverness cape. He had hustled me onto the train, making a tremendous fluster out of finding a window seat and stowing the black tin box and a cardboard carton on the rack above.

Smith stood on the platform, not ten feet away. Typically, he dared not turn and face my indignation but looked the other way as if his responsibility lay with the comfort of the passengers on the train standing at the next platform. A cardboard carton instead of a leather suitcase and a celluloid collar instead of a linen one!

They had done nothing to give me confidence to carry off my part nor, of course, to nurture optimism that once again Madam Fame would seek me out. I was given that pauper's carton instead of a suitcase because it had no value should I try to sell it; and I was wearing the offensive, cheap, white celluloid collar because, as Smith pointed out, it could be laundered simply by wiping with a damp cloth.

Whistle in mouth and lamp in hand, the train guard marched down the platform. Doors slammed; the whistle shrilled; goodbyes rose to a crescendo; the train jolted into motion; Smith, without a wave or even a smile of relief, slipped out of sight. We were rolling northwards into the night.

Added to the degradation of a third-class compartment was the discomfort of overcrowding. Every inch of seat had flesh crammed on it. I examined my third-class travelling companions in the black glass of the window.

Sitting opposite me, her shoulders covered with a shawl and her legs with a long black skirt, a plump lady burrowed in a canvas satchel, disgorging its contents onto her lap. Next to her a nun looked with patient serenity across at her wimpled sister sitting by my side. At the other end of the compartment, six sailors – three on each side with their heads bunched together in the middle – whispered and laughed. Beyond them, the corridor was thronged with khaki-clad soldiers.

Her lap heaped with homely trash, the plump lady sat back and beamed to all her readiness to enter into conversation. Encouraged perhaps by a beatific smile, she addressed the nun at my side. 'Fair knocks ye up, this travellin'!'

The nun acknowledged the observation with a gentle inclination of her head.

'Train's packed oot,' the plump lady went on, 'lucky tae get a seat. Oh the war's tae blame I suppose. Everything's blamed on the war these days, sure it is?'

A doubtful penguin, the nun dipped her head.

The plump lady picked up her knitting, made five stitches then looked over again. 'Goin' far?' she asked, and not waiting for an answer, went on, 'Tae Edinburgh, masel'. Awfy long journey! I canna' sleep on trains. Can you sleep on trains? Passes the time right enough. My man's away back tae France. I just hope tae God – oh, I beg yer pardon sister! Didn't mean tae offend ye but I hope he comes through it all right.' She stitched the hope into her knitting then with a sigh, shook her head sadly, 'One week oot the trenches he got. Just one week. Couldn't have him wastin' two days of it travellin' tae Edinburgh and back so I came doon tae London so's we could be together as long as possible. Got tae do things like that for yer man, sure ye have? Her face glowed scarlet, 'Oh not you, sister! But if ye had a man – well anyway, ye get my meanin'.'

I flicked a speck of soot from my grey pants. My place was centre stage under the lights, not at the back of the tent among the two cent gawpers.

I shut my eyes because, even on that last morning, I had been roused at six o'clock to do exercises and to practise the codes and signals yet again. My thoughts mingled with the clickety-clack rhythm of the train wheels.

I tried to believe that every turn of those wheels carried me further from the reach of the old spy in London, but his daunting influence clung to me much as the smell of mothballs did to the old black overcoat I had been given. He had set cautions and uncertainties about me like mantraps. I feared – and I was meant to fear – the terrible consequences if I dared to step aside from the path on which he had set me.

I had been put on the train without a farthing in cash – something I must remedy at the first opportunity. A good story alone would not get me passage to a safe neutral country. However, be the amount little or large, I must acquire it discreetly, if not honestly. Arrest by the police would bring upon me the calamity of the old spy's vindictive threats.

I pondered just how real those threats were. Was the black box and its contents not the only evidence of my treacherous purpose? Were I to throw the box from the train, would I not then be free and safe? I felt sure the old devil had somehow incriminated me in other ways. Almost certainly he had sent someone to accompany me; someone armed and disguised as an ordinary traveller. Although I had recovered my little pistol, it offered no protection against an armed adversary I could not recognise.

Were I able to take the police to that house in London and expose what was going on inside, I had nothing to fear. I would be a hero. But the black box on the rack – the condemning evidence against me – was also the only evidence I could produce of that nest of spies. Of the house itself, I knew only that it was large and within earshot of a ship's horn; of its occupants I possessed nothing which would mark them out from London's loyal citizens. I needed better odds than that before I gambled my life on a confession!

One of the sailors gave a laughing shout. I opened an eye. They were playing cards on a greatcoat folded on their knees. A flicker of hope kindled in me. I had but to change places with the nun sitting beside me, chat my way into the game, and I would surely have coins to jingle by the time we reached Edinburgh. But how did I get into the game without first having money to stake? Further, an expensive grey suit with empty pockets might prompt awkward questions.

Watching half-pence being tossed onto the coat, I decided the return did not justify the risk. I consoled myself with the thought that when I was settled in the Ghillies' Croft and knew my neighbours, card games would get me the money I needed. Those straw-chewing hicks were going to find, as others had in Mistress Pettyleg's backroom, that having the company of the Great Melnikov at their table turned an innocent game of whist into a costly adventure.

I let my thoughts dwell on a happier future. South America, by all accounts, was a safe and sunny place to live. The compartment had become warm and the coach rocked gently. Yes, South America with Rosalind as a caring, adoring companion ...

A judder of brakes and the clatter of doors being opened pitched me from my sleeping paradise back into the dimly-lit, stale-tasting discomfort of the train. The two nuns in their long robes were stumbling over my legs. Passengers who had already alighted were hurrying past the window. My fuddled brain strove to make sense of what was happening. Had we arrived in Edinburgh? I rose to get my things from the rack.

I had taken down the carton and was reaching for the tin box when a porter walked past shouting, 'York! This is York! This train stopping at Newcastle and Edinburgh only! York!'

I let the box stay on the rack and looked at my watch. The time had just gone midnight. York? Newcastle? Smith had said nothing about the train stopping at these places. I hustled my wits: was this an opportunity to slip off into the night?

While I weighed my chances of escape, two perfumed ladies were boarding the train. A porter slammed the door shut behind them – which seemed to settle the question of my bolting.

The first of the two ladies was without luggage and sat where the nun had been by my side. The other stood holding a small valise and scanned the filled luggage racks with frowning annoyance.

I was returning my carton to its place beside the black box when one of the sailors sprang to his feet. He took the valise from the lady and, pushing me aside, held it up expectantly. I left my carton in its place beside the box and sat down. The smart lad had grabbed the lady's problem; his the privilege of solving it.

By the time the valise had been found a place and everyone seated, the train had left York and was picking up speed. I studied the two who had joined us. They were of an age with myself. Of the lady by my side I could see only that her hands were tucked into a fur muff on her lap. Her companion on the other side wore a large flower-decked hat and sat very erect resting her gloved hands on the handle of a parasol. I watched as she cast her eye over the sailors and dismissed the plump lady's presence with little more than a sideways dip of her eyes. As if that were merely a prelude, she turned her attention to me. Beginning with my shoes, she contemplated each item of my dress with a tiny frown as if setting a value on it. Our eyes met. She held my gaze boldly, yet with a sort of indifference. I looked away. With a little sigh, so did she.

The sailors had given up playing cards and the plump lady's hands lay idle on top of her knitting. A restful tranquillity seemed to be settling on the compartment. I stretched my legs and lit a cigarette.

Over the flaring match I saw the lady in the flower-decked hat stiffen with indignation. Her red lips crabbed with malice. She drew a sharp breath through her nose and, leaning across the plump lady's lap, said primly, 'Pardon me!' Reaching down, she picked up the window strap, gave it a violent tug, cast it away and, with a tight little smile, resumed her erect posture.

The window dropped with a crash and driving wind peppered my face with icy rain and needle-sharp particles of soot. I bent into the hurricane, grabbed the strap and slammed the window shut again. I made no protest as I ground out the cigarette under my shoe. No doubt she reckoned she had levelled the score in the matter of finding a place for her valise.

For several minutes she rested her cheek on a long, gloved forefinger and regarded me thoughtfully before laying aside her parasol and withdrawing a paper bag of candies from her handbag. She presented the open bag to her friend, to the plump lady at her side and then to each of the sailors. Turning in my direction, she did not quite offer the open bag to me but, holding it between us as if she just might, she leaned forward and asked, 'Are you by chance in mufti, sir?'

'Mufti? Not sure I have your meaning, ma'm.'

'Are you a serviceman in civilian clothes?'

'No ma'm. I'm from the United States of America.'

'Are you indeed!'

'Yes, ma'm.'

'And being from the United States of America, does that mean you cannot wear a uniform and do your duty?'

The question hushed the compartment. All eyes were now focussed on me.

'My duty, ma'm?'

'Yes indeed. Surely it is the duty of every English-speaking gentleman to rally to the colours and fight for the king. Australia, Canada and New Zealand did not waver.'

'The U.S.A., ma'm, is no longer a British colony.'

'But, I understand, bravely taking the profit while our boys face up to the Bosche!'

'If you will pardon me ma'm, there happens to be many good German citizens in the U.S.A.'

'Aha! One of those, are you?'

Perspiration trickled down my back. The train had become a steamy jungle and that lioness was intent on a kill. 'No ma'm, my origins are Russian.'

She sat back smiling too sweetly. 'Then surely you are travelling in the wrong direction for the Russian front? Or perhaps you are perfectly aware of that!'

In every part of that jungle the other creatures watched this savaging, glad they were not her prey. My false position made dealing with this mischief-maker a delicate business. My face felt as if it had been scrubbed with a wire brush. I turned to the window, pretending indifference and hoping to end the exchange.

'With all those Germans and Englishmen – and of course Russians – in the United States of America, I'm surprised there is not another civil war. Wouldn't you think so, Clarissa?'

Beside me, Clarissa withdrew a hand from her muff and replied, 'I shall enquire, Hilda.' She delicately tapped my knee with the case for her spectacles. 'Perhaps sir, you can enlighten us. With such a confusion of enemies, is there not a danger of civil war in America?'

I turned briefly, and said, 'No, ma'm.'

'No Hilda, it is seemingly not the case. Perhaps the Germans just snatch the dear little Belgians as they did in Europe and make them into slaves like the niggers. One wonders what a brave Russian would do in that event.'

Hilda raised the point of her parasol and prodded my thigh. There was a desire to inflict pain in the force she used. 'Would you try to stop a German killing a Belgian in the United States of America, sir?'

'Ma'm, I don't know many Germans or Belgians and those I do know get along just fine.' I tucked my head back into the corner and shut my eyes. No hope now of receiving a candy!

'Can you imagine, Clarissa, how simply awful it must be for a fit young man to find himself travelling away from the scene of action and valour?'

'Unless of course he were a German spy travelling to Scotland.

I'm told the police regularly catch spies coming off trains at Inverness, turn them round and send them right back to the Tower of London for shooting.'

I knew that was no more than a jibe, but nevertheless a maggot of doubt squirmed in that all too tiny portion of assurance I possessed.

A sailor's voice butted in, 'Aye, ye may hiv something there, missus. Heard that meself like, and me mate that's stationed at Invergordon says civvies hiv got tae carry permits now. If ye don't hiv a pass ye'r in real bother. A special military zone like. Been that way since August.'

I longed for the train – for the whole embattled world – to stop so that I could re-assess my undertaking. But the train and the world hurtled on relentlessly. As if in a deep sleep, I let my head drop forward hoping thus to conceal my dismay from those two hunting cats. I would have given a great deal to know where in Scotland Invergordon was, and Inverness too, and if either lay between Edinburgh and Dunmallach.

If what the sailor said was true, then the old spy would have known it too, for that was not the sort of intelligence he missed. Yes, that was why the cunning old man had seen in me just the piece he needed to make his plan work! A German, as he had half admitted, would have little hope of getting through a security screen, but a Russian or an American would be much better placed. Moreover, until I had been kidnapped into his organisation, my life, in espionage terms, had been innocent. At worst, even if my purpose were discovered and I was arrested, tried and shot, what had he lost? A suit of clothes and a signal lamp! By cutting me off from all assistance and yet retaining the means to expose and destroy me, he was coercing me – if I wished to survive - into using my utmost ingenuity in his cause.

Listening to Hilda's braying voice intimidating the compartment I once again felt like that tethered chick in a coop of polecats. To get free I had to behave with such caution I aroused the suspicions of no one. Yet I must also act swiftly and decisively the instant an opportunity presented itself. Top of my list, then, must be to find out if I had an escort on the journey. In doing so, however, I must not reveal my intention to escape.

My posture had become cramped and uncomfortable so I opened my eyes and sat up.

I had scarcely raised my head when Hilda's sarcastic voice cut through the rattle of the wheels, 'Ah, our American adventurer – or is he Russian – has rejoined us! And at such an opportune moment! We have decided, sir, that we shall all subscribe to the price of a glass of rum for each of our brave jack tars. You would not wish to be left out, I'm sure. A shilling each, I say!'

'No need for that, missus. An' less than a shillin'll get us a rum,' a sailor protested.

'Nonsense! Our Russian companion – or is he American? – will probably insist on nothing less than a sovereign!'

Had my pockets been filled with five pound notes, I might have refused with dignity and firmness. But my pockets were empty. The Great Melnikov, dressed in traitor's clothes – oh, fine elegant clothes – did not have one red cent with which to buy off his shame. Mortification snatched away the props of any brazen show I might have put up leaving me helpless and exposed to their ridicule. Jeering eyes stared at me from every quarter. My face stung as from the blast of a furnace, a furnace in which my honour was melting like rancid butter.

'Come, come, sir. A shilling cannot mean that much to you!'

My numb lips moved and pitiful words stumbled into the mocking silence. 'Won't have any British money until I get to Edinburgh.'

'Really? How very, very remarkable ... and convenient!'

The hush of sneering disbelief seemed to go on and on and on. If my heart had been a wad of dollar bills I would have torn it from my chest just to prove my lie. In the stillness of their derision my fiery ears heard the homespun lady facing me say, 'Dinna fret sir. I'll put in a florin – that's from us both – and ye can pay it back at yer convenience.'

Words gurgled from my throat, but whether of gratitude or of indifference, I knew not. My right hand fumbled in my pocket for a bottle which was no longer there and retrieved instead the pack of cigarettes.

The sailor who had taken the lady's valise leaned forward truculently, 'Ah don't think ye should light another fag, mister.'

With as much domination as I could muster, I asked, 'Why not?'

'Why not? I'll tell ye why not. 'Cos them boxes ye've filled the rack wi' are more'n likely goin' tae drop on top of ye if ye do, man!'

'How very gallant of you!' Hilda exclaimed with delight. 'But really, we leave the train at Newcastle and we are almost there now.' She turned disdainfully to me, 'I'm so very, very relieved that despite having no English money you appear to have been able to purchase English cigarettes. Now I must get my valise.'

I made up my mind then that whatever the consequence, I was getting off the train at Newcastle. The assignment I had been forced to accept was beyond my endurance. The English were an odious people, puffed with insolence and quite without kindness. I would take only the cardboard carton and leave the black box on the rack. I stood up and turned, intending to take down the carton.

Instantly, the sailor was at my side, 'No ye don't,' he said, pushing me back and placing possessive hands on the lady's valise. 'Ye hivna shown much consideration up tae now so ye can just sit down again!'

I certainly had no desire to contend for the lady's gratitude, so I resumed my seat. In any event the prospect of my making a quick getaway vanished when a line of soldiers from the corridor crowded into the compartment, blocking the way to the door. Soon there was general commotion as bags and overcoats were retrieved from the luggage racks on both sides. But I did not miss seeing the gallant sailor nudge a mate, cast a mean look in my direction and arrange himself last in the file waiting to depart.

The train came to a halt with a crashing of doors being thrown open. I remained in my seat because the floor space was taken by those already on their feet and looked out on travel-crumpled passengers straggling by. Last in line leaving our compartment, the gallant sailor swung a heavy kitbag on to his shoulder and came forward. I was ready and the vicious kick he lashed at my legs as he passed struck only the seat support.

It was my turn then. I felt I owed him for more than a badly timed kick. I half-rose, put my hand on the bottom end of his kitbag and gave it a mighty push sideways. Its weight and momentum corkscrewed his body so that while his boots stayed pointing to the open door, his head and trunk turned to face me. I placed my right shoe in his stomach, straightened my leg and ejected him, spinning backwards, out of the door like a champagne cork.

He landed on his back on the platform beside his kitbag, from which a smashed bottle of rum poured its contents over the concrete. Fast as a jack-in-the-box he was on his feet and pushing his sleeves up over muscular arms. Before he could reach the carriage door, his mates took over. Two caught and held his arms, stopping his forward thrust, two slammed the compartment door shut and gripped the handle to prevent me from getting out, while the fifth tried to salvage the contents of his kitbag.

I stood at the window laughing at him – a dividend of my superiority – until I glimpsed a tall, elderly figure dressed in a black coat and a top-hat standing near to the train. He had evidently watched the fracas and was now turning to board or re-board. Uncertain whether I had recognised an austere countenance or just imagined I had, I sat down, surprised to find how hard I was breathing.

The encounter with the sailor should have put new heart into me. Instead, all my uncertainties returned.

Across from me the stout lady had lifted her legs out of the way on to the seat. 'My, my,' she said, her tone a blend of admiration and rebuke, 'An' yer no' the big softie ye look. But ye shouldna' have done that to the wee sailor laddie; it wasna' him that was gettin' at ye. An' if ye'll excuse me being personal, dae ye ken your collar's fleein' away.'

I turned to the window and discovered that one end of the celluloid collar had unfastened itself from my front stud and was flapping at the side of my head like the wing of a wounded seagull. While I fastened the collar the stout lady swung her feet down to the floor. She leaned over in a motherly way and patted my knee, 'Don't let they two harridans from the white feather brigade get at ye, sir.'

I smoothed my rumpled hair, 'White feather brigade, ma'm?'

'Oh aye, they were from the white feather brigade all right, even if they didna' give ye one. But, believe me, they know nothin' aboot it. If they did, they widna' be sae daft. It's all right them shamin' lads into the trenches so long as they dinna' have tae go themselves. My man's oot there, and my brother wis one of the first tae go. And where is he now? I'll tell ye, sir: he's lying in a military hospital wi' both his legs blown awa'!'

Dialogue with the lady was beyond me for it took ten minutes to gather her meaning whenever she spoke. I smiled politely, picked up a newspaper which had been left on the seat and gave my attention to advertisements for lozenges which would invigorate our brave boys at the front and for cider which would ward off gout. When next I looked over, the stout lady's hands lay still on her lap and her eyes were closed. She could after all sleep on trains.

For two hours an agreeable silence filled the compartment then, with a crash like thunder, a southbound express charged alongside. The noise woke the stout lady. She rubbed the window with her sleeve and peered out. 'Musselburgh,' she announced, rising, 'Twenty minutes and I'll be home!' She buttoned herself into a tweed coat. 'Mind what I said now. Join up if ye want to, but dinna' let them two bitches bark ye into it.'

My brain had not been idle while the stout lady slept. I reasoned that I could desert and be sure to escape retribution only if I abandoned the black box and gave my escort – if indeed I had one – the slip. To flush him out, I decided that when we got to Edinburgh I would stay on the train after the other passengers had departed. Ultimately he must take some action, if only to confirm that I was still on board. In doing so, he must surely disclose his identity.

Once I had identified my man, eluding him should not prove impossible. Having lived all my life in cities, given a fifty yard start I could hide myself beyond any man's discovery.

Wearily the train snaked into the station and, venting a deafening blast of steam, stopped. The stout lady bid me good-day, good luck and was gone.

I pulled on the old black overcoat and sat in the corner of the compartment furthest from the door. My enemies, whoever they were, must sooner or later disclose themselves because I had been given no directions regarding the next part of my journey.

Chapter Eleven

I WAITED FOR SEVEN MINUTES during which time no one appeared to manifest any interest in my whereabouts. The more optimism swelled inside me, the more I ground my knuckles together. Whatever I did next would decide my future.

I stood up and searched beyond the open carriage door. The passengers from my train had long since departed. I was about to turn away and collect my boxes when the tiny movement of a head, half-hidden by the platform railings, caused light to glint on the glass of a pair of steel-framed spectacles. Behind the spectacles and below a green bowler hat, two eyes were steadfastly watching me. I realised that I had lost my advantage. They knew where I was but I did not know how many they were or where.

If I left the train without the black box, what kind of end was I making for myself? Doubts of every sort shattered my confidence, as the old devil in London intended they should.

In the end I decided I would take both the black box and the carton as far as the ticket gate. If no one accosted me there, hell, I'd take my chance, ditch the box and run. If nothing else, I now had a reason to get off the train. I pulled the metal box from the rack and picked up the carton. When I looked out again, hat and spectacles had disappeared.

Once through the ticket gate I paused to scan the scene for anyone remotely resembling an escort. No one was about except two old porters and a burly lounger propped by a pillar who swigged beer from a bottle. A tug on my sleeve caused me to turn. I found myself looking down on a green bowler hat sitting on a nest of silver hair. Two anxious blue eyes looked into my face from behind steel-framed spectacles. An Irish voice asked, 'Would I be mistaken, sir, if I addressed you as Mr Yetstone?'

Expressionless, I regarded the shabby little man who stood at my side clinging with one arm to a wicker basket. I dismissed his question with a growl, 'Why the devil should you or anyone else seek to address me as Mr Yetstone?'

He was taken aback. 'You're not Mr Yetstone? Then indeed I'm sorry in more ways than one for troubling you.'

I moved on but he followed me, staying close by my side. Had

I been certain that he had no accomplice I would have abandoned the box and made my getaway. Too much was at stake. 'And if my name were Yetstone, what of it?'

His blue eyes twinkled. 'Ha! Teasing me were you, sir? Dangling me at the end of your little joke, eh? The name's Norton. Brought your breakfast. When they told us you hadn't got off the train at York or Newcastle, we knew you must be our man.'

'Who told you I had not got off the train at York or Newcastle? And who the hell are we?'

'And I'm to stay with you, Mr Yetstone, and to see you safely on to the six-fifteen to Oban.'

'Are you indeed!'

'On that sir, my instructions are specific. From the lips of Mr Hart himself.'

'Since it concerns me, pray tell me where does Mr Hart come into this?'

'Field and Hart, solicitors. My employers in another city. We acted as your agent in the matter of renting the property on the west coast.'

'Well then, Mr Norton, as my agent I shall be obliged if you will now advance me a sum of money. A modest amount will do for the moment.'

He cocked his head on one side and wagged a finger at me. 'Ah-ha, that I would and happily if it were for me to decide, but there again, y'see sir, my instructions are specific. They tell me you're an ... you've had a hard time of it lately and 'tis for your own good and nothing else that you're to receive no money. No, not in any form. You understand my position, sir? Now here is a seat. Rest yourself on it and eat your breakfast.'

Looking at his ink-stained hands reaching from threadbare cuffs, I knew it was indeed pointless hoping for money from him. I doubted if he even possessed the cost of a penny omnibus fare. I tried another line. 'They tell me one needs a permit to get into some parts of Scotland. Is that true?'

He displayed no great interest. 'Do they say that now?'

'Yes they do, Norton, and I don't have a permit. What do your specific instructions say about that?'

He spread the contents of the basket on a white cloth which he had laid on the seat at my side, then he went along and sat at the other end. As if I no longer existed, he pulled a short clay pipe from his pocket and proceeded to stuff the bowl with tobacco. That done, he looked up at the smoke-filled roof, pulled on his nose then tilted his face in my direction. 'There was no word about permits sir, no word at all.'

'Then me boy-o, had you not better go and find some words?'

'Ah now d'ye see, Mr Yetstone, there's a difficulty there. Mr Hart will be sound asleep in the comfort of his bed at this hour and 'tis more than my job is worth to disturb him with the telephone.' He put the pipe in his mouth, struck a match and then solemnly watched the flame until it burned down to his fingers and he had to toss it away. He took the pipe from his mouth. 'But if the matter is giving you concern, I'll take myself down to the Stationmaster's office and make enquiries.' He rose from the seat wagging the pipe stem at me. 'Now you will please stay here and get on with your breakfast.'

The caution alone was not enough for I saw him nod to the ruffian with a lurcher dog who lounged against a pillar close to my back.

What other forms did their lack of trust take, I wondered as I cracked the shell of a hard-boiled egg.

Norton came back.

'Now sir, is your breakfast to your liking?' he asked, pulling out his pipe and sitting down.

'Fine, just fine. And?'

'Oh the permits! Now there you were both right and wrong.' He pushed the short pipestem between his teeth and struck a match. With his cheeks going into deep hollows, he puffed and puffed and puffed.

'Are you not going to tell me then where I was right and where I was wrong?'

He waved clouds of smoke away from his face. 'Nothing for you to worry about, nothing at all.' He tossed the spent match away. 'Rumour has it they picked up a German spy – or maybe it was two – trying to get into a naval base up north. There's plenty of rumours about if you're making a collection.'

The oat cookie crumbled in my fingers. I tried to hold my voice steady and to show no more than a mild interest. 'And about permits, Norton, did you find out about permits?'

'No permits needed where you are going. Not to Oban. That's the word just now, anyhow.'

I could get neither information nor reassurance from Norton on anything which really mattered. Like a cagey old bird, he kept fluttering just out of reach of my questions. He pretended to misunderstand me or else answered with some irrelevant, droll anecdote. By the time I had breakfasted I knew no more of the hazards of my journey and, if it were possible, less about the measures taken to secure me. I shivered and blamed the bitter wind which thrust itself between the folds of my clothes.

Just on six o'clock, Norton tapped the dottle from his pipe. 'Now then,' he said, 'let me discharge my duty by seeing you onto the train for Oban.' He must indeed have thought me in wretched mental condition.

The sky was shedding darkness and tradesmen were already going about their business of lifting and dispatching goods. After accompanying me to public toilets, Norton found me a seat on the train, shook my hand, winked familiarly and swaggered off.

Although a full ten minutes before departure time, I was not the first to board. A traveller, muffled in a dark blue overcoat, was already curled deep in a corner seat of the compartment. His face was concealed by a thick woollen scarf, up-turned collar and pulled-down hat, but I fancied the fellow watched me settle myself in the corner furthest from him.

The little train chuff-chuffed out of the station. A shell of silence encased each of my early morning travelling companions so, gratefully, I viewed the smokey procession of spires and tenements, mills and mansions, shops and parks as they loomed up and then vanished behind us.

City streets gave way to fields and farmhouses. The light of day spread over the land exposing its patchwork of fields and plebeian peasantry: a labourer plodding behind his plough, a peasant girl feeding steaming mash to hens, a shawled crone carrying two baskets of cabbages.

Any hamlet comprising a mansion, a cluster of cottages and a church was reason enough for the train to stop. At every such halt an interchange of passengers took place, but the muffled fellow - whom I suspected of being my escort – remained lodged in his corner. His body was young. I guessed the coils of woollen scarf, the upturned collar and the pulled down hat most probably concealed one of the guards from the house in London. The wall which really held me prisoner, however, was the wall of ignorance.

Fields gave way to a more rugged landscape. Mountains, massed against the northern sky, formed the backdrop to a castle built on ramparts of craggy rock. The train turned westward. The sky cleared and shafts of sunlight danced in treetops or splintered on wet rocks in boisterous rivers. Sometimes the twigs of silver birches brushed the windows of the train, flickering their shadows along the walls inside.

I had set out from London buoyed with the prospect of escape, but I knew now that even were I to open the door when the train slowed and jump out, I would not survive in that wilderness of heather, forest and flooded glens for more than a day.

I had no story ready should I be challenged on the contents of the black tin box. It had never occurred to me that I might be. Oban drew nearer by the minute and every minute increased my conviction that I would be challenged. Nothing I could think of seemed plausible.

There were four of us left in the compartment: myself, two old ladies and the silent man who had been first on the train. I held a belief that every man, if the right words were used, could be inspired to deeds of heroism, persuaded to betray or moved to acts of compassion. Of all the words I knew, which combination would that fellow barter for my release?

He sat so still and quiet I thought he must be fast asleep. I searched in the folds of his scarf and upturned collar for a glimpse of his features. When at last my gaze penetrated the shadows below his wide-brimmed hat I was shocked to find two very hostile eyes looking out at me.

For the first time throughout the journey he stirred. I heard the shuffle of his feet and from the corner of my eye saw him rise, his great bulk blocking the light. He came towards me, swaying ponderously between the seats like a drunk. Even when his shadow settled over me, I went on looking out of the window with what I hoped seemed unconcern. I braced my legs and my left hand gripped the butt of the pistol.

He stood right in front of me, his feet between mine and so close I could smell his clothing.

I did not look up, even when he dashed his felt hat on to the seat at my side. He made a sound something between a growl and a snarl.

His long woollen scarf fell like a thick rope before my face, coiling itself into a heap at my feet. A seal-like bark challenged me. I held my right fist ready and raised my eyes.

Above me, two watering eyes looked down from a grotesque skull. Most of his head was hairless. Stubs of gristle represented his nose and ears. The skin covering his face was like a puckered mask of mottled, cracking leather with fiery crevices where it had been stitched together. A white scar dragged the corner of his mouth upwards, making him seem to leer. He wiped the saliva which trickled from the corner of his mouth with the back of his hand and spoke as if his tongue were held in a clamp.

'Ish what you want to see, ish it?' he slobbered. 'Been spying and gawping since you got on the train. Seen you!' He paused, gasping, 'Have a bloody good look then! Go on! I'll take off the hospital blues and show you the rest. Want me to do that? Make you feel handsome? Think maybe I'll get a job in a circus, do you?'

He reached up and gripped the rack with both hands to get support while he recovered his breath. His awful disfigurement shocked but it was the discharge of his bitter emotion which suffocated the compartment with inexpressible embarrassment and compassion.

After a few minutes he let go of the rack and sank back onto the seat facing me.

I looked out, unseeing, at the sunlit trees and sparkling water and heard myself say, 'Thought you might be someone I know. Mistaken. Sorry.'

I heard him sigh as he leaned back on the seat. His voice was a trace less harsh or perhaps he was simply exhausted. 'Not mishtaken. I am shomeone else but God knows who.'

I gathered up his scarf and hat and laid them on the seat at his side. One of the old ladies, her voice cracking emotionally and tears streaming down her cheeks, asked, 'Och my poor boy, my poor, poor boy, what have they done to you? Was it in Flanders?'

'Not in France. Bloody U-boat in the Bay of Biscay.'

'Oh my! Terrible things the submarines!'

'Diabolic! Rats of the sea! Sunday morning. Bang! Then he sneaks away leaving us to roast in the flaming oil we'd been carrying.'

A wailing chant of outrage and sympathy gushed from the old women but I sat absolutely still and silent, made voiceless by the thought I had almost addressed the fellow as my escort. A single word could betray me. I was convinced my black box beamed out its guilty purpose and I knew then that the inscription on my watch, stolen from the war wounded, was enough to hang me from the nearest lamppost. How that evil old man in London had shackled me to his service!

The disfigured sailor leaned forward and raised an apologetic hand, 'Shorry about the outburst. Folk can't but look. But y'see, I'm terrified by the thought of getting off the train at Oban. Strangers like yourself I'll get used to in time no doubt and even my wife ... well, she's seen me in hospital. But, oh man, it's my three lovely wee girls. Will they ever bear to look at me again? I'll not dare steal a kiss even as they sleep lest they wake and die of terror.'

He bent forward, covering his face with his hands, and he did not raise his head again until the train came to a standstill in Oban station. 'Get you and the ladies off the train,' he said, 'I'll follow when the place is quiet.'

Discovering that he was not my keeper and listening to the man's anxieties had somehow eased my own. I could do nothing to help him and it would be foolish to involve myself. I strode down the platform with the black box on my shoulder, the carton swinging at my side and breathing cool sea air. Not until I had pushed into the slow-moving funnel of passengers converging on the ticket gate did my bravado desert me. Standing, one on either side of the gate, a massive police sergeant and a constable examined each of the passengers as they passed through.

The constable cast a glance over those of us still to come, a glance which first passed over me then swiftly flicked back. He studied me for a few seconds then spoke to the sergeant. Impassive as agents of doom, they watched and waited as I was jostled towards them.

Chapter Twelve

ALTHOUGH I LOOKED ALL around me in hope, I knew that I was the one for whom those two policemen waited. I stopped breathing. A faintness threatened to overcome me. The station swung like a pendulum. I stood still, gasping for air and bracing myself against the press of the crowd. It was too late to simply abandon the box; too late to do anything but pretend to be half-witted. Innocence, however, was not so easily mocked and I thought it wise to move the box on my shoulder so that it hid my face from the policemen. Yielding to the push of the mob, I moved on again.

At the gate, I set the carton down, handed over my ticket, picked up the carton and, holding my breath, stepped through. One, two, three, four paces: a heavy hand fell on my shoulder and a stern voice intoned, 'Are you the man from London?'

It was a daunting question. Unslept, unshaven, unkempt and panic-stricken, I tried to compose some lie to uphold denial. My brain throbbed with perplexity while the police sergeant searched my face remorselessly for an answer. Guilt dried my mouth. I set the carton on the ground and mopped my forehead with my sleeve.

'Have you travelled to Oban from London?'

The only words in my head were, they turn them round and send them back to the Tower of London for shooting, 'No ... yes ... I think so.' I shivered involuntarily.

'Then you are the man we are waiting for. The constable will escort you.'

They were the words I had half-expected, yet I stood bewildered. The sergeant had not asked to see a permit, he had not sought to examine the contents of my boxes, he had not enquired my name or purpose. They already knew all about me. I strove to gather my swirling wits. Had the old spy in London delivered me for execution? Surely I had given him no grounds to do so? Then it came to me. The Turk! The treacherous Turk taking his revenge had betrayed both me and his master! Only the Turk could have done this!

The police sergeant gripped my arm and repeated with stern solemnity, 'Take your boxes and go with the constable.'

The old constable waited with corpulent dignity until I had picked up the carton then, like a great ship getting under way, he sundered the ring of spectators that had gathered and I followed close in his wake through the rising growl of questioning voices. He neither stopped nor turned, but left me to struggle with my burden as best I could.

Outside the station, my senses recognised the sunlight, the hard road under my feet and the smell of tarry rope and fish, but nothing had any real meaning. I could not comprehend how men and women went about their business with so little concern for the calamity which was overwhelming me.

I was not only hungry and thirsty, my thoughts were slithering about like a duck walking on ice. The world was coming at me faster than I could handle it. But, little by little, the constricting grip of fear on my reason relaxed and I realised I had but a few minutes in which to contrive my escape. The seafront promenade was busy enough to impede the old constable were I to make a dash for freedom. I surveyed my surroundings. The half-circle of shops and houses round the bay would not conceal me for long. Somehow I must get back to the railway and hide myself in the station buildings, sidings or wagons until I could stow away on an outward bound train.

The constable was a pace ahead of me so, as if taking a moment's rest, I put my boxes on the ground – they were unnecessary baggage now – and rubbed my shoulder, thus letting the distance between us increase.

As if divining my thoughts, he too stopped and hailing a workman in faded blue overalls, half-turned in my direction. The wind carried his words back to me.

'I've got the American drunk for you, Wattie. The one for Dunmallach. You'll need to keep an eye on him for he's in tremendous bad shape.'

'Dammit!' the man in overalls replied, 'The last thing we need is trouble from a drunk!'

'You'll have no trouble with this one. He's sober for a start and looks as harmless as a sick rabbit.'

I stood dumbfounded. The drunk for Dunmallach, the policeman had said. What did that mean? I had not been drunk for nearly two weeks.

The two men turned and the constable, as if I were a backward child, waved me on while Wattie came forward to meet me with his hand thrust out. 'Well! Well! Well! So you're the gentleman from America! Let me help you with your boxes then.'

I put down the cardboard box and his hand gripped mine in a crushing, vice-like grip which took the very breath from me.

'You've had a long, long journey. All the way from London! By jove and you'll be tired! Come away now and we'll get you settled down.'

I was more than ever bemused. Even when he released my hand and the blood throbbed back into its bruised tissues, I could find no words of reply. We were standing on the sidewalk close to the sea wall. The jostling townspeople going about their affairs gave us not the slightest attention. Wattie nudged me towards the sea wall. Moored below, a little steamer not seventy feet long belched black smoke from its single funnel. A ladder with its foot on the deck was propped against the quay beside us.

'Give Wattie your boxes. You'll break your neck if you try to take them both down yourself,' the constable said, and Wattie bent as if I were an infant and gently prised the string on the carton from my fingers.

The policeman stood at my back, Wattie stood at my side and seagulls hung in the sky above. No one seemed to think any further explanation was needed so I walked towards the ladder. Steadying the black box on my shoulder with one hand, I swung a foot over and on to the top rung.

As I set foot on the gritty deck, Wattie finished his conversation with the constable, put the carton on his shoulder and with practised ease started to follow me down. While I waited for him to join me, a burly figure in a soiled blue uniform with tarnished brass buttons emerged from the sulphurous smoke that swirled round the base of the funnel. Ignoring my presence, the black-bearded face at my shoulder turned upwards, 'Is that the best speed you can move yourself, Wattie? You're not waiting for one of the gulls to lay an egg in your pocket, are you?'

'It's Mr Yetstone for Dunmallach, skipper,' Wattie shouted back, continuing to descend at a leisurely pace.

'Has he any more luggage to come?'

'No, just the two boxes.'

'Right. Show him to the foc's'le and come you back on deck right away.' For the first time, the skipper acknowledged my presence. Without introduction of any sort he said gruffly, 'We are engaged on government business. Wattie will show you below.' And with that for a welcome, he disappeared into another down-draught of smoke.

As we made our way forward, Wattie spoke over his shoulder. 'The skipper's in a bad mood. Doesn't like navigating at night but there's nothing else for it now. It wasn't just waiting for yourself that is to blame for us being late. The coalmen weren't ready for us either.'

Scarcely listening to his words let alone understanding them, I followed him down into the warm fo'c'sle.

'You can sleep on the bottom bunk on the starboard side, Mr Yetstone, and stow your boxes on the one above,' Wattie said, throwing my carton on to it. 'Settle yourself down and I'll be back in ten minutes to get you some dinner. He can be very unreasonable when he's in a bad mood can the skipper.' He looked into my face with concern. 'Aye, you've had a long, irksome journey, I can see that. If you want to relieve yourself, the place is up on deck, aft.'

I stood where I was until I heard him go up the companion-way then I put my black box on the top bunk beside my carton, took off my overcoat and stretched my weary, muddled frame on the bunk below. I had slept but two hours in the previous thirty and my world was a turmoil of doubts and questions.

Smith had bundled me out of the house in London and into a waiting cab without one word of explanation or direction concerning the journey which I was to undertake. I had gone forth with such burgeoning hopes of escape, I had asked for none.

I lay perspiring in the overpowering heat of the fo'c'sle and looked at the underside of the bunk above. I had all along supposed that my safety and the security of what I was engaged on depended on keeping the fact of my existence hidden from the police. Yet the police had been asked to meet me off the train and now I was on a ship engaged on government business. Was I being carried to an island prison? Was that the government business the ship was engaged on? Or had I missed the key to the purpose of my journey while I had been daydreaming during Smith's dreary lectures? If I had, it must forever remain a mystery.

The heightened rumble of the engines and a shuddering vibra-tion of the ship's frame told me that we were under way. There was little I could do now but allow myself to be carried to wherever they chose to take me.

As I lay dozing, words drifted in my mind like flotsam. The word, mystery, bobbing about like a cork, became entangled with other words and formed the combination, 'you will remain an alien mystery until people have met you'. The dry, emotionless intonation of the words sparked recollection. They were among the words of advice the old spy had given me before I left the house in London.

The din of the engines seemed to diminish. I spoke the words aloud and the astonishing truth dawned on me. By asking the police to meet me off the train, that crafty old fox had virtually nullified their interest in the stranger who had come to live in the Ghillies' Croft and put a gloss of drunkard's innocence on everything – however unusual – I might do. To them I was the pathetic American drunk; a comical figure perhaps, but harmless as a sick rabbit. So no one need tell them that I acted strangely. They had seen it for themselves! Moreover, he could be sure that I would see the covert threat of exposure which lay behind the act. The desiccated old tyrant was a master of his craft!

The mixture of admiration and relief produced a sort of exhilaration in me. I threw my legs over the side of the bunk and rocked forward and back. Now I wanted that old man's respect and admiration more than anything on earth – and I would get it! I would get it by showing him that I was the more brilliant performer. While he thought I was dancing in his ring to the crack of his whip, I would, with a quicksilver leap, vanish as if I had never existed.

Breathlessly I mopped my brow and sat back. Wattie was standing at the foot of the companionway. He kept one foot on the bottom step and looked at me with a mixture of alarm and concern. I waved him in. 'It's all right,' I said, 'I just remembered the words of one I thought held me close.'

'Did you now?' Wattie replied in his slow way, and still watching me warily, edged towards the stove. 'The words of the departed can make sad remembering. But sit you in to the table. You'll feel better with a bowl of broth and a plate of tatties and herring inside you. The skipper will be down in a minute.'

Even as he spoke the skipper of the little steamer came down the companionway. Black-bearded, burly and overbearing, he tossed his cap with a sweep of his arm onto the bunk beside my boxes.

'Aye! Aye! Aye! They tell me you are from the United States of America, Mr Yetstone.' He shouted as if the length of the table which separated us was six cables of wind-torn sea. 'And what part of the great U.S.A. would that be?'

His bombastic manner served only to encourage me to demonstrate his provincialism with a show of indifference. I spoke the first place which came to mind. 'New York.'

'New York! By jove and many's the time we have sailed into New York.'

Amused by the ruffian's boast, I laughed. 'You're not telling me that you cross the Atlantic Ocean in this old—,' I was about to say tarboiler, but seeing his face darken, I finished, 'in this little steamer?'

'So you're an expert on crossing the Atlantic, are you, Mr Yetstone? Let me tell you then, this wee puffer will take you anywhere in the world you could ever want to go, but it was not in her I went to New York. It was when I was an officer on the luxury liners. But that's not what we were talking about.' He leaned back to let Wattie place a bowl of steaming broth on the table in front of him. 'You were going to tell us all about yourself and your adventures in New York were you not?'

I was going to do no such thing. Echoing his cadence, I parodied his words. 'New York is as fine a city as any you could find in the world, but I did not spend my life there.' I said to Wattie, 'My, that broth smells mighty good!' and bending over the steaming bowl, I scooped a brimming spoonful.

I was conscious of a strained silence as the scalding liquid passed my lips and boiled on my tongue. The silence was broken by the skipper saying with weighty emphasis, 'Will you please say grace, Mr Yetstone.'

I spluttered and choked on the broth.

'Very well, if you cannot manage it, I will say it myself.'

While he intoned a long, sanctimonious grace, I decided to change the subject of our conversation from my affairs to his. Echoing his amen, I asked, 'You're on charter to the government, are you skipper?'

'When they need a ship they can rely on. Do you know, Mr Yetstone, without ships like this – aye, wee tarboilers you may call them – the Grand Fleet, dreadnoughts and all, would never get out of port.'

'Ah yes, the business you spoke of. What's that about?'

'It's best you don't know these things,' he replied cryptically.

Wattie spoke off-handedly from beside the stove, 'They riveted some deck plates together in one of the Glasgow shipyards for a supply vessel up north and then discovered the thing was too wide to go on the railway and too heavy to go by road.'

The skipper shook his head. 'Wattie, Wattie, you've no business to be giving out confidential information to all and sundry. Would I not have told him myself if it was proper for him to know?'

'Huh! Confidential? And do you think Mr Yetstone or anyone in Dunmallach gives a hoot what is in the hold?' Wattie replied, stung by the public rebuke.

'Man, man, you're missing the point as usual. It's just that there's a matter of trust and principle involved when a ship is engaged on the government's business.'

'Principle, is it?' Wattie looked over his shoulder and spoke with a laugh. 'And what kind of principle are you talking about, Captain? Have we not twenty tons of coal on board for Sir John Harris at Glenannack Castle that the government knows nothing about? And is the engineer not shovelling Sir John's coal into the ship's boilers this very minute? For that matter, would we be holding this conversation at all if you had not taken Mr Yetstone himself as an unlisted passenger? Och, you are a fine one to be talking about principles!' Wattie turned back to his stove, confident he had won the argument.

Not greatly put out, the skipper leaned back in his chair with his arms folded over his broad chest. 'You have learned nothing - nothing at all – about the way business is conducted. If you can't break yourself of this habit of telling the world what it doesn't need to know, we'll have to consider your position on the ship. Aye, it's something I'll have to think about.'

'Then you'll have plenty of time to do your thinking when you're standing at the wheel all night making up for the time we have lost on your other ploys.'

The skipper looked over at me and shook his head sadly. 'The poor man just cannot grasp the economics of the shipping trade, and that's a fact.'

I smiled agreeably for it seemed I had hit upon a diverting topic – nor had I forgotten the spoonful of scalding broth. 'Sounds like you run an intriguing business, Captain. Sometime I'd like to learn more about these economics and principles you were speaking about just now.'

His heavy black eyebrows came down and he glowered at me steadily, trying to work out if I was mocking him. Then, without a word, he began supping his broth. The rogue, I supposed, realised that if he said anything at all he must confess to his unprincipled greed.

The skipper finished his broth, put his spoon down and said to Wattie with surprising appeasement in his tone, 'Not bad! Not bad at all! Now I'll have the fish if it's ready, Wattie.' To me he said, 'So you're interested in my principles, are you? And yourself, Mr Yetstone, are you in the way of business? Maybe one of them financiers I hear them talking about?'

'No Captain, just got an enquiring mind.'

'Now there's a fine thing to have: an enquiring mind! My poor principles can be no match for your enquiring mind. A simple man, I act with the innocence of ... of a new-born babe.'

There was nothing I could imagine less like an innocent babe than the devious, scruffy, black-bearded pirate facing me.

He held up a hand as if to stop me praising his artless honesty. 'There's no doubt I get taken advantage of from time to time, but that's just the way I am. Everything I do is done to make someone happy. That's my principles, Mr Yetstone.'

I pretended to ponder these pious remarks before asking, 'And how does loading your ship with a cargo of coal that's not on the manifest together with an unlisted passenger make other people happy?'

'Och, maybe not your financiers, Mr Yetstone, but I would have thought a man like yourself with an enquiring mind like a super Swiss watch would have seen it for himself.'

'Just not got it clear yet, Captain.'

'Then the mainspring of your enquiring mind must be wound down after your journey.'

I laughed. 'A philanthropist of the high seas! Is it morality or modesty which inspires you, Captain?'

'Philanthropy! Morality! By jove Wattie, and what was it you put in the man's broth? We'll be on to theology next! No, no, Mr

Yetstone, I'm a simple old sea-dog. If I can pass on a bit of happiness it doesn't concern me who it is that benefits. Man, I got vast gratification just watching the clever wee Admiralty clerk stuff the charter papers into his pocket and skip away like a spring lamb to tell his masters he'd talked me into signing for one pound twelve and sixpence less than the going rate! I ask you, what is one pound twelve and sixpence against that man's happiness?'

'What indeed, if Sir John What's-his-name is going to pay you three pounds – or whatever – to carry his coal.'

'The three pounds is nothing! But think you, Mr Yetstone, about the pleasure Sir John and all his family and servants will be getting from blazing fires in that draughty old castle in the winter. And am I not right, Wattie, the ship is a lot more comfortable for the crew and her passengers with some ballast to trim her?'

'You're right, skipper, but the engineer says Sir John's coal is poor quality for steam.'

'There again, d'ye see, engineers is only happy when they've got something to complain about! And yourself, Mr Yetstone, I couldn't be letting them welcome you into the Highlands of Scotland by way of the terrible long journey by road from Oban to Dunmallach. So here you are sitting in magnificent comfort exercising your enquiring mind!'

'And do you yourself get no reward out of all this, Captain?'

'Did you not hear me say grace? All I ask is to gladden the lot of my fellows and for good sailing weather.'

'Captain,' I said to flatter him, 'The way you've worked things out, you're also a brilliant financier.'

He laid down his knife and fork. 'Well I'll be blowed! You haven't understood one thing I've been saying. Am I not the very opposite? Not one bit of happiness does your financier create! He comes up from Glasgow or London, just like yourself, buys up a poor widow's croft for twenty-five pounds, sells the house, the cow and the land for fifty, and back he goes to the city grumbling that he only doubled his money. Me a financier!' He pushed his chair back. 'I'm away up on deck. I'll get more sense talking to the seagulls!'

'I told you,' Wattie said when the skipper had gone, 'he's in a bad mood, and it's started to rain.'

Chapter Thirteen

IN ONE THING THE SKIPPER was right. I should not have cared to make the journey by road. When I went on deck next morning we were, according to Wattie, still an hour's sailing from Dunmallach. Wattie had called me from the fo'c'sle to where he sat forward on the hold covers. I was none too pleased because I had dressed to make an impressive entrance to Dunmallach and a fresh wind whipped spats of salt foam onto my grey suit.

'You should not be stewing yourself down there and missing all the fine scenery,' Wattie told me, pointing to the land on our starboard. 'Look you at the magnificent colours on them trees: red and yellow and brown and green.'

I could not match his admiration. Hills and trees there were in plenty but signs of civilisation were rare. I searched the coast: six lime-washed cottages strung like beads round a lonely bay. When they slipped from sight astern, I turned to go below again.

Wattie jumped down beside me. 'We'd best be getting your boxes. Dunmallach Point will be coming up soon.'

So we brought up my boxes and went again to stand in the bow of the ship.

'See yonder!' Wattie shouted into my ear, 'The green tip coming out from behind the headland – that's Dunmallach Point. Summer and winter the grass down by the sea is green but the hill we'll be seeing in a minute, changes every month. A few weeks back it was glowing purple like it was lit from the inside.'

As I watched the emerging spit of land increase in length and height, the waves into which the ship had been heading began to slap against its side.

'We're turning into Dunmallach Loch,' Wattie explained, 'Your house is on the other side of the peninsula by Loch Dorch. We could just as easily have put you off in Loch Dorch close to the Ghillies' Croft but your man in Glasgow said you were to be dropped this side, near to the Post Office. Maybe you've a telegram to send when you arrive; but it will mean there's a long walk over the hill ahead of you.'

I studied the peninsula as we steamed into the loch. Even without Wattie's assistance I would have identified the untidy cluster of steadings as Dunmallach farm and the little greystone cottage with its green wooden lean-to as the Post Office. They were indeed the only buildings within sight. They sat, as Smith had told me, about half a mile apart in a fringe of fields bordering the shore. Behind them, and dominating everything, was the hill I had to cross to get to the Ghillies' Croft; and I had never climbed a mountain in my life! I guessed I was being put ashore on the Dunmallach side so that I would know the location of the Post Office and so that everyone who wished to view the American drunk would have an opportunity to do so without crossing the hill.

As the ship's engines cut back, I looked across the short distance to the farm and the Post Office. I knew the little steamer's arrival would have attracted attention and I prepared to make an entrance to the community befitting the Great Melnikov. I dusted my polished light shoes, displayed my pale blue handkerchief attractively from my breast pocket and adjusted my tie over my white shirt.

The ship heaved-to less than a hundred yards from the shore. 'We can't get in to the landing stage because the tide's out,' Wattie informed me, 'but I expect John MacInnes the farmer will row out for you. Aye, there you are, a boat is being pushed out now.'

Long before the rowing boat came alongside it was obvious the person pulling on the oars was a mere boy. The ragged urchin shipped the oars and deftly threw a line from the bow up to Wattie. As Wattie caught it, the skipper joined us.

'I thought it was you at the oars, Malcolm.'

The boy, who could not have been more than eleven years of age, pushed a grubby hand through light brown hair and his freckled face grinned up at us. 'Aye, Captain. My father's not off the hill yet but Ma says I've to give you this.' He pointed to a sack which lay between thwarts on the bottom of the boat. 'I think there's a haunch or two of venison in it.'

'A haunch of venison!' the skipper exclaimed with exaggerated delight, 'By jove and be sure to give your father my thanks, Malcolm. And don't you try lifting it. Mr Yetstone, get you over the side into the boat and hand that sack up to Wattie.'

I flushed at the man's presumptive insolence and stood still.

His blue eyes looked inquiringly at me from their surrounding fuzz of curly black hair. 'You are going ashore here, are you not? Right then, Wattie will hold the boat steady and over you go!'

I knew I would have to get into the rowing boat sooner or later and it was in fact but a few feet below the steamer's gunnel, but I resented the man's insolent manner and I considered that a more dignified arrangement than scrambling over the side might have been made to transfer me. With ill-grace I climbed into the rowing boat and lifted the sack up into Wattie's hands.

The skipper, ignoring the fact that I had indulged his wishes, offered not a word of thanks but spoke to the child. 'Have you heard from your cousin Neil since he joined the army?'

The child's face lit with eagerness, 'Aye. He's coming on leave next week.'

The skipper turned to me. 'Now there's good news for you, Mr Yetstone. Malcolm's cousin who lived in the Ghillies' Croft before he joined the army is coming on leave next week. He'll show you what's what.'

I concealed my alarm as best I could. 'Just hope he's not planning to put up with me.'

'He's going to live with us at the farm,' the child proclaimed proudly.

'But if I know Neil, he'll be delighted to help you settle in. Knows the place and he'll be company for you for a day or two,' the skipper added.

'Don't need help and don't want company. Settle in in my own way and in my own time.'

'Perhaps you should wait until you see the Ghillie's Croft before making up your mind on that. What with Neil being an orphan, I expect he'll have time on his hands.'

The man was being deliberately obtuse. 'Then Captain,' I said, 'I don't plan to adopt him or to make calls on his time.'

The skipper folded his arms across his chest. 'It's like that, is it? Now that I come to think of it, there's maybe not many that would want you to adopt them.'

A strained silence followed which, feeling ill-used, I was reluctant to break. Nevertheless I was conscious that Wattie was taking an inordinately long time to hand over my boxes. Risking further rudeness, I was about to prompt the skipper when the sack which had contained the venison was again balanced on the ship's rail above me. It was covered with a thick layer of black coal dust and plainly held a hundredweight of Sir John's coal.

'There's a teaspoonful of coal, Malcolm. Present it to your

father with my compliments. Hold it there, Wattie, until Mr Yetstone is ready to take it from you,' the skipper shouted.

I looked down at my white shirt, my pale blue tie and my light grey suit and then up at the soot-covered sack which I was expected to embrace. 'I'm not a deckhand, Captain.' I said, reasonably, 'I'm a passenger.'

'You are mistaken, Mr Yetstone,' the skipper spoke with equal moderation. 'You are no longer a passenger and so of course you are free to please yourself. But as captain of this vessel, I am the one who says how and where her cargo will be discharged. Now I don't care how that bag of coal is got into the rowing boat but, until it is, your boxes can sit where they are until we get back to Glasgow. There I'll sell their contents to pay for the freight.'

The fury which boiled in me was made impotent by the realisation that while I was separated from the black box I had lost control of the menace its contents held for my life. With jaw muscles grinding my teeth, I reached my arms up for the sack.

When I had my boxes safely at my feet, I looked at my coal-stained, crumpled and dishevelled clothing and I almost wept. I turned round from where I sat in the stern of the rowing boat and shouted, 'You're worse than any financier ever was, you hypocritical, swindling hustler!'

The skipper cupped his hands round his mouth, 'And you're a bit of a character yourself, Mr Yetstone, but good luck to you! Keep in mind my ship will be passing Loch Dorch on the way back to Glasgow in ten days' time: Sunday week. If you have any business for the city – even a sack of rabbit skins – give us a shout!' His laughter echoed over the water.

Chapter Fourteen

THE BOY PULLED THE rowing boat up onto the shingle. He tried to lift out the sack of coal but finding the task beyond him, left it where it was and ran up to where I waited. 'It can stay there until my father gets home,' he said, tilting his freckled face and grinning.

Side by side we looked out to sea. The little steamer was already buffeting her way out of the loch with the wind tugging the black smoke of pilfered coal from her stack. I could not deny it, the old spy in London had succeeded in getting me into his goldfish bowl!

We turned and made our way up to the Post Office – a timber lean-to on the gable end of a small stone cottage. Because the cottage sat on a low bank, the Post Office had a wooden veranda along its short front, reached from the road by three wooden steps. A notice above the door read: POST OFFICE. TELEPHONE. GENERAL STORES. TOBACCO. POSTMISTRESS K. MORRISON.

A buxom, but not unattractive girl, of about eighteen, lazed against the wall beside the Post Office door. Her heavy brown hair cascaded to the shoulders of a white blouse which was tucked into the waist of her long black skirt. An amused rather than a welcoming smile played round her lips as she watched my approach. Black and dishevelled like a miner fresh from the coal-face, I no doubt presented a comic figure.

Where the single-track road ended in front of the Post Office, it had been widened enough for horse-drawn vehicles to turn around. As we crossed this hard, flat area Malcolm said, 'You're to leave your things here and come down to the farm for something to eat. When my father has done the milking, he'll put paniers on the horse for your boxes and go with you over the hill.'

I saw the old spy's hand in this arrangement but by now I longed only to end my journey. Moreover, I was well rested after the voyage. 'How long does it take to walk to the Ghillies' Croft?' I asked.

With an uncertain glance towards the girl, Malcolm shrugged. 'Two hours.' He looked at me again. 'Maybe two and a half.'

'Then, if you'll point the way, I'll get there by myself.' Not only did a two-hour walk over the hill seem a trifling imposition on the forty which had gone before, but at that moment nothing appealed to me less than being subjected to hours of inquisitive small talk. 'Present my compliments to your parents and thank them for their kindness,' I said, hoping the formality of my words would establish a safe, distant relationship.

Whatever else it did, my reply upset Malcolm. He spoke at length with the girl in their native language. She answered almost with indifference. The boy bit on his knuckles. Lazily the girl kicked the hem of her skirt and pushed herself off the wall.

'I take it you don't speak Gaelic, Mr Yetstone. It is Mr Yetstone, isn't it? I was saying to Malcolm that if you have no more luggage than what is at your feet, it's scarcely worth taking out the horse. On the other hand, we can't have you falling into a bog on the day you arrive. So, since the boy has had his dinner, he'll show you the way.' She cocked her head, 'It's more than just a stroll, you know. Are you sure you're up to it after your journey?' Without waiting for my answer she added to Malcolm, 'Right, I'll tell your ma you've gone with the gentleman.'

Once more I hefted the black box on to my shoulder and gripping the cord which bound the carton, I strode after Malcolm through a wicket gate at the side of the cottage, up a grassy bank and across the meadow which lay behind it.

Beyond the meadow and a stretch of spongy land tufted with rushes, the path began to ascend. I filled my lungs with soft, fragrant air. The drag on my thighs of what was no more than a gentle slope should have warned me of what lay ahead. Soon the hard edge of the black box began to sear the flesh on my shoulder and the fine cord to cut into my fingers. We had scarcely climbed a hundred paces before I was obliged to call a halt. The exertion made me quite breathless and I was starting to perspire. The boy watched as I set down my burden.

'My father and Neil once carried a horsehair mattress from the Post Office to the Croft without once stopping,' he said, his soft lilting voice denying any criticism of my prowess. With an upward look at the hill and a backward glance over the short distance we had come, he added, 'You'd best put your cardboard box on my back. We'll need to be getting on.'

Now stooped, but with undiminished pace, the little figure went ahead. We climbed steadily. The soft grass underfoot became springy, peat turf. My knees and thighs ached. My lungs dragged for air. I shifted the box from one shoulder to the other at ever shortening intervals. At first I watched the laden child above me with admiration. As my agonies became less and less bearable, I saw only the calves of his remorseless brown legs. Eventually pain and exhaustion blocked out everything but his advancing boot-heels. I called out. We stopped. His face was red with the effort of climbing but I could hardly speak. 'How ... how far?' I panted.

'We're maybe a quarter of the way now,' he replied, 'but it'll be downhill when we're over the top. My father says going down a steep hill is worse than going up.'

I had to believe his father was also a joker.

While we climbed I had been thinking about the soldier's return and the dangers it might present. The child's thoughts, too, were on the previous tenant of the Ghillies' Croft for, without prompting, he announced, 'Neil's been in the army three months now. My father says he wouldn't need much training because he was a crackshot with a rifle before he joined up.'

'Well son,' I gasped, 'you tell Neil to keep his crack-shooting this side of the hill.'

Malcolm laughed, 'He'll be shooting Germans soon!'

'Likewise, tell him I'll take care of Germans my side.' Guessing an explanation was called for, I went on, 'Listen boy, it's not my concern what your friend does or why he chose to leave the Ghillies' Croft, but—,'

Malcolm cut in, 'Didn't they tell you on the boat? Neil's father and mother died of flu last year. My father says it was living alone in the Ghillies' Croft that drove Neil into joining the army.'

'Sure, your father's a wise man and I'm willing to bet your friend is a truly patriotic person but, from now, I live in the Ghillies' Croft. So tell your buddy: no visiting, right?'

'Och, my father says it will be a pleasure for Neil—,'

It was my turn to interrupt. 'I don't give a cuss what your father says. No visiting! Got that?' Looking down on the child's hurt and puzzled face I deemed it wise to add, 'Got to get away from people for a bit. It's my trouble, see. You tell him that.'

Twice more on the way up we stopped for a rest. As the lad stood silent with his back to me, I became concerned lest I had made too much of being left alone; for neither did I want my need of privacy to become a matter of curiosity.

Although my smooth-soled shoes slipped on the path and caught on heather roots, I had my eyes shut for much of the time in a futile attempt to repel pain and fatigue. I knew the heather growing beside the path was knee high only because from time to time I stumbled into it. Tears of perspiration trickled down my face. Beneath the black overcoat my wet shirt clung to my back and the sharp edges of the metal box tortured my body wherever they made contact. I tried to focus my mind on one thought: each racking step was a step nearer deliverance.

The child stopped without warning and I collided with his stationary form, almost collapsing on top of him.

'We're over the top now,' he said, 'Do you want to rest for a bit before we start down?'

'If you need the break, son.' Gratefully I lowered the black box and lifted the carton from the boy's shoulders. I threw myself down where the heather was short and springy. My legs trembled after their exertion and my shoulders were aflame from the chafing of the box.

Malcolm looked down on me. 'You can see the Ghillies' Croft from a rock over yonder.'

A cool wind caressed my fiery face and whispered through the heather round my head. In an ecstasy of relief I floated serenely on the brink of unconsciousness. The clouds sweeping across the sky seemed to pause in their flight and my weightless body then glided effortlessly under them. I would have been happy to lie there for ever but the wretched child was standing over me.

'I can show you the croft,' he started eagerly, ending plaintively, 'if you would like me to.'

I looked at the appealing little figure shivering in the wind and pulling down the sleeves of an old, darned jersey. A fragile, freckled grin tested my resolve.

I struggled to my feet. What a bleak scene met my eyes! The clouds I had been looking at were so low that trailing wisps brushed the rolling banks of heather which stretched like an endless, tempestuous brown ocean on every side. The child was standing on a mossy tuft watching me. He pointed down the peninsula. 'It's down there that my father cuts the peats.'

We left the boxes on the path and I followed Malcolm along the crest of a ridge which ended on a narrow platform of promontory rock overhanging the hilltop. Standing beside the child I understood why he had insisted on taking me there. We were on the very edge of the world.

Poised high above land and sea, and with my coat-tails spread by the wind, I became an eagle scanning new territory. Near vertical cascades of scree flanked the rock on which we stood, seeming to defy gravity by not tumbling down onto the trees which grew along the shore hundreds of feet below us. Beyond those wind-twisted trees and on the other side of the dark waters of Loch Dorch, cliffs of slate rock rose perpendicular to meet a sullen sky.

'Down there, see!' Malcolm was tugging my sleeve and shouting against the wind.

I looked where his finger pointed to a tiny, squat, stone building standing by itself just beyond the trees and close to the lochside. Much smaller than I had imagined, the Ghillies' Croft seemed already to be crumbling into the ground and oblivion. No light shone from its single window, no smoke rose from its chimney, and nothing moved round it.

The boy was shouting again, 'My father was going to take the slates and roof timbers back to the farm because we thought no one would ever live in it again.'

'Well for sure lad, it's not best placed to catch a streetcar to the opera!' Beyond that I could think of nothing, for nothing so forsaken had ever been in my experience. Not wishing to contemplate it a second longer than I had to, I drew my coat close, 'Let's get off this goddamned mountain.'

The path as it descended the hill made a succession of turns, going diagonally in one direction then turning sharply in the other to lessen the gradient. Each dropping footfall jarred my knees and spine and bounced the metal box on my raw, bruised shoulders. Even when we reached the lower slopes where heather gave way to dying bracken and grass, I sought yet another halt to gather my strength. Finally, when we came into the trees behind the Ghillies' Croft, the track was wide enough for me to walk alongside the boy.

'My father says you should use the windblown trees in the wood for firewood. It's safer than felling and it'll keep the place clear. Neil's father kept goats and a few hens, but until you get settled in we'll give you as much milk and eggs as you need, and in the spring my father will let you have half a dozen chickens and a bag of seed potatoes. You're not to be making a stranger of yourself and feeling lonely. Whenever you fancy, come over to the farm for a cooked dinner or a game of whist or just for a crack by the fireside.'

He was older than a grandfather. 'Son,' I replied, rumpling his hair with my free hand, 'say no more. Hens! Potatoes! Whist! Give me time to get accustomed to such an exciting prospect. Tell your dad I'm mighty grateful for his interest. Perhaps sometime I'll take up his invitations, but not for a week or two.'

Malcolm twisted his head below the carton and looked up at me. 'Are you not going to miss having folk around at all?'

Before I could frame an answer, he suddenly stood still and, steadying the carton with one hand, pointed with the other. 'Yon rock, Mr Yetstone, is where you get water for the house.'

We came up to the little building from the rear. The dark stone of which it was built was stippled with orange and grey lichen. Dying weeds collapsed on brittle, whitened stems against its walls. The door of an empty henhouse swung creaking in the wind. Sheets of rusting corrugated iron rattled above a stack of firewood logs. The dusty glass in the curtainless window at the back of the house seemed to me to reflect resentment rather than welcome.

We went round the side of the house to the front. I knew from the plan I had seen in London that the first door we came to led into the byre with its four stalls and hayloft above. The second opened into the livingroom of the house. A few feet along from the door, the livingroom window faced out onto the sea and, like the bedroom window at the rear, it was without curtains. Two small doors built into the roof above the byre gave access from the outside to the hayloft. From gable to gable, byre and house, the length of the building was no more than fifteen paces.

I put my box down at the door of the house and relieved the boy of the carton. 'I don't have a key, so how do we get in?' I asked him.

He stepped forward confidently, lifted the latch and pushed the door wide.

I went in and examined the door. 'Say, sonny, the lock appears to be missing.'

'Lock? Will you be wanting to lock yourself in then?'

'Might just do.'

Malcolm was shuffling his feet, anxious to be off. Embarrassed by having nothing with which to reward him, I spoke gruffly. 'That's it then. What you waiting for?' In truth, the Great Melnikov was never so humiliated.

'Mind I told you about coming to the farm for your dinner.' He backed a few steps and then, turning on his heel, scampered off like a puppy unleashed.

I stood in the empty house listening to the boy's running foot-steps crunching on the gravel round the croft. When they reached turf and I could hear them no more, a little surge of elation raised my spirits. My journey was over! But I was not my own man. At my back, in the silent shadows of the house, I knew that a fiend more terrifying even than the black spy in London lay in wait for me.

Chapter Fifteen

I DRAGGED THE TWO BOXES into the house and shut the door. The windows being small and deep-set did not admit much light so I saw only a dim reality of what I had seen on plans in London. Nor had Smith's drawings prepared me for the claustrophobic smallness of the rooms: a living-room some twelve feet square, a larder cupboard, and a bedroom even smaller than the living-room. Malevolent shadows sulked in every corner.

The house was furnished with whatever its previous tenant had chosen to discard. A deal table and two wooden chairs filled the middle of the room. An old armchair sat in front of the fireplace and a box of logs to one side of it. Above the mantelshelf a mould-speckled mirror reflected my travel-worn face. In a varnished cabinet behind the door I discovered an unmatched collection of dishes and cutlery, a lantern, a can of paraffin and an assortment of tools.

The musty smell of an unventilated house permeated every room and a damp chill rising from the stone floor seeped through my clothing. I tossed a pack of cigarettes onto the table and put a match to the fire, ready set in the grate. Flames crackled through the dry kindling, splashing light on the walls and giving me the only welcome I would get.

Tired though I was, I made an effort to respond. Singing a Russian song, I picked up the pail which I found beside the cabinet and went out to where Malcolm said I would get water. There a crystal stream tumbled from an overhanging rock and fell splashing and bubbling into a tub formed by large boulders. The sky was heavy now and even as I filled the pail, specks of rain glistened on the black fabric of my overcoat.

By the time I returned to the house and set a pot of water to heat on the fire, my little burst of liveliness had leaked away. Yet I feared idleness. While waiting for the water to boil, I trotted out to the back of the house and returned with an armful of logs; removed my coat and jacket and hung them from a nail behind the door; carried the carton into the bedroom and stowed its contents in an old chest of drawers.

Everything I did, I did with self-absorbing haste, striving to construct a barricade of industry against the legions of temptation. These legions of smooth-tongued traitors had been clamouring for me to open the larder door from the moment the child had turned and run off. Inside the larder I knew that two bottles of whisky, like two disreputable old cronies, were waiting to reunite me with the degradation of my past.

When eventually I did go into the larder to get something to eat, I found it well stocked. My eyes were inevitably drawn to the two bottles standing on the top shelf but my resolve held and I removed only a loaf of bread, a can of corned beef and a canister of ground coffee.

I threw a handful of coffee into the pot of boiling water and opened the can of beef. Sitting in the armchair in front of a blazing fire, I shut my mind to everything but what I ate and the flaming, hissing logs.

My hunger satisfied, I moved the pot to one side of the grate. Re-heated, what remained of the coffee would do for breakfast. Hours and days of lonely inactivity lay before me.

I faced a contest, a contest so daunting that a part of me begged for instant capitulation. Nothing stood between me and those two repulsive, seductive bottles of spirits. Were I but to remove the cork from one, by dawn both would be empty. Then would come the raving of a disordered brain, the spewing sickness of a body convulsed with poison, the terror of insane hallucinations and, eventually, suicidal self-contempt. There was no cruelty which that sadistic, craving madness had not inflicted on me.

Although I ached with fatigue and the chair snugly supported my body, I squirmed and fidgeted. I could neither content myself nor sit composed knowing that a supply of alcohol lay within reach of my hand. With relief so readily available, where was the point in this self-torture? My restraint began to slip. My legs trembled uncontrollably.

I got up and went to stand by the window with my back to the room and looked out at the curtains of rain now sweeping over the sea in the gathering dusk. A tic twitched the corner of my eye and my hands fluttered from my trouser pockets to my face and back again. I pounded my right fist on the window ledge and began to count aloud.

I reached two-hundred and seventy-two before the unrelenting magnetism of the spirits drew me back from the window. Still struggling against compulsion, I went the longest way round the room, making every sort of excuse for surrender as I went.

I could scarcely see the bottles in the dark cupboard but their ruthless temptation reached down like tentacles and strangled my power to reason. Honeyed arguments oozed from the crevices of my craving, cloying my effort to resist. Was the whisky not my contracted wage? Ought I not to take what solace I could get? Would one final, hideous binge not be the best start to a new life of abstinence? The mirage of a blissful, tipsy intermission in my strife-torn existence at length beguiled my only half reluctant hands to reach up.

Even as my fingers touched the nearest bottle, repugnance exploded in my skull. My whole frame shuddered. I slammed the door shut and staggered in choking frustration to the fireplace where, my wits in turmoil, I clung to the mantelshelf for support.

While I regained composure, darkness deepened round me. I lit a lamp, piled logs on the fire and threw myself into the armchair. I had faced similar ordeals many times and in passing through, had suffered unimaginable distress. The wickedness of the old man in London was not just that he was using my weakness for his own ends, nor even that in doing so he would destroy my health and happiness. It was that, having scooped out all that remained of my sense of decency and pride, he would discard a worthless shell. The shame of treachery would finally douse that tiny spark of aspiration to be the greatest in my field which alone gave my life purpose.

When asked which side I wanted to win the war, I had answered truthfully that I was indifferent. I had little attachment to Russia, and Germany had been an unhappy refuge. However, because of that accident of birth, what I might honourably do for Russia I could not do for Germany. If that night I traded treachery for two bottles of whisky I was no more a man, let alone the Great Melnikov. I was forever a despicable wretch hiding in the skin of a traitor called Yetstone. I would be tainted trash, despised by myself if not by the world. This time then, the Great Melnikov was truly fighting for his existence.

I sat alone. The hellish rabble of tantalising devils closed in again. Their seducing chant rang in my ears. No one was there to put an encouraging hand on my shoulder; no one even witnessed my courageous stand. Tears trickled down my cheeks. How, oh how was I to defy my own persecution?

The utter hopelessness of my plight compelled me to seek consolation in my imagination. In reverie, I searched for some miraculous, invincible tactic. Uncritically I clutched at notions founded only on bravado. I made yet another solemn covenant with myself. I swore that before opening a bottle of whisky, I would first brand each of my hands with a burning faggot, forever to remind me of their betrayal. Surely there could be no greater deterrent! Oh yes, in my frothy fancies I was resolute, heroic and noble! The flames leapt with delight into the chimney.

So fortified was I now with self-confidence, so elevated above mortal frailty, that as I passed the larder on my way to bed I opened the door and looked with derision at the two bottles. Their complete indifference enraged my vanity. I snatched them down and with a flourish, set them in the middle of the table like ornaments. I blew out the lamp and went to bed content in my conceit.

I did not sleep. The witches on the train and the satanic skipper on the steamer harangued my fevered brain. I rolled from my right to my left side and back again until the blankets were lashed round my body like a lumpy corset. Cramp seized my leg and I had to pitch myself off the bed to stretch the rigid limb on the cold floor.

Clad only in my shirt I sat on the side of the bed, crushed and utterly worn out. Through the open door the translucent amber liquid in the bottles caught the radiance of the flames still flickering in the grate and winked a genial invitation. 'Surely ... surely,' temptation whispered, 'there can be no conceivable merit in a life of self-denying torment?'

Stripped of its quixotic aura, I saw that my pledge to brand my hands was as feeble and as useless as the thousand other pledges which had gone before it. There was only one thing which I could do to keep myself sober enough to see the light of day and that was to smash both bottles of whisky – there and then.

I got up, hobbled over to the table and grinding my teeth with resolve, gripped the bottles by their necks, one in each hand. I raised them above my shoulders meaning to hurl them at the wall. I could not. Though I strained until the sinews in my neck were taut to breaking, my hands and arms were strangely paralysed. I could neither cast the bottles nor yet unclasp them to shatter on the stone floor.

Groaning – for at that moment I fervently wanted to be free of the curse which forever crippled me – I slumped down onto a chair, fell upon the table and wept. Sobs lurched from my body and I tore hair from my head.

At length, my emotions discharged, I stopped sobbing and the room was silent. I might have slept then with my head on my arms but in the absolute quiet I distinctly heard someone snigger outside the window.

In an instant I was upright, the back of my neck prickling. Wide-eyed and motionless I stared at the black glass, straining to pick up the least sound. In the chimney, the wind sighed; outside, a blob of water splashed to the ground; near to the window I heard a soft footfall and a stifled cough.

Whoever had come through the darkness to that lonely house, and who had no doubt pressed his face to the glass and watched me, was still out there. And the door had no lock!

Night in such a lonely place is a swamp from which primeval terrors crawl to strangle sanity and paralyse reason. I knew two things: whoever was on the other side of the door intended me no good, and I must act before my blood congealed.

Watching both door and window, I slipped forward and down off the chair until I was on my hands and knees. I crawled to the wall below the window and stood up only when I was behind the door and within reach of the pistol in my jacket pocket. The little weapon revived my courage. I held it ready with the safety catch off. A foot scraped in the gravel on the other side of the door. I watched the latch, waiting for it to lift.

Minutes passed. The coldness of the stone floor at last convinced me I had to take the initiative. I pressed my back against the wall, gripped the pistol ready to fire, raised the latch and flung the door wide. From out of the drizzling darkness, a goat pushed into the firelit room.

I dropped the gun, grabbed a chair and with it in front of me, charged the beast. Its horns locked in the spars of the chair and then, head down, it began to push against me.

But I was the stronger and I was compelling it backwards, step by step, towards the door when a second goat pushed its head and shoulders into the room. Like a screaming dervish in my white shirt, and brandishing the chair, I raced round the table to stop a numberless herd from entering. The second goat threw up its head and wisely backed out. Being then behind the first animal, I battered its flanks with a chair. Three times we cantered round the table before that stupid goat found the door.

I put the chair down. The goats had made evident what I should have done earlier: secured the house. What a primitive place it was! I rummaged among the tools in the cabinet until I found a hammer and some nails. With these I nailed the sashes of the windows to their frames in both living-room and bedroom. That done, I ripped a blanket in half and tacked a piece to cover each window. Finally, I drove four three-inch nails half their length into the doorpost and secured the door.

Ash was now smothering the last glowing ember in the grate. I let the hammer drop from my fingers, threw myself down on the bed and knew no more.

Chapter Sixteen

DAYLIGHT, FILTERING THROUGH THE blanket covering the window, wakened me. Never had my body felt so ill-used. My bones had fused together so that I could neither bend nor move without pain. My shoulders had been peeled to raw flesh. Defying the protest of every muscle, I pulled on the trousers of the old black suit which I had been given when I first went to the house in London. Stiffly, like a badly constructed wooden figure, I went into the livingroom and hitched up the blanket covering the window. Beyond the window a leaden sea receded into a grey mist. I raked cold ashes from the grate and relit the fire.

The day being Thursday, I had no reason to wash or shave because I did not have to go to Dunmallach until Saturday when I went to take my first telephone call. While I waited for the coffee left over from my supper to re-heat, I removed the nails round the door and stepped outside.

It no longer rained but water lay in puddles everywhere. The air smelled of dank vegetation and rotting seaweed. Only the rhythmic crash and swish of the incoming tide scrubbing the shore disturbed the silence. Even the high pearly clouds promised nothing. I returned to the house and shut the door.

The bottles of whisky were still on the table. I scowled at them. Why should alcohol, I pondered, draw me, as the edge of a cliff drew some men, to consign myself to self-destruction. I kicked the empty corned beef can through ash dust on the floor. The Great Melnikov, whom thousands had watched with admiration, was made serf and dumped in that god-forsaken hovel. And for what? For two bottles of cheap liquor! Once I had given their value as a tip for having my shoes cleaned. Far away in the living world, men were laughing, gambling, quarrelling and singing while I, so often the focus of their interest, sank miserably in the quicksands of my own betrayal.

I had deceived myself in London when I had supposed I would be beyond the old masterspy's control in Scotland. As with everything else, he had used the remoteness of the Ghillies' Croft to his own ends. Pennyless, I could neither pay for transport nor yet survive walking to freedom. A four-mile tramp over the hill would take me no further than Dunmallach. From Dunmallach there was possibly another hundred miles of townless road before I reached the safety of a city. I might well indeed have been on the planet Mars!

I sat in to the table and blew on the coffee. Nor had that black-bearded skipper doled out any of his happiness to me by involving himself in my affairs. How much, I wondered, had the rascal been paid to carry me to Dunmallach. I had no answer to that but the question spawned another. How much would it take to persuade him to carry me away? Now that was something worth thinking about!

Was his ship not transport to a city, to a seaport to boot! Given the chance, the greedy rogue would surely break any agreement if he saw an opportunity to double his profit. Had he himself not invited me to avail myself of his vessel on its return voyage in ten days' time, if only to transport a sack of rabbit skins?

I cut a slice of bread and spread it with jam. Whatever his price, how could I possibly raise it? Nay better, how could I deceive him into thinking that I had access to even greater sums?

My only possession of value was the German signal lamp. But to disclose possession of that would stir dangerous questions. What of my talents as a gambler? If Malcolm's darned jersey signified anything, it signified I would be lucky to raise the cost of a box of matches playing whist with his parents and their neighbours. As for the two bottles of whisky I received each week, that cunning old man in London knew that in my afflicted predicament, I would not long resist the solace that they offered. Had I not, in less distressing circumstances, swallowed turpentine?

I set the cup down. The notion that I could win my freedom by using the greedy instincts of the skipper, clung to my mind. The old spy was relying on my addiction to secure me. But suppose ... just suppose I found some way to suppress or overcome that addiction? The fare to Glasgow by the steamer must surely be less than the value of two bottles of whisky. Even if the grasping pirate demanded more, I would have collected another two on the Saturday before he was due to return.

My heart palpitated. With willpower, and bottle by bottle, was it yet possible to pull myself out of that pit? Willpower! How many times had I tested that rope and found it rotten? Hope and doubt wrestled in my head.

I sucked on a cigarette, then ground it under my foot and lit another. Once the little steamer was in Loch Dorch and once her skipper's avaricious eyes were fastened on an array of bottled spirits, I was certain that I could persuade him to grant me a berth to Glasgow.

If nothing else, I had devised a way of escape. Whether or not I would muster my ransome, I ought not to deny myself the opportunity at this stage by dismissing it out of hand. I would therefore write to the skipper at Glenannack as soon as I could procure the means, and invite him to call in to Loch Dorch on his return voyage. The means - paper and postage – I could surely obtain by bartering cigarettes at the Post Office.

Engrossed in my plan, I sat back. I would need to word my letter convincingly because the rogue must know that I possessed little of value with which to trade. Were I successful, however, and I left on his ship on Sunday, I would be safely in Glasgow, if not on the high seas to South America, before my next telephone call from London was due on the following Wednesday. Everything fitted so perfectly!

Then doubt, like a great sea roller, swamped me again. Was I being realistic, or was I once again merely weaving dreams to cover my unhappiness? Could I possibly live through ten dreary days and ten lonesome nights with free whisky for a companion and not succumb to the solace it offered? Even as I looked at the bottles my tongue hankered for the biting sensation of the spirits they contained.

I thought of all the feeble, talentless men in the world who could live a lifetime in a distillery and never taste the product. Yet I, the Great Melnikov, could not stop at one measure. I had to go on, and on, and on stupifying myself until, in the end, that hateful old man in London – or someone else – would put me down like a rabid dog.

I looked about me. What a detestable kennel! I fingered my second-hand suit. What a despicable cur I had become! Was the Great Melnikov nothing then but a braggart's fiction; a blustering, cheapskate traitor?

That was not what Rosalind saw. Suddenly my heart ached with tenderness. That dear, dear child ... that sweet, innocent - yes, and lovely – princess had seen in me someone she could love and risk her life for. Had I, on my part, truly fulfilled my pledge to honour that love and trust? No one else in my life had ever given a cuss what became of me ... except perhaps Schnorr. Schnorr was the ringmaster who had taught me when I was a child how to back-somersault and to walk the slack wire.

The terror and the exhilaration of that learning came back to me ... and the grim determination. One breath-taking step ... then another ... and another; and with each a tiny increment of confidence. Once again I saw Schnorr's brief nod of approval – his only reward – and once again my heart swelled with pride. One step - one minute – then another and another and another. Could I outface the whisky minute by minute, hour by hour, day by day for the near eternity of a week on Sunday?

I shut my eyes and revived Schnorr's presence. Whatever stubborn, sweating, screwed-up perseverance it took, I meant to compel myself to abstinence until I had stumbled or shuffled along the length of high wire which stretched between the Ghillies' Croft and the Halls of Fame! My phantom ringmaster would watch expectant, until I did. My darling Rosalind would be waiting for me with arms outstretched. If, however, weakness overcame me and I fell, there would be no safety net. The Great Melnikov would be no more.

I opened my eyes and looked with contempt at the bottles. Worthless glass and detestable poison!

No! Oh no! No! No! That had too often been my fool's conceit! Those bottles of whisky were not worthless. They were the most precious things I had ever possessed. They were the key to my prison. I laid a finger on one: the smooth glass pressed back on my skin. I cradled it in my arms and kissed the seal which capped its cork. Setting it down beside the other, I gazed like a mother - no, not like a mother, like a miser – upon my treasure.

Like a miser too, I sought a place to conceal my riches. I found it in the bedroom. Dragging the chest of drawers away from the wall and using an iron spike, I prised up one of the heavy slate slabs which formed the floor of the house and scooped a hollow in the dry earth beneath. Gently – oh so gently – I laid the bottles side by side in their soft bed and replaced the slab and then the chest of drawers.

Freedom now seemed a real prospect and I wanted to be ready to take full advantage of it when it came. Old acts would have to be revived and work started on new ones so that I would possess a repertoire with which to captivate the widest possible audience.

In a delirium compounded of resolve, fervour and exultation, I skipped round the room laughing crazily. Had I not changed dread and despondency into optimism and purpose? The old spy had dealt a knave from the bottom of the pack but I was going to trump it with an ace from my cuff! Even the fine clothes he had provided would serve my purpose. I must sponge my suit and boil my white shirt. I would do that now!

I picked up the pail and putting my arms around it, waltzed out through the door. I went spinning past the byre door lustily singing a Viennese melody until, with stunning impact, I collided with the solid body of a man coming in the other direction.

We were equally winded and equally startled but I was first to recover. I bowed low, and said, 'A very good day to you sir, whoever you are, and goodbye.' I turned about and walked into the house, firmly shutting the door behind me.

I stood back from the window and looked out. A tall, thick-set man in old tweeds, heavy boots and a cloth cap stood a few yards out from the corner of the building. He carried a folded coat over one shoulder and rested a hand on top of a shepherd's crook. Two black and white dogs sat at his heels. I was looking, I supposed, at the sage of Dunmallach, Malcolm's father.

For three minutes the man rubbed his chin and frowned at the closed door. One of his dogs moved forward wagging its tail. A muttered command and it dropped flat to the ground. He pushed his cap back, scratched his head then, turning on his heel and with the dogs following, went off the way he had come. I ran to the bedroom and watched from its window until he was beyond the trees and on to the hill path.

I was pleased with the way I had handled the incident. Any offence my behaviour may have given was as nothing to the danger such unpredictable visits might confront me with. Another occasion could find me engaged in some less innocent activity than fetching water. I smiled. For sure, I had added to my reputation as an eccentric.

A miser's mistrust spawned the thought that there would be others in the district who, knowing I received a regular supply of whisky, would seek to help me dispose of it. Well, if they came to the croft I'd see to it that they left with a dry tongue and sore ears. The whisky was mine and inviolate!

The farmer's visit reminded me that I had still to hide the black box in the hayloft. I carried it outside, drew back the bolt on the byre door and entered. The place was without windows and stank of cow dung.

Picking my way past the empty cow-stalls in semi-darkness, I climbed a near-vertical ladder into the hayloft and set the box down. This was to be my operational post. I opened the two small doors in the roof and sitting on the floor, looked out across Loch Dorch to the now sun-glistered cliffs on the other side.

For some minutes I felt in harmony with the universe. Then a resurgence of the sense of urgency got me to my feet. I concealed the box under a mound of hay which was piled in a corner, shut the doors and returned to the house.

Although I had been told to practise signalling twice every day, the farmer's visit made me fearful of being caught doing something which would disclose the real reason for my being on the penin-sula. That at any rate was how I explained to myself why I occu-pied so much of my time with other activities. Indeed I had pushed the living-room table to one side, swept the mess of cans, crusts and cinders on the floor into a corner and started creative work before the farmer and his dogs had reached the top of the hill.

Sometimes a terror gripped me that my craving for alcohol would take advantage of a lapse in vigilance and I would find myself in the bedroom gulping down the whisky. At such times I conjured up the vision of Schnorr and had him stand over me, dri-ving me relentlessly to work harder. Behind him, Rosalind smiled encouragement.

Developing the initial concept of an act into a stage presentation had always been for me a heady and a dispiriting business. A dance or mime which made me gasp with delight or laugh or weep would, when done again, seem merely contrived or mundane. I was in poor physical condition by professional standards and often found that I could scarcely execute even the most basic techniques. From my first days in Hamburg, I had aimed, not merely to show off my dexteri-ty but to convey by seemingly effortless antics the elegance of bodi-ly movement, and to pick out by pose and gesture the comedy of everyday life, so that even old man Rott the accordian mender, obese and asthmatic as he was, would feel agility in his wasted sinews and laughter in his heart. Yetstone, the German agent, had but a small share of my waking hours and for long spells the impending arrival of my first U-boat never entered my head.

Chapter Seventeen

ON SATURDAY I PUT ON my sponged and pressed grey suit, my white shirt and that accursed celluloid collar. It was, I thought, regrettable that my new city shoes must again survive the rough walk over the hill but the second-hand ones I had worn in London did not fit well enough. This dandy turnout had less to do with impressing my neighbours and more to do with nurturing a belief in my own success.

As I slipped and stumbled along the rough, windy, moorland path I was compelled to acknowledge that Smith's choice of studded brogues had had much to commend it. My thoughts, however, were mostly occupied with rehearsing what I would say on the telephone to conceal my plans to get away. The old spy thought that my weakness bound me to his service and I wanted him to go on thinking so. I would, therefore, imply that I had consumed all of the whisky. I must also try to convince him that, although perhaps not filled with enthusiasm, I was, never the less, complying with his directions. More than that would be suspiciously out of character.

I entered the Post Office at two minutes to five o'clock and for the first time breathed its blended smells of paraffin, ham and plug tobacco. Three matrons cluttered what little space there was for customers inside. My presence among them caused a flutter of embarrassment. They ceased warbling in Gaelic and, whilst still covertly scrutinising me, bade the old dame behind the counter goodbye. Despite their hasty departure, each old crone dipped a respectful curtsy and gave me a 'good-day, sir'. This, I felt, went some way towards justifying my best suit.

The woman behind the counter held out a podgy hand. 'I'm Mistress Morrison, the Postmistress, and you will be Mr Yetstone from the Ghillies' Croft. I was expecting you about now.' She waited until the last matron left and the door was closed before adding with a chuckle, 'You will be well talked about round the fire tonight.'

She was so fat I was sure the rolls of flesh which circled her neck bounced one on top of another all the way down to her ankles. We shook hands. When she spoke, her words slithered from between toothless gums. Her eyes, however, sparkled with merriment which somehow made everything about her seem wholesome.

She was going to add another pleasantry when the telephone bell rang. After a brief word in the mouthpiece she pushed the instrument towards me. 'You are to speak to the lady. I know it is private so I'll take myself into the house.'

When the door between the shop and the house was shut, I said, 'Hello, this is Abe Yetstone speaking.'

A woman's voice came from the earpiece, 'This is your sister, Abe. We confirmed with the postmistress on Wednesday that you had arrived. You are, I suppose, settled in post now. Have you discovered any difficulties or anything else which we should know about?'

'Yes,' I replied, 'I was very sick on Thursday. My head throbbed like an iron foundry and my guts ached all day. How am I to get a doctor if I need one?'

'Sick?' Then guessing at the reason as I hoped she would, she laughed. 'Heavens, you didn't drink the two bottles of whisky straight off, did you? For goodness sake, can't you exercise any restraint? To answer your question, you cannot get a doctor. We want no one taking an interest in you, medical or otherwise. In that you are no worse off than you were in Trafalgar Square two weeks ago.'

'Two bottles are not enough. I want four.'

She laughed again. 'Ah, so you now plan to skip the doctor and go direct to the undertaker! You must show that you can cope with two bottles and be effective.'

'Old Rottenguts knows damn well I have no choice but to be effective until he gets me out of this pit in the wilderness. And do you know the house door has no lock?'

'Yes, we do. Fitting one might imply that you distrust your neighbours or that you have something to hide. Keep the black box hidden in the hayloft and carry the watch on your person at all times. Now, are you practising regularly with the lamp and codes?'

'Yes, I'm practising – more than I'm scheduled for because I've nothing better to do with my time. So why don't you reward me with four bottles?'

She stopped speaking into the telephone but I could hear her voice in the background. Then she said clearly, 'We are making arrangements for your first operation to take place next Saturday ...

that is one week from today. If that goes well, you will be rewarded with an extra bottle in your next batch of stores. Now, lest someone can overhear you, lift your voice and be less surly. Put on a performance!'

'Ma'm, I have put on many performances in my life but none has come near to my achievement these past few days. You have all but nailed me in my coffin – and for so little! A night and a day last a century in that God-forsaken hovel. Yes, lady, I do need that extra drink! Do you know, I might even bring myself to throw my arms round the neck of Old Ho Ho Rottenguts himself were he to turn up on the door-step bearing gifts of bottled alcohol.'

'I'll convey your respects. Is there any other way in which we can help you?'

'Yes there is. Pickle the Turk and send him to me in small glass jars.'

'Then your next telephone call will be five o'clock on Wednesday. Please be on time to take it. Goodbye.'

Our conversation ended with a click.

I hung up the earpiece then rapped on the counter. When the door from the house opened, it was not Mistress Morrison who came in but the buxom girl I had met on the day of my arrival. I felt less comfortable in her presence.

'It's yourself, Mr Yetstone!' she exclaimed with mocking familiarity, 'And how is your sister today? More to the point, how is yourself? I can see you've survived the first few days in the croft. Now you'll be wanting your provisions, I expect.' She swung a sack on to the counter.

'Thank you ma'm.'

'Are you giving a party then?'

'No, ma'm.'

'You disappoint me. When I saw the whisky and all the fancy things in the sack I said to my mother that you must surely be going to liven the place up with a party.'

I pulled the sack across the counter. ' 'Fraid not, ma'm.'

She sprawled her arms on top of the counter and looked up into my face. 'My name is not ma'm, it's Morag. Well then, if you're not giving a party, how would you like to come to a dance in the village hall next Saturday? The village is four miles up the road but one of the boys from the estate will pick us up in a gig.'

'Happens I'm busy Saturday.'

She laughed disbelievingly. 'Is that so now? Ah well, and if you're not giving a party, I'll never discover what that big red sausage in your sack tastes like.'

'The red sausage, ma'm? If you consider it of equal value, I shall be happy to exchange it for a sheet of paper, a pencil, a postage stamp and, if you know it, the address of the skipper of the little steamer. I have a duty to write and thank him for his kindness.'

'We don't have loose sheets of writing paper but you can have this exercise book, an envelope and a stamp without exchanging anything for them. And I'll do better than give you the address, I'll write it on the envelope.'

'Then I'd be more than grateful if you would take the sausage in exchange.'

'It's more than the stationery's worth, but you can have another exercise book whenever you need it. Come on now; change your mind about the village dance.' She pouted, 'Just to please me! You'll go mad in a month if you never leave the Ghillies' Croft. A fresh face will do us all good and you can be my partner.'

As she addressed the envelope, I put the notebook and pencil into my pocket and gathered the sack under my arm. Taking the stamped and addressed envelope from her, I said simply, 'I'm grateful for your help in the matter of the letter, ma'm. Goodday.' I went out.

Four children were gathered round the veranda steps, no doubt waiting to view the new tenant of the Ghillies' Croft. Among them, Malcolm smiled shyly and risked a small wave. I took two cans of peaches and a can of pears from the sack and beckoned him. As he came forward, I tossed the cans up, juggled them a few turns and then let them drop one by one into his waiting hands. 'Mighty grateful for the trouble you took on Wednesday, son.'

My heart was light as I set off for the Ghillies' Croft. I had established a system of barter at the Post Office; I had salvaged my pride by rewarding the boy; I had the means to get in touch with the skipper of the steamer; I had convinced the old spy in London that he had me safely pickled in whisky; and I had another two bottles of whisky – two bottles I had not been expecting so soon after my arrival. Assuming I got paid again next Saturday, on Sunday I would have six bottles of whisky with which to bribe the skipper and, I feared, I might need them all.

The extra bottle that I was to receive if all went well was more than a bribe to make sure that I was effective. Pickled in alcohol, I could never escape the old spy's goldfish bowl.

I too wanted things to go smoothly for the next eight days, so I made up my mind to practise with the lamp and codes every day. I also decided to assist my memory by writing down the codes and signals in what was left of the notebook after I had written my letter to the skipper. If any pages still remained, I would use them to take down the information on target shipping as it was given to me.

When I reached the summit of the hill, I left the sack on the path and visited the promontory rock to which Malcolm had taken me on the day of my arrival. The barbarous isolation of the tiny abode which sat far below where I stood was just the inspiration I needed to compose the first draft of my letter to the greedy blackbeard. I meant to work on that draft until my bait was irresistible.

As I went on my way down the hill, I thought about the wench in the Post Office. I reckoned her a meddlesome coquette and I would be wise to take care that she did not imperil my life. Were I to respond in the least to her advances, she was the sort who would then assume privileges and liberties I dared not grant to anyone. Without encouragement she already spoke to me with a familiarity bordering on disrespect. The wench had none of dear Rosalind's self-doubts. Morag was already confident that her smile could procure the attention of any local lad and now she wished to test her charms in a wider field. I fancied she was not done with me yet. A sharp rebuff would be good for her character.

* * *

Strangely, it was not when I was tired, lonely or frustrated that I was most tempted by my buried treasure, but when I was replete and relaxed after my evening meal. A small tot then seemed an agreeable and harmless reward. At such times, I discovered that my best protection lay not in fleeing temptation but in pulling out the chest of drawers, lifting the slab and gloating over my hoard.

I thought a lot about Rosalind and my affection for her increased with each passing minute. Her beauty, like that of an uncut diamond, had to be uncovered. One could only search for flaws in someone of near perfection: but my Rosalind would reveal more and yet more aspects of goodness, kindness and love with each passing year.

Although I now practised with the lamp every day, I was really living inside my vision of the future. Thus, coming down off the hill to Dunmallach Post Office on the following Wednesday, I was so absorbed in planning new acts and in plotting how to increase my allowance of spirits to fund my first few days of freedom that I was more than halfway across the meadow before I became aware of Malcolm and a lad in khaki uniform striding up the lane from the farm. Wanting no truck with Neil, the previous tenant of the Ghillies' Croft, I stood still hoping to let them pass ahead.

What a comic pair they made! Neil's slight frame went nowhere near to filling his uniform and the heavy boots at the ends of his long putteed legs gave him a foal-like clumsiness. He marched along swinging his arms and with his chest so thrust out his spine was bowed. Malcolm imitated him in everything, stretching his shorter legs to match the soldier's stride.

They were almost beyond where I stood when the child, finding the business of marching too much, ran ahead, and turning to look up at his hero, caught sight of me. They stopped and waited for me to reach the lane.

I made to go ahead but Malcolm called, 'Mind I said Neil was coming home? He's here!'

'I see that. Good day to you, sir,' I answered with cool civility and I would have walked on but the soldier fell in step beside me.

'You're Mr Yetstone? Neil MacInnes.' He offered a hand which I ignored. 'They'll have told you I had the Ghillies' Croft until three months ago.'

'Yes.'

'A right lonesome place it is too.'

His freshly washed face was shining and scarcely needed a razor. Where his cropped fair hair showed below his cap, it glistened with brilliantine. I lengthened my stride but he did likewise.

'You'll need to be thinking about firewood for the winter. Malcolm's father stacked some logs at the back of the house to start you off, but I don't mind coming over the hill and giving you a hand to cut some more. A day and a half would just about see you through to the New Year.'

Whatever his motives, I had to make clear that I wanted neither his presence near my house nor his interest in my affairs. 'Keep your hand. I'll take care of myself.' I spoke sharper than I might have done had enforced sobriety not tightened and frayed my nerves.

My bluntness took him aback. He tossed his head with a snort.

'Like that is it? Well, I expect I'll be on the hill helping my uncle while I'm home so I'll maybe visit the croft for old times' sake.'

His persistence was irksome. I was not going to have him put my first treacherous operation in jeopardy or do anything which would make the old spy in London suspicious before I got away on the steamer. I spoke dismissively. 'Use your time to visit folk who want to see you, soldier. Now goodbye.'

We arrived at the Post Office. I went up the steps, Neil went with Malcolm to where some ragged urchins were kicking a small ball on the flat area of roadway in front of the Post Office. The youngsters abandoned their play and gathered like yelping puppies round the soldier.

Morag looked up from the newspaper she was reading on the counter. 'It's yourself, Mr Yetstone! And have you been admiring our brand new soldier?'

'No, ma'm,' I replied, placing my letter to the skipper of the steamer beside her hand, 'There's plenty around to admire him without assistance from me.'

She franked the stamp on the envelope and tossed it into a canvas bag. 'You mean the boys? Now you've had time to exhaust the diversions of the Ghillies' Croft, I hope you've changed your mind about the village dance.'

'No, ma'm.'

She made an exaggerated display of disappointment. 'And I've been telling everyone that you're going to show us the new American dances. You know, the turkey trot, the tango and the fox-trot. You'll not have me tell them now we're back with reels, quadrilles and twosteps!'

'I no longer dance, ma'm.'

'I've heard different. So how do you pass your time?'

'At this moment, waiting to take a telephone call from my family in London.'

'A sensitive girl might be discouraged by that sort of answer. Just two telephone calls a week for company is surely neither proper nor healthy.'

'Suits me nicely.'

'Then we'll have to change what suits you. As I said, with all the lads in khaki or blue, we're short of men. So what will it take to persuade you? Ah, there's the telephone bell now. If it's not for you, give me a call. I'll be out at the front doing my share of admiring.'

When she went out and shut the door, I lifted the earpiece off its hook. There was a brusqueness in the voice of the lady in London. 'Give me your full attention. I have intelligence for you to pass on and there are some changes to our procedures. Firstly, final preparations have been made for an operation to proceed on Saturday night. Let me repeat: all being well, a U-boat will be in Loch Dorch on Saturday. Do you understand, and do you foresee any exceptional risks?'

They had absolutely no concern for my personal wellbeing. I was nothing more than a makeshift cog in their carnage machine. I willed that little steamer to come into Loch Dorch on Sunday and take me away.

'Are you there?' she asked sharply.

'Yes, sure. Saturday will be perfect. Happens all the folk round here who could climb the hill are going to a village dance.'

'Good. I shall now give you the information we have on shipping. Do you remember the order in which you are to memorise it, or shall I recapitulate briefly?'

'I've been working on it so I guess I'll get by.' I opened the notebook and laid it on the counter.

For the next six minutes she intoned the names, courses and tonnage of ships with estimated times and positions. When she came to the end of her list, I repeated the information she had given me, deliberately making minor slips to cover the fact that I was reading it from my notebook.

'Well done! You've a good memory. Now here are the changes I spoke of. Your telephone call on Saturday will be at four o'clock, not five. This will permit you to start signalling to the U-boat one hour earlier and so reassure its crew if they're already waiting in the loch. I'll repeat the information I've just given to you on Saturday so that it will be accurate in your mind. Remember, you are to continue signalling until the U-boat surfaces or until late on Monday night. Got that?'

'Yes madam!'

'We must take every possible precaution to ensure that nothing goes wrong with this operation. This includes making certain that you are fully in command of your faculties. You are not, therefore, going to get your bottles of whisky with your provisions on Saturday but, if all goes well, you will get, not two, but three bottles on Wednesday. All right?'

Perspiration stood on my brow. If I did not get my wages on Saturday I would have accumulated only the four bottles I already possessed by Sunday, two less than I might require to bribe the skipper. 'No, lady,' I said flatly, 'it is not all right. Tell Frozenface that if he wants this pony to trot, he's got to feed it first. And tell him he'd better make it four, and on Saturday. Now, you got that?'

Her voice subdued, she said, 'I have. Please wait a moment.'

Almost instantly I heard the frigid, angry voice of the old masterspy. 'Do not ever again attempt to blackmail me or to challenge my instructions, Yetstone. I have invested considerable resources in this enterprise. You and your wishes are of insignificant consequence when compared to its success. Remember that. I shall protect you only as long as you are compliant and successful. If you are negligent in your duties I shall have you destroyed. You shall, as you were promised, get your reward when the business is complete. Return to your place now and comply with my orders to the utmost of your ability.' On the last syllable the earpiece clicked and the line went dead.

My face stung as if it had been struck. I, the Great Melnikov - for I had again come to regard myself as such - rebuked and mortified like a tiresome child! The blossoming of my new life was at risk. A destructive but impotent hatred choked me. Rage made me clench my hands so that I crushed a cigarette as I lit it. I pulled smoke into my lungs until it hurt.

I would have brushed past Morag where she lounged against the doorpost talking to Neil who stood on the road below, had she not put a detaining hand on my sleeve. 'You've forgotten your groceries. Hold on and I'll get them for you.'

I stood on the veranda looking over Neil's head. Pent-up frustration churned inside me. Neil's face hung slack with the stupid smile of a love-sick calf as he watched Morag disappear into the shop.

A ragged scamp trickled the ball up to Neil's feet and appealed plaintively, 'Aw never mind Morag, Neil. Come and play with us.'

With a big sigh, Neil turned, and said, 'Might as well.'

I sensed he was grateful for any excuse to move away from me. Within minutes he had forgotten his military dignity and joined in the melee. Their game scarcely touched my interest but, professionally, I noted that Neil was surprisingly quick and well-balanced.

Morag dropped the sack at my feet. 'They think he's amazing good. What do you think?' She whispered from close behind me.

My thoughts were not on Neil. I kept silent.

'He plays the melodian too. Did you know that?'

That bit of information too, seemed irrelevant, so again I made no reply.

'Tell you what!' she exclaimed close to my ear, 'How about some of us coming over to the Ghillies Croft on Saturday night instead of going to the village dance? Neil could provide the music and you could show us the new dances.'

On Saturday night – the night of my first treacherous operation! Her proposition dazed me like a blow on the chin. I drew on the cigarette and heard myself say, 'For sure, I got to teach someone something round here.' I wanted revenge for the humiliation I had suffered at the old spy's hands and I wanted it more desperately because my body was starved of alcohol. I ran down the steps.

For just a minute I was a stranger in their game but soon my polished light shoes were accepted among the battered old boots chasing the ball.

In the beginning I let my performance be no better than that of the ragamuffins who shrieked round me. Then, when one of them got the ball, I took it away from him and, without seeming to do so deliberately, let Neil take it from me. One by one the youngsters, finding themselves excluded, retired from the game and joined Morag on the veranda to watch. Eventually, as I had intended, the contest lay between Neil and myself only.

Because Neil possessed some natural ability, it was easy to make him seem more accomplished than he truly was. By observing his more practised tricks I manipulated the game so that, drawing on his utmost skill, he seemed just to dominate the play. The children saw how close the contest was and screamed their delight every time Neil won the ball. Once, when he trapped a spinning ball with his heel, I heard Morag clap her hands and call out something in Gaelic.

'So you're the lady's champion, are you?' I asked.

'Huh, some champion I'd be for anyone!' he laughed.

I would have preferred a little more conceit to heighten the effect of the lesson I was about to teach. I leaned over him. 'And she sure is no lady.'

'What does that mean?'

'Peasant trash ain't she? A bit of a slut too, I'd guess.'

With a word in Gaelic he barged in, lungeing a boot for the ball and heedless of how his elbows bruised my ribs. I fostered his rashness by letting him get the ball just once more so that he still thought himself my master. Then, closing with him, I took the ball back and rolled it six inches to the left of his heavy boots. Again and again I did that, making him turn round and round following it while I circled with him. Thus we gyrated like rehearsed dancing partners for a full minute. The spectators were quiet, puzzled because they did not yet realise they were being presented with another form of entertainment.

I moved closer still and nurtured the hesitant laughter by putting an arm round his shoulders. 'You hear them laugh, Dobbin? For sure they think you're a comical oaf.'

He shrugged off my arm and blundered against me, determined to regain control of the game. I slipped the ball between his boots, ran behind him and flicked it high over his head before he turned. Hearing more laughter as he searched for the ball, he flushed scarlet.

'You dumb clodhopper. Lost the ball now? It's right behind you!' And I stepped round him to where it had landed.

He rushed to beat me to it but I flicked the ball above my head so that, in dropping, it rolled down my back. I caught and held it between my heels. Neil knew then that he could not match my act and he would have retired in sulks. I had to end the lesson quickly. Letting the ball trickle a yard in his direction, I mocked him, 'Sure, you can run away now, baby boy, but what will you do when you meet a Prussian with a bayonette and you don't have your strumpet's skirts to hide under? Cry maybe?'

He stepped up and drove a fist at my face. I backed off, leaving the ball where it was. 'Don't think you should change the sport sonny, do you? The ball's there, go for it if you're not yellow.'

He took a swift pace in my direction and everyone knew the target of his viciously driven boot was not the ball but the middle of my leg. Anticipating a splintering of bone, the spectators gasped but I had slipped my leg aside. As his right foot swept harmlessly upwards past my thigh, I leaned down, gripped the ankle of his foot which was still on the ground and hoisted it beside the other.

For a moment the soldier seemed to recline in the air three feet above the ground then he crashed down, landing head and shoulders on the hard roadway. His hat rolled in the dust.

Half-stunned by the impact and shaking his head, Neil struggled to raise himself onto his elbows but I stood over him and, putting the sole of my shoe on the tip of his nose, I pressed his head back and down onto the hard surface. I pressed on his nose until tears started in his eyes. 'You got my meaning now, kid?'

I swung the sack over my shoulder, took the cigarette butt from my lips and flicked it to land at the girl's feet.

I did not look round until I reached the far side of the meadow where the land began to rise. Head down, Neil slouched back along the lane to the farm like a whipped dog. Two condolatory yards behind, Malcolm carried his hat like a funereal wreath. No one from Dunmallach was going to visit the Ghillies' Croft for dancing lessons or for anything else on Saturday. On Sunday, if the skipper of the little steamer demanded my soul, by God, it was his because I meant to leave that wretched place whatever the cost.

Chapter Eighteen

I WAS NOT WITHOUT REMORSE for the way I had treated the soldier. The world had never been liberal with its goodwill to me yet events had driven me to trample on Neil's offer of help. I made up my mind that should we meet again, I would speak kindly to the boy and praise his skill with the ball. My conciliatory intentions were, however, thwarted by those boorish peasants.

I first supposed that my earlier arrival on the Saturday at the Post Office accounted for the absence of gawping children but, though I glimpsed a face at the window as I ran up the steps, no one came from the house to greet me when I entered the shop. My sack of provisions was already on the counter and when my telephone call was over, I left without anyone acknowledging my presence.

This incivility mattered little because, if all went well, I would be leaving that accursed place for good. More vexing was the fact that the skipper of the steamer had not replied to my letter. With or without the prospect of gain, the man was disobliging and boorish by nature. I fretted too lest the U-boat was late and did not arrive in Loch Dorch until Sunday. There was the possibility that if her commander witnessed the little steamer leaving as he entered the loch, he would sink it.

The sum of those anxieties burdened my mind as, coming down the hill to the croft, I searched the surface of the sea for signs of a periscope – and fancied I saw a score among the waves.

The time had almost arrived when I would perform my first - and with luck, my only – act of treachery. I wanted to get the business over and done with. So, tired though I was, I tossed logs on the fire, hung my jacket behind the door, checked the slab covering my treasure had not been disturbed and then hurried out to the byre to begin signalling to the U-boat.

The unexpected visit of Malcolm's father had left me apprehensive about using the apparatus. I therefore scanned the shore and the hillside before entering the byre. No one was about.

The byre door was ajar, but then I generally left it open to keep the place fresh. I climbed into the loft and set up the signalling apparatus. A reluctant eagerness had my fingers tripping over themselves as I charged and lit the lamp. I sat on the floor with my legs astride the tripod and with the notebook resting on my knee. It was scarcely credible that, below the white-dappled surface of the sea, someone was watching and waiting for my signal. I drew a deep breath and placed my hand on the signalling lever.

Yes, I felt sick with guilt – guilt which flashed with frightening brilliance through the open hayloft doors as I made the signal that it was safe for the U-boat to surface and for her crew to land. I repeated this signal a score of times before deciding to break off for supper. The back of my neck ached. I turned off the water supply on the lamp, stuffed the notebook in my pocket and got to my feet.

I was about to descend the ladder when I heard something heavy thump against a stall partition in the byre below. Guessing that a goat had strayed into the byre in my absence, I clambered down the ladder to evict the animal.

In the farthest corner of the first stall which I looked into I discovered the child, Malcolm, curled up in a terrified ball. When I told the lady in London that all who were fit to climb the hill would be at the village dance, I had not thought of the boy. I beckoned him to me.

Malcolm unravelled his limbs and came cowering out of the stall. Even in the poor light of the byre I could see that his face was greenish-white with terror. His eyes brimmed with tears and his chin quivered.

I spoke not unkindly. 'So, my lad, what are you doing here?'

'Please sir, we came to kill rats.'

The, 'we', rang a warning in my head but since the boy was almost beyond coherence, I asked gently, 'We? And who are we, Malcolm?'

'Me and Neil.'

Knowing that I had just put a terrible weapon of revenge into the soldier's hand, I held my breath. 'And where is Neil right now?' I asked softly.

From behind me, and harsh as the rasp of a metal saw, Neil's voice said, 'Stand just where you are, Yetstone. Now give Malcolm the notebook you have in your pocket.'

I had no wish to make myself target practice for the crackshot of Dunmallach so I stood quite still. It was, of course, possible that the soldier was bluffing. Watching the boy's face closely, I asked, 'What will happen, Malcolm, if I don't give you the book?'

The child's eyes flickered apprehensively and I imagined Neil's finger tightening on a trigger. 'He's going to fire it at your head.'

I drew the notebook slowly from my pocket. Grabbing the child and using him as a hostage was altogether too risky.

Malcolm took the book as if it had fangs.

'Run you home,' Neil said, 'and I'll follow when I've dealt with this twister.'

The boy edged round me, then scampered off.

'Put your hands on your head, Yetstone. Go into the stall and kneel with your face to the wall.'

Gambling that I could give myself a couple of seconds of thinking time, I drew a weary sigh before raising my arms. Surprise and agility were my only weapons. I guessed Neil was standing close to my back so I made as if to walk forward but instead pitched myself into a back-somersault. I caught him off-guard. As I landed, my shoulder struck his thigh.

Neil stumbled to one side, recovered, and stuffing a catapult - not a gun – into his pocket, squared up to me like a fairground pugilist.

I was so confident the soldier had learned a lesson from our last encounter that I strolled forward with a laugh, expecting him to turn and make a dash for the door.

Instead, he advanced a long, swift stride, dropped to one knee and rising, drove both his fists upwards into my stomach. His knuckles, like steam pistons, rammed every gasp of breath from my lungs.

Reeling back, I tried to club him down with my right fist but I missed his head and struck his shoulder only a glancing blow.

He came at me again with outstretched fingers clawing for my face.

Unbalanced, I could do little to protect myself but try to duck his flailing arms.

His left hand grabbed my shirt, his right a fistful of my hair. His heavy boots smashed into my legs again and again like sledgehammers.

Had I not been winded, Neil would scarcely have survived five seconds. As it was, the best I could do was to gasp for breath and try to throw him off.

His clumsy weight dragged me down.

For me this was more than a bad-tempered brawl. I was fighting for my life. Neil had only to land one lucky blow and I would be trussed up and on my way to a firing squad in the Tower of London. The lessons I had learned in prison came to my aid. I wrested an arm free and then locked his head under it so that, by pushing out my hip, I would break his neck. As I gathered my strength, he savagely tugged my hair, pulling my head back. His hot, wet breath deafened me as he sucked my left ear into his mouth and his teeth began to close over its base.

Alarmed, I threw him back to prevent my ear being bitten off and slammed both my fists into his chest, thus forcing him to release my hair.

He rushed at me again. This time it was his knee which pounded my stomach.

I slashed at his throat with the edge of my hand and caught his cheek.

Falling, he wrapped his arms round my legs and together we rolled on the ground.

Together we scrambled to our feet. Panting and snarling, we faced each other in the half-darkness of the byre.

I edged round him, meaning to make a break for the door and then to bolt him inside the byre. Once I had my little pistol he would not last long.

As if knowing what I planned, he leaped high onto the loft ladder.

I would lose my advantage if I let him jump on top of me from the hayloft doors, so I grabbed his left foot and tried to haul him down.

Neil lashed backwards with his right leg and his boot-heel struck my face. In doing so, however, he lost his footing.

I charged out of the byre, not taking time to bolt the door behind me. As I entered the house, I heard the signal lamp being knocked over. Then a rattle of slates and a heavy thud on the ground told me that the soldier had escaped.

I might possibly confuse the child about what he had seen and refute any tale he might tell, but if Neil got away, I would need more than a mish-mash of falsehoods to save me.

With the gun ready to fire, I opened the house door and charged out.

A stone from the catapult shattered the paint on the doorpost and then whined past my ear.

I slipped back, pulled off my jacket and holding it spread out in front of me to protect my face, advanced towards the gable of the building.

When I turned the corner beyond the byre door, I saw Neil, sixty yards off, running across the meadow towards the hill path. On the other side of the meadow, close to the trees, Malcolm stood waiting for him.

I had been within twenty-four hours of getting away on the little steamer. Why, I groaned, did events constantly conspire to make my life turbulent and perilous? Head down, I raced after Neil. Sixty yards and my lungs were dragging for air. My heart pumped in my chest, and my legs trembled. I had gained but twenty yards on the soldier.

With a vague notion of holding both soldier and child prisoner until the steamer called, I raised the gun and, although my heaving chest swung my aiming arm from side to side, I fired to bring the soldier down.

Neil leapt forward and stumbled. But it was no more than an instinctive reaction to the gun's report for, head down, he then increased the length of his stride.

Not only had I missed my target, I had further incriminated myself. They now knew that I had a gun and I had lost the advantage of surprise.

I would, I think, have given up then, but another means of escape came to mind. The U-boat which was due, and might already be lying in Loch Dorch waiting for darkness to fall, must now take me away. The U-boat, however, might not turn up before midnight, by which time, if Neil got away now, he could cross the hill to Dunmallach, gather together a posse and return to take me prisoner. I must better my chance of escape by somehow delaying their return to the other side of the peninsula. I pocketed the pistol and loped after them.

They had made for the bottom of the hill path which, because it came down on a slant, was taking them away to my right. I changed direction and galloped through the trees directly for a point high on the hill. Dying bracken tangled my feet but I kept going. I stumbled on up and up the hill as far as my thighs and lungs would take me.

Neil saw that I would get to a point on the path above them. He shouted to Malcolm and together they turned from the path and headed towards the end of the peninsula.

I too, turned in the direction they had taken, but I went on climbing to keep above them on the hill. I no longer hoped to capture Neil and Malcolm. They had but to part company and run in different directions and I could follow only one. Heather and bog and the coming of darkness were on their side. If the Germans were at all punctual, however, the Great Melnikov would have vanished, leaving behind only the mystery of his disappearance.

A heather-clad shoulder jutting from the hillside loomed above me. Neil and Malcolm, being lower on the hill, passed on its underside and soon disappeared from sight. I was not much troubled by their disappearance because I meant to climb to the top of the shoulder so that they could not pass back over the hill without my seeing and obstructing them.

I was now preoccupied with the arguments I would use to convince the commander of the U-boat to take me off. In the circumstances it was clearly his duty to rescue me.

Yet another thought set me fretting. If the U-boat had not arrived until after I had ceased to signal, it would not surface at all. I was perplexed. Should I detain Neil and Malcolm on my side of the peninsula as long as possible lest the U-boat did not show up until after midnight, or should I return immediately to the loft and resume signalling in case it came and went while I was on the hill? I went on climbing.

There was no easy path to the summit of the shoulder so my tired legs dragged me up, step by step, through knee-high heather. Anguished in mind and tortured in body, I cursed the rat in Trafalgar Square who had sold me into this slavery!

When I did attain the summit, I was dismayed to discover that another hump of hillside, higher and steeper than the one I was on, faced me. A steep-sided valley lay between. As I surveyed the gully I had first to descend and then climb again, I caught sight of Malcolm some two hundred feet below. He was standing near the base of the hill with his back to a small tree. His face was upturned as he scanned the hillside. Neil, I guessed, was in the nearby wood, for they would not be far apart. He had misjudged my wisdom if he thought I could be lured into a hide-and-seek chase through the concealing shadows of the forest.

I was sure that Malcolm saw me, for he abruptly abandoned his search and tried to hide behind the slim tree.

It was not yet dark but a soft evening haze was settling on the higher parts of the hill. A sheep path, like scraps of black thread, traced an erratic course down my side of the valley and then back round the shoulder of hill which I had just climbed. Every passing minute reminded me that a U-boat might be awaiting the signal that it was safe to come to the surface. Nor did I want to get lost on the hill after dark. I made up my mind to let Neil and Malcolm go wheresoever they pleased. I would follow the sheep path down and return to the hayloft. Neil was a stubborn customer but surely, knowing I had a weapon, he would not try to tangle with me again.

The sheep path was little more than a greasy parting in the heather. In places it clung precipitously to the hillside. In others it scarcely existed at all. Often my safety lay in clinging to the heather above my head and moving hand over hand. When I could, I kept an eye on Malcolm where he stood behind the sapling. I could see Neil nowhere but I guessed they were waiting for me to pass them by on my way back to the Ghillies' Croft before themselves crossing the hill to Dunmallach. No doubt they felt sure that I was safely confined on their forsaken peninsula.

Darkness was settling everywhere now but I was within sight of the bottom of the hill. I looked back over my shoulder, checking for the last time that Malcolm was still standing where I had first seen him. I think I heard a movement at my back but, before I could turn, I was clubbed to the ground.

I was only half stunned. Neil had taken possession of my gun and stood over me swinging a rotten branch of a tree in his hand. Had the wood been heavier or not so rotten, my brains would have been pulped. I feigned unconsciousness but he swung a kick at my thigh and growled, 'Get up!'

Still hoping to take him by surprise, I lay on my back moaning.

He listened to my groans with indifference as he examined the weapon in his hand. 'Get up!' he said brutally.

I groaned more loudly.

Without warning, he pointed the gun in my direction and fired.

Before the bullet hit the ground between my legs, I was on my feet.

'If I'd meant to hit you,' he said with contempt, 'I would have. Just checking that it's not loaded with blanks.'

I had been too ready to see the soldier as a khaki-clad bumpkin. He had guessed that I would come down by the sheep path and he had arranged for Malcolm to distract my attention from where he lay in wait. Had he used a sounder piece of wood, I would not have survived.

I was standing on the path. Neil stood above me. Malcolm came panting up from the trees to where we were on the hill, his young face scrunched up with anxiety.

'Take off your jacket and throw it down to Malcolm,' Neil ordered.

'There's a bitter cold wind, soldier.'

The barrel of the gun came up and his finger tightened on the trigger.

I slipped off the jacket.

He waited until the boy caught it. 'Empty the pockets, Malc.'

Kneeling on the ground, Malcolm went through the pockets of my jacket and removed a pack of cigarettes, a box of matches, a pencil and a can opener.

'No other weapons? Right, put it all back,' Neil said, 'Roll up the jacket and throw it up to him. No! No! Don't go close. He'll take you hostage if he can.'

I had already dismissed that idea. Anyhow, the child had done me what kindness he could.

I had expected the soldier to kill me in the cow-shed. Now I wondered if perhaps he was uncertain about what I had been doing. If so, it was something I might turn to my advantage. 'Can't say for sure what you think you saw me doing in the hayloft, Neil,' I said pleasantly, 'but I reckon you've got it all wrong.'

He made no answer.

'Don't blame you for jumping to the wrong conclusion. Would have done the same myself.' I had no time to plan my piece of fiction. 'What you saw, son, was an inventor testing his invention. I'm working for the government, y'see. Mighty confidential business it is too, so now I got to swear you to secrecy. Better you hadn't got involved. Tried to scare you off with the gun. But you surely don't imagine that I'd want to harm you.' I waited for him to say something – to give me a clue as to what he was thinking. He said nothing.

'You saw me using a signal lamp, right? So, who could I be signalling to? The empty sea? The black cliffs on the other side of the loch? Ah, there's the magic of my invention. Now this is top secret, laddie. I was signalling to a Royal Navy warship six hundred miles out in the Atlantic. Some invention, eh kid?'

Neil spoke as if he had not heard a word I said. 'Start walking down the hill, Yetstone, and then back to the croft.'

There was nothing for it but to keep on with my story. I started off down the hill a pace ahead of him. Over my shoulder I said, 'You must see why I tried to stop you. Now I'll have to work out what's to be done. The Admiralty ain't going to be any too pleased at having you interfering with them fighting the war. But don't worry, lad, I'll explain you did it for the best. Just give me a bit of co-operation now. I got a lot of influence, y'know.' He said not a word.

'As I just said, you interrupted a test I was conducting with a ship in the North Atlantic. So, when we get back to the Croft I'll have to let them know that it wasn't the machine that failed. While I'm doing that with my magic lamp, you get back over the hill to the Post Office and make a telephone call to the Admiralty in London. Mind, you speak about this to no one but the Admiralty in London. The Hun mustn't get to know what we're up to. I'll give you the number you're to call and the message you're to pass on.' I laughed as easily as I could. 'Well, now I've explained the way things are, you can quit levelling the gun on me. Sure, keep it if you must, but let's stop behavin' as if we were enemies.'

Neil was not listening to me. He was talking to Malcolm.

'When we come to the hill path,' he was saying, 'You get back home as fast as you can. Tell your Da what's happened and tell him to bring Dougal the gamekeeper with a couple of guns and Dr McAllister and the horse over to the croft. When I get Yetstone back to the house, I'm going to put a bullet in his leg. That way, even if he's got someone else hidden over here and they do for me, he's not going to get far. Can't risk taking him over the hill in the dark tonight by myself.'

My attention was on what Neil was saying and not on where I was treading. I must have stepped on a patch of slimy peat for my foot slipped below me and I pitched sideways. My limbs were wrenched and my body jarred as I flailed about trying to keep upright. My heart pounded against my ribs as I waited for a bullet to smash into my spine. But Neil did not shoot.

For an instant I was grateful to the soldier. Then I realised that I could use to advantage his hesitation to press the trigger. I saw a heather root ahead and deliberately made my foot catch on it. Lurching sideways, I threw out my arms again as if striving to keep upright. I hoped by this to condition the soldier not to open fire instantly, should I make a sudden and violent movement.

Darkness had now cast a black veil over everything below the skyline. Only because our eyes had adjusted to the decreasing light were we able to proceed safely. This ambiguity of shape and form, I thought, must be to my advantage in what I planned.

We were by this time only some thirty yards from where the ground levelled and not more than sixty from the trees. A short but steep grassy bank would finally take us off the hill. As I started down this bank, I made my foot slip, swivelled my trunk and, as I fell, I reached back and grasped one of Neil's ankles.

I did not bring him down but, staggering to keep upright, neither could he level the gun on me. I rolled down the bank dragging his limb with me. Neil stumbled over my body then dropped on all fours with the gun on the ground under his hand. I released his ankle, rolled my body, slashed his hand off the gun and recaptured my little weapon.

Even as I scrambled to my feet, Neil was hurling himself at me. In pushing him off, I sent myself staggering backwards down the last few feet of sloping ground. I was near to the trees before I was able to check my involuntary retreat. When I did, I could see no one on the path above me. I cared not where they were. I had my protector and I would not be tricked into losing it again.

The soldier had a lot to learn about this unprincipled world. He had put himself at a disadvantage by carrying the gun with the safety catch on. I did not, and I kept my wits about me, walking midway between the trees along the shore and the base of the hill to lessen the risk of being concussed by a stone from Neil's catapult. I was sure, however, that he would not attack me again in the open. The child, I guessed, was already on his way home. There was just a chance that the soldier would run ahead and conceal himself in the darkness of the house or the byre and there lie in wait for me.

The ground between the hill and the trees was more or less level, spongy and covered with tufty grass. Anxious now to summon my rescuers from their hiding in the sea, I was loping along when I came to where water welled and spread out from a spring close to the bottom of the hill. The ground became mossy-soft and wet. Suddenly I was squelching through a black paste which reached over my ankles. I tried to leap forward and in doing so lost a shoe. Before I retrieved the shoe and struggled clear of the bog, my trousers and the arms of my jacket were slimy with mud.

I came at last to the gap in the trees through which the path to the Ghillies' Croft passed. Never had I thought I would so welcome the sight of that hovel.

I started to run. Because of the darkness, my eyes were down searching the ground where my feet would land. I could not have been more than fifty yards from the croft when I looked up. A cry of astonishment – no, of fear – burst from my lips. A huge, black, monstrous shape lay on the water close to the shore in front of the Ghillies' Croft.

Panic seized me. How long had the U-boat been there? The waves were breaking over its bow. Was it departing? Oh, why had I ever left the hayloft on that fruitless pursuit on the hill? I howled on the Germans to wait for me.

Now, heedless of what might lie in my path, I charged headlong for the byre door. And careless, too, of whether or not the soldier was waiting to ambush me, I burst into the byre and clawed my way up into the hayloft.

Chapter Nineteen

NOTHING IN MY LIFE GAVE me reason to suppose that Dame Fortune looked on me with special favour but when I struck a match in the hayloft and saw the signal lamp lying on its side in a pool of water, I knew her to be a vindictive bitch. Of the hundred other ways that lamp could have fallen when the soldier knocked it over, none would have drained the water so completely from its tank. It was water dripping on to carbide which produced a gas that gave the lamp its brilliant white flame.

With the match burning down to my fingers and half my attention given to the U-boat, I righted the tripod. The waves breaking over the submarine's bow fired my imagination into seeing her disappear under the waves. 'Wait!' I sobbed, 'Please wait five minutes! Just until I fetch water to re-charge the lamp!'

I hurled myself across the floor of the loft, tumbled down the ladder and staggered, breathless, into the house.

Inside, the house was dark as a coffin. I squatted in front of the open doors of the cabinet. My distracted fingers snapped the head off the first match I tried to strike. I scraped another. For a second, its flaring brilliance dazzled my eyes. Then by its yellow flame, I found and lit the lantern. I made to rise but, without sound or warning, ice-cold steel touched and then pressed into the back of my neck, holding me down.

It was not self-control but nerves shattered beyond responding to anything which saved my life. That cold steel could only be the muzzle of a gun. But whose gun? I was close to fainting when a thick voice said, 'If you move, I vill shoot.'

'Do not think to do something foolish is to be brave,' a second voice added.

I put down the lamp and gripped the shelf with both hands to steady myself. The accents were unmistakably German and I should have been cheered but the muzzle of the rifle kept pushing my head down into the cabinet. On the verge of toppling forward, I spoke in German, 'If you don't take that thing off my neck, I'm going to fall on my face.'

'Who are you, please?'

'I'm Abe Yetstone, the man you are to meet. So what the hell way is this to greet me?'

'What is the name of the girl in the house in London?'

'Rosalind.'

'Stand up and put the lamp on the table.'

I rose and turned around. A small German sailor with exceptionally long arms levelled a rifle at my chest and watched me with suspicious eyes. I had seen apes just like him holding sticks in the circus. Close to the bedroom door, an officer in a black greatcoat held a pistol which followed my every movement.

The officer stared at me then pushed back his cap. 'God in Heaven!' he exclaimed, 'Are you a man or an animal?'

'Stinks like a polecat too,' the monkey sailor added.

I could afford to ignore their insults. Passing between them I said courteously, 'Permit me, gentlemen, to light another lamp.'

With both lamps lit, I looked at myself in the mirror above the fireplace. I did indeed resemble a swamp savage. My eyes stared wildly from my sweating, bruised and mud-caked face. My hair was matted and tangled. My celluloid collar swung at the back of my head like a drunken halo. Grass and mud spattered my crumpled grey suit and my shirt was torn open, exposing my bare chest. It was scarce believable that the self-same mirror had reflected an elegant gentleman less than six hours earlier.

'I've suffered misfortunes, captain,' I said, brushing myself down and fastening my collar.

The officer came forward, pushed the lantern aside and sat down at the table. 'I am not a captain and we all have our difficulties. You have information on shipping for me? Good! I shall write as quickly as I am able then depart.' His pen was poised over a notepad. 'That is what you want too, is it not?

'Well ... not exactly.'

'Have you different instructions then?'

I smiled in a friendly way. 'My problems, Mister Officer, are such that I must leave this place right now. It's best I leave in your ship.'

'Oh no, Mr Yetstone, that is not the arrangement! Now please give me the information on shipping.'

I made my smile vanish. Placing both hands on the table, I leaned over it so that he had to look up. 'The information you most need right now, Buster, is that your London masterspy's half-baked plot has come apart at the seams and the thing we must all do is get the hell out of here.'

The sailor, thinking I was about to assault his officer, stabbed my ribs with the muzzle of his rifle, 'Stand back from the table. Schnell!'

I held my pose and spoke with measured annoyance. 'And get your bloody monkey off my back!'

'We are discovered?' The officer's eyes were wide with alarm. 'You have betrayed us with your signal that it is safe to bring the U-boat to the surface!'

'I shoot him and we go.' The monkey sailor took a step back and raised the rifle.

'Give your performing ape a banana. Far from betraying you, Mister Officer, I've fought off British soldiers to make sure that you are safe - well, safe for the time being. I've risked my life and, as you can see, lost blood in your cause. No, I don't want a medal. I want a berth on your ship.'

Mystified and worried, the officer put down his pen. 'For how long are we safe?'

'Perhaps four or five hours.'

'Good. Now you give me the information on shipping. As you may be mistaken about how much time we are safe, it is best that you stay here and delay our enemies. You will know best how to do that. You may have to sacrifice your life.' He bent over the notepad. 'The information, please.'

'Not in the contract, Buddy. Besides, I've received information on other matters from agents in Sweden which will be of interest to your government.' I just had to compel him to take me off.

'German agents in Sweden? What has this to do with me?'

'With you, nothing. With your admiral, a lot. German agents are being captured at Inverness and—'

He interrupted me. 'First you give me the information on shipping then, if we have time, you may tell me what you know of other matters. When I get back to Germany, it will be passed on. Now—'

It was my turn to interrupt. 'I have also some very technical information on a secret signalling device the British are making.'

The officer threw himself back in the chair and thumped the table with both fists. 'God in Heaven! But not the information on shipping which is my reason for being here! A U-boat is not a luxury liner, Mr Yetstone. It is the most uncomfortable of all ships. And dangerous too. You may never reach Germany with all this ... this information you have.'

'Better still, old son, drop me off in any neutral country which suits you. I'll find my own way from there.'

'We have neither room nor food for passengers.'

I waved a generous hand. ' I can supply my own chow.'

The officer threw up his hands and jumped to his feet. 'One thing is certain. Every minute we remain here our ship is in danger. It is for the commander to decide what will happen to you. I promise nothing.'

I sighed with relief and nodded. 'Good decision, mister! Right, let's get some cans of grub into a sack and be off.'

I went over and opened the larder door. Prison had taught me that there are places where cigarettes are worth more than gold. A U-boat, I guessed, was one. I dropped a carton of two hundred cigarettes into the sack and I was reaching for another when I overheard the sailor whisper, 'This man looks as if he has just escaped from a lunatic asylum. He may be armed too, sir.'

'He is all we have and yes, we will search him before we leave. I am more troubled because I have no authority to remove him from his post.'

I left the second carton where it was and dropped my hand into the pocket which held the pistol. Where, I wondered, could I conceal and yet retrieve it after I had been searched.

The officer, thinking I stood idle, came over to investigate. 'Please, Mr Yetstone, we must return to the ship as soon as possible.' He took the sack from me and looked inside. For an instant, I thought he would strike me. 'Are you indeed mad?' He tipped the carton of cigarettes on to the floor and kicked it across the room. 'We do not eat cigarettes, you fool! Get out of my way!' He gave me a push and taking my place reached an arm behind the cans on the shelf and swept them into the sack. 'That must be enough!'

I dared not give them cause to doubt me more than they already did, so I handed over my little gun to the monkey sailor rather than have him discover it. He in turn passed it to the officer.

I was not only searched by the monkey sailor, he tied one end of a length of cord to my right ankle. The other end he wound round his hand. Giving the cord a light pull, he warned me, 'It is dark outside. If we are attacked by anyone – be they your friends or your enemies – you will not run away, you will be the first to die. Now carry the sack.'

I put on the old black overcoat, slung the sack over my shoulder and followed the officer out into the night. I walked always prepared for the sailor to snatch on the cord and trip me up. He waited, however, until we came upon a small, black rowing boat hidden among the rocks on the shore before snatching the cord and sending me headlong with the sack. A rowlock gouged my ribs and a thwart bruised my shoulder.

I was made to sit in the middle of the boat and to pull on the oars. The officer sat in the bow, while the monkey-sailor sat in the stern directing me. As I rowed out from the shore, I looked back at the black and solid mass of hill – the hill which had so tortured me on the day I arrived in Dunmallach – and at the receding light shining from the open door of the Ghillies' Croft. Suddenly the full meaning of what I was doing burst into my mind. From the moment I stepped onto the U-boat I was embroiled in a bloody, brutal and merciless war. I who had no cause to fight for; I who had no quarrel with any man or nation; I who wanted only to entertain and to grace the world with my art. I was now part of that brawling, maiming, slaughtering madness.

We swept into calm on the lee side of the U-boat and the sailor called for me to ship the oars.

Chapter Twenty

BEFORE THE ROWING BOAT quite touched the hull of the U-boat, the officer climbed out and strode off towards the conning tower. I was hauled on board like a sheep, the cord cut from my ankle, and then harried over the deck grating like a wayward ewe by two seamen. I pushed them aside and climbed at my own pace up to the conning tower.

Even as I introduced myself to the officer on watch, a hand gripped the back of my neck and thrust my head down. A greasy finger pointed to a brightly lit hole at my feet.

I prised the fingers off my neck, stood erect and then, gathering my black overcoat about me, lowered a foot onto the first rung of an iron ladder. The instant my head passed below the deck hatch, a foul smell of rancid food, stale sweat and hot diesel oil filled my nostrils.

The ape-like seaman followed me down to a bright but cramped space at the bottom of a second ladder and, pushing me to one side, said, 'Wait here in the control room. Touch nothing and don't get in the way.'

On the other side of the control room, two men in faded overalls, each seated on a swivel stool in front of a large spoked wheel, swung round and studied me with dislike and curiosity.

'Good evening,' I said affably in German, 'I am a guest of your captain.'

The younger of the two grinned and pinched his nose. 'One speaks of old friends, Petty Officer, but our captain has surely kept this one too long: he's over-ripe.'

'Don't be uncivil, Wilhelm,' the petty officer replied, then he laughed, 'Perhaps the commander keeps his friends as my brother keeps turnips - covered with earth and straw.'

The diesel engines started with a rumbling thump-thump-thump and, vibrating throughout its length, the U-boat got under way. A cold draught of night air blew down on my neck from the open hatch above.

'Don't we travel under the sea?' I asked the petty officer.

'Faster on the surface. Charging the batteries too,' he called back.

Officers came and went, stood at a chart table, looked at gauges and spoke to one another. I might not have existed ... until I lit a cigarette then, scarcely glancing up, one of them struck it from my fingers. 'Outside on deck only!'

Standing motionless made my spine and legs ache. I was looking about for a place to sit when the officer who had come to the Ghillies' Croft entered through a bulkhead door. He jerked his thumb over his shoulder, 'Commander wants to see you.'

Grateful for the opportunity to exercise my limbs, I followed the officer through the bulkhead door and into a small cabin furnished only with a bunk, a locker, a chest of drawers and a table. The commander, a man younger than myself, sat at the table.

'My second officer tells me you insisted on abandoning your post.'

I let him get no further. 'Compelled to. Let down by the incompetence of the London section. Indeed, sir, I had to fight off soldiers to make certain your ship would be safe.'

The commander raised his hand. 'Please. That is something you must tell the court of enquiry or whatever court you may face in Germany. For now I want only the information you have on shipping.'

I thought quickly and spoke gravely, 'It would be most unwise to act on the information which I have been given. As I said, I can no longer trust my source in London.'

The commander drummed his fingers. Then, with a brisk shrug, he said, 'If the information is good we shall use it; if it is not good we shall either have no target or a British warship will be waiting for us. Now we are ready for either. A British warship would be a plump bird to bring down!' His eyebrows lifted optimistically, 'Yes, give me the information. How it is used will be my responsibility.'

Having relied on the notebook and with all the distractions which had befallen me since I was given the information, I could remember almost none of it. Confident, however, that I had covered myself by implying the information was unreliable, I threw out a random stream of names of ships, times, courses and tonnages akin to what I had been given.

The commander ran his eye down the list, then looked up smiling. 'This would be excellent if it were not suspect. Do you know, Mr Yetstone, the greatest anxiety which afflicts a U-boat commander is that he will traverse endless miles of empty sea until his fuel runs out and never sight a target?'

'Unfortunately, sir, I may not have helped you there. Now, I've had a strenuous day so I'd be grateful if you'll arrange to have me shown to my cabin.'

'Your cabin?' He laughed. 'Yes, yes of course. Sleep well.'

The second officer led the way forward along a narrow passageway – a rattling, roaring tunnel of hell, cluttered with gauges, pipes and greasy machinery. He stopped beside a bunk no wider than a shelf which had somehow been fitted into this confusion and shouted above the noise, 'Your cabin, Mr Yetstone.' Before I could protest, he went on, 'And you'll have to give it up when the man to whom it belongs comes off watch.'

'And then what am I to do?'

'Oh, we'll find something for you to do - helping in the galley, if nothing else.' He patted my shoulder reassuringly as he squeezed past me on his way back.

The commander's reference to a court of enquiry set me worrying. I would now have to make a credible case for leaving the Ghillies' Croft. Luckily, no one in Germany, nor indeed London, could check on anything I might say. By tomorrow Dunmallach and the Ghillies' Croft would be swarming with policemen. An enquiry, however, was better avoided because the old spy in London must have had some means of making contact with German Intelligence. I decided that in the morning I would concoct a story with which to persuade the commander to put me ashore in a neutral country.

I was, in fact, over-tired and the noise of the engines together with the coming and going of men along the passageway constantly disturbed my sleep. It was almost with relief that I opened my eyes to find a seaman standing over me shouting, 'Please, my bunk now!'

In the galley a sweaty, toothless sailor grudgingly let me have a hunk of mouldy black bread and a mug of oily tea which I carried forward until I came on an alcove at the side of the central aisle. In the alcove there was a table with a bench seat on each side.

I had not only slept badly, my whole nervous system had been deprived of alcohol and tobacco for too long and now looked for a scapegoat on which to vent its spleen. Although I sensed the antagonism of the three sailors already sitting at the table, I pushed myself onto the bench beside one of them. I had experienced that kind of resentment before: on my first night in an overcrowded prison cell.

'You a British traitor, then?' the man facing me asked, his voice slimy with truculence.

I stared into his eyes with cold anger. 'Are you addressing me, sailor?'

'No one else round here smells like a traitor.'

I lifted my chin and asked with sharp authority, 'What's your name and rank, man?'

Taken aback, he blurted out, 'Stoker Schmidt.' Then surliness returned to his face. 'If you're British, you must be a traitor.'

'I am an American, Stoker Schmidt, working for German Naval Intelligence and my rank is higher than that of your commander. Do not be insolent if you wish to avoid trouble.'

He blinked for two seconds, then burst out, 'Not on this ship, it isn't!'

'What is not on this ship?'

'Your rank isn't higher than the commander's – and I don't give a damn who you are or where you're from!'

I had been dealt a poor hand but I could easily outplay the stoker. 'Do you always behave like a bad-mannered oaf to guests on your ship, Stoker Schmidt, or, for that matter, in your home? Married, are you?'

I had caught him wrong-footed. 'What's that got to do with you.'

I looked pointedly at the ring on his finger. 'You are, of course. Not ashamed of your wife, are you? Perhaps it is she who is ashamed of you. Tell us her name.'

He was now confused and defensive. I flicked a wink to his companions as if we were all together in teasing him and so increased his feeling of isolation. 'Come, come Schmidt, can't you answer? My God man, you must know her name! Pretty is it, or funny? All right, how old is she?'

These cooped-up sailors were like prisoners; their home life was sacred and utterly private. My questions threatened to expose to ridicule something Schmidt no doubt cared about deeply and tenderly. I was making him pay for his insolence.

He stabbed an angry finger at my face. 'My wife's name or age is none of your business, you ... you stinking pig!'

I shrugged carelessly, 'Could be if I choose to visit her while I'm in Germany.'

Almost choking on his words, he reached out and grabbed my shirt front. 'You ... you ... go near my wife and I'll kill you! I'll beat you to pulp. Yes, you rotting garbage heap, you'd better keep out of my way while you're on this ship!'

Yawning, I smoothed my shirt where he had creased it. 'On one condition will I keep out of your way, Schmidt.'

'What condition?'

'That you keep right out of mine.'

I was relieved when a seaman came up to the table and addressed me. 'Mr Yetstone? Commander and first officer want to speak to you in the control room.'

I gave an off hand nod. 'Expect they want my advice on something. Tell them I'll be along shortly.' But I rose immediately because I knew that it was only a matter of time before one of the three sitting at the table had another go at me.

In the control room a young, fairhaired officer wearing a white polo-neck jersey, and whom I took to be the first officer, sat at the chart table. The commander stood beside it. Waving the list he had made of the information which I had given him, the commander asked, 'Why do you suppose this will place us in danger, Yetstone?'

With sinking heart I noted that he no longer addressed me as, Mr Yetstone. 'Seemed logical that your enemies would want to entice you into a trap.'

'Our enemies, yes. And it's true the first position you gave us would indeed have put my ship on the rocks. But we are puzzled. If the British knew we were about to call into Loch Dorch, they surely had time to prepare something better than a few misleading bearings. They must know I have charts to keep me off rocks.'

'Perhaps they weren't able to lay the trap they intended. I told you I fought off soldiers to keep your ship safe.'

'Yes you did – and with one small pistol. One wonders why our boys are finding things so difficult in Flanders. The second position on this list is more preposterous. It places the target vessel three miles inland on the coast of Ireland.'

He tossed the list onto the table. 'I first supposed that you had neglected your duties and simply given us a random selection of ships, courses and so on. But my first officer points out that we know the real Yetstone received and memorised sound information.

Are you withholding that information or do you not possess it because you are not in fact Yetstone?'

I could think of no story but the true facts which would account for my position and for what had happened. I took a deep breath and spoke with my utmost conviction. 'Sir, I am Yetstone, but I do not have the information you seek.' I went on to describe everything which had happened since I first saw the rat in the brown coat in London's Trafalgar Square.

When I ended, the commander looked sourly at the control room chronometer. 'I do not believe one word of your story but in the time you have taken to relate it I have come to realise that you may possibly be of some use to our intelligence service in Germany. They, I am sure, have ways of extracting something of the facts and will discover why this excellent plan has failed. They may also find out what happened to the real Yetstone and if any other agents are at risk.'

'Captain,' I appealed, 'I have told you the truth. Please put me ashore anywhere in Europe except Great Britain or Germany. I do not want, and have never sought, any part in this war. I beg you, sir, let me live my life out in peace!'

He levelled his unsmiling gaze on my face and spoke harshly, 'Ninety-nine percent of my crew could, with more sincerity I am sure, make that appeal. We are at war, and war both annuls sentiment and abolishes the concept of neutrality. You are either an ally or you are an enemy. If you decide you are an ally, you will be subject to the discipline of this ship and you will obey orders given by any member of its crew, irrespective of rank. If, however, you decide that you are our enemy, there is a short walk with a cold and wet end ahead of you. Now, which is it to—'

A shout from the conning tower, 'Smoke on the horizon!' stopped him.

One foot already on the ladder, he spoke to me over his shoulder, 'Wait here.'

Although the routine of the ship did not vary to any great extent and the engines rumbled evenly on, I sensed the atmosphere had become charged with tension. It was as if everyone was awaiting some portentous event. Twice the chief engineer came into the control room, looked at instruments and went aft. The first officer tidied papers then drummed his fingers on the chart table. The petty officer and his mate sat motionless on stools, their waxy faces turned upwards as they watched the gauges and dials. Orders seemed brisker and briefer.

Having no part in whatever game they were playing, I let other things occupy my thoughts. My passage on the U-boat was now likely to be an uncomfortable one.

'Action stations!' A brief flurry of activity subsided to what seemed routine movements. Not a moment too soon I eased myself behind the iron ladder. An alarm bell sounded in the control room and crewmen came tumbling down from the hatch above.

With the topside hatches made fast, fresh air and daylight were shut out. The noisy clatter of the diesel engines was replaced by the whining hum of electric motors. Waves no longer splashed against the hull and the ship ceased to pitch and roll. I shut my eyes and gripped the sides of the ladder. We were being carried down to the depths of the ocean in a frail, sealed canister.

Finding I could still breathe, I opened my eyes and found myself looking at the back of chief engineer's head, framed between the rungs of an iron ladder. He was standing just to the right of the petty officer on the stool, his feet apart and his arms folded over his chest. Although his eyes roved anxiously over the instrument dials on the walls of the control room, his overall expression was one of alert eagerness. He glanced over his shoulder and made a light-hearted comment which the first officer, who was standing close by my side, added to, sparking a chorus of laughter. I felt excluded from their brotherhood. Above me in the conning tower, the commander pushed his cap to the back of his head and pressed his face to the periscope. His commands were repeated like an echo in the control room. 'Steady at periscope depth.' ... 'Steady at periscope depth!' 'Port fifteen, slow ahead.' ... 'Port fifteen, slow ahead!'

I tried to picture what he saw. A great cargo vessel perhaps, its crew stoking boilers, playing cards, standing at the wheel or sleeping, but all of them unaware of the satanic monster skulking beneath the waves and furtively creeping closer and closer with fangs bared to rend their lives. 'Rats of the sea,' the disfigured man on the train had said.

Remembering that man's anguish made me feel exasperated by the quickening thrill of excitement around me. That was the moment I disassociated myself utterly from everyone in the U-boat and from everything she was intended to accomplish. I was in the wrong place.

Beside me, the first officer unscrewed two small brass caps and stood with his thumbs over the red buttons which they had protected. The caps, dangling at the end of short chains, made a bell-like, tinkling sound.

'Fire one!' the commander ordered, and in the next breath, 'Fire two!' He removed a hand from the periscope handle and wiped its sweaty palm on his thigh.

The first officer pressed one red button and then the other. The ship rocked briefly. The chief engineer uttered a succession of orders. Then only the high-pitched whine of the electric motors disturbed the silence. That was how destruction, disfigurement and death were delivered.

The commander turned around and leaned with his back against the periscope. The petty officer and his mate sat very still on their stools. The first officer wrapped his arms round his chest and hugged himself. They were all like wax figures except the chief engineer who seemed more alert than ever. Seconds ticked away.

Two thumps like muffled beats on an empty metal drum, echoed off the U-boat's hull. The chief engineer uttered a brief command, The first officer threw back his head and with ballooning cheeks, released his pent up breath. The petty officer and his mate bent over their wheels, the commander had turned to face the periscope.

'Up periscope.' ... 'Periscope up!'

'Two hits!'

Round me excitement exploded into fragments of laughter. Then, almost abruptly, discipline returned. Brisk orders were given and acknowledged.

I started to walk out from behind the ladder. Without warning and close to my head a high-pitched screeching, as if the hull were being ripped open, made me crouch with my hands over my ears. The first officer, one hand resting on the ladder, pulled on my arm with the other.

'Steady, Russian. Only compressed air going into the saddle tanks to lift us to the surface.'

When the hatches were opened, I made to follow the first officer up but the second officer pushed me aside. I went instead to the galley and got myself a mug of coffee. When I came back to the control room, the commander and the first officer were standing beside the chart table. I heard the commander say, 'Note the log. Eleven thirty-five. Four-thousand ton tanker, S.S. Nightingale, hit forward of midships and below the bridge. Breaking up and burning. Stern section going down. Some lifeboats launched. Black smoke.' He put his hand on the first officer's shoulder and shook his head sadly. 'Looked a new ship too. Hope they have radio to call for assistance.' Then he spread his hands and shrugged. 'That column of smoke will surely bring something to investigate. Yep, better we move away from the scene.' And he walked forward to his cabin.

Chapter Twenty-One

THE S.S. NIGHTINGALE WAS one of the few ship's names I had remembered and given to the commander. Whether I had recalled her course and position accurately and thus contributed to her sinking, I would never know. The possibility that I had, and was thus partially the cause of torn and bleeding bodies screaming and wallowing in salt water and blazing oil, left me sick and trembling.

The first officer, coming through the bulkhead door, saw me standing idle. He thought for a moment then jerked his thumb over his shoulder, 'You need exercise to liven you up, Yetstone. Into the bow section and report to petty officer torpedoes.'

The bow section, when I got there, seemed already over-crowded – everywhere on that ship was overcrowded - so I stood on one side and watched men lowering a torpedo which had been suspended from a beam under the roof, down through lashed hammocks on to a cradle in front of an open torpedo tube door. I was no innocent, and nothing I could say or do would stop them preparing that package of suffering ready for delivery, but I wanted no part in it.

The petty officer in charge – aptly, the monkey-sailor who had come to the Ghillies' Croft – climbed through the hammocks, along racks and finally dropped to land in front of me. 'What the hell do you want here?' he asked.

'Merely admiring your jungle skills, Petty Officer.'

His little eyes narrowed, 'Told to report here, were you?'

'For sure, if you need advice I'll be happy to give it.'

'That so? Well lads, what do we want the Russian's advice on?'

A ferret-faced man muttered, 'Lost my brother on the Russian front. Put the bastard and his advice up the tube and fire them.'

'Not yet Schiller. Not yet.'

'Could show us how to grease a torpedo,' another suggested.

'A selfless thought, Muller, since that's your task. But perhaps you're right; just be in the way doing anything else. Okay, grease the fish, Yetstone. Now lads, let's get the damn thing into the tube.'

Muller pushed a can of grease and a piece of rag into my hands. 'Spread it evenly where its been rubbed off by the hammocks and see you don't leave any bare patches.'

The torpedo was larger than I supposed one to be and probably weighed more than a ton. Ferret-faced Schiller - the one who had lost his brother on the Russian front - worked beside the cradle while in the bow the petty officer and the rest of the squad prepared tackle with which, I supposed, they meant to pull the torpedo into the tube. They worked efficiently and with urgency. I saw this because, having spread grease on such bare patches as I could see, I felt free to look on.

Schiller snarled, 'Under it too, Russian. And get the parts you've missed as it moves forward.'

I lay on my back under the torpedo. Schiller worked on the cradle beside me. Suddenly the cradle, rocking unsteadily, jolted forward. Realising that I would be crushed to death if the torpedo toppled off and fell on top of me, I began to wriggle out from under it. Before I could so, Schiller got to his feet. He put a boot on the back of my neck and endeavoured to force my head back under.

My hand found a spanner which he must have left on the deck. I dropped my neck and shoulders clear of his boot and lashed out at his shins with the spanner. He jumped back with a howl and I sprang to my feet. For a moment we stood face to face, each holding a spanner. I advanced. Schiller threw down his spanner and shouted to the petty officer.

The petty officer ducked under a cable and came back. 'What's going on here?'

'Caught him tampering with the torpedo and then he tried to kill me,' Schiller lied.

I rolled my eyes heavenwards to imply Schiller was mad.

'You try too hard to be funny, Russian,' the petty officer said.

'And some don't have to try at all,' I replied. 'Just think about it. Why should I want to tamper with a torpedo and how could I possibly know what to do even if I did?'

'You certainly know how to make yourself unpopular! Right, Schiller, show me what he was up to.'

They got under the torpedo and in less than a minute crawled out again. The petty officer spoke to one of the squad. 'Fetch the first officer. Torpedoes are his responsibility.'

The men began to shuffle round me in a muttering circle and each had a spar of wood or a metal stay in his hand. Somehow I found myself with my back to the forward bulkhead, facing them. Led by Schiller, they began to close in. The petty officer stood outside the ring with his back to it, pretending that he was unaware of what was going on.

I knew that, at best, I was going to end up with broken bones and bruises. My only way of escape was to pull myself up into the hammocks and torpedoes slung under the roof, cross above Schiller's gang, then drop to the deck and make a bolt for the control room. I was getting ready to jump up for the nearest hammock when the first officer broke through the ring.

'What's this about Yetstone disarming a torpedo?'

'Not disarming it, sir. But have a look.'

The petty officer did not even lower his voice as he crouched beside the first officer. 'We'd have a damn sight less trouble now if we'd shot the Russian in his stinking hovel as I suggested. What he's done is taken the hawser off the torpedo and then fixed it to the cradle. Instead of pulling the torpedo into the tube, we'd have pulled the cradle from under the torpedo and it would then have smashed its tail fins on the deck.'

Everyone heard what he said. Hostile words like poisoned darts flew in my direction.

The first officer stood up. I appealed to him. 'You must surely know that's a tale concocted because I happen to be Russian. If the torpedo had come off the cradle it wouldn't have smashed its tail on the deck, it would have crushed my skull. I was lying under it. No, if anyone did anything to it, it was Schiller.'

'He's a liar, sir!' Schiller blustered. 'I knew he'd been up to something when I caught him getting out from under as fast as he could. Then he tried to kill me with the spanner.'

The petty officer looked at the spanner in my hand. 'So, what were you using that for, Yetstone? You were told to grease the torpedo.'

The first officer gave me no opportunity to defend myself. 'Schiller, take Yetstone to the control room and both of you wait there. Carry on arming the ship, Petty Officer.'

As we pushed through the circle of seamen, one of them muttered, 'You'll feed the fish yet, Ivan.'

We were only a few minutes in the control room before a chief petty officer stuck his head through the bulkhead door. 'Schiller, report to the bow section. Yetstone, the commander's cabin.'

The commander was lying on his bunk. He raised his head and shoulders and rested on an elbow. 'I can't imagine what you're up to, Yetstone, but clearly I've got to treat you as a hostile prisoner. I'm putting you in irons.'

'I never tampered with the torpedo. It was Schiller—,'

'Silence! This is not a discussion. Whether for the safety of the ship or for your own safety, you will be kept under guard until we return to port. Escort him back to the control room.'

In the control room I found Stoker Schmidt waiting for me. He held a wooden stool, a short length of light chain and a padlock. He placed the stool behind the iron ladder, then he took my left wrist and clamped it in a manacle which was attached to the chain. 'Only guests with a rank higher than the commander's get this decoration,' he gloated, 'And Schiller says to tell you the conger eels are waiting. Another of your old friends, is he?'

The chief engineer asked, 'Done yet, stoker?' To me he said, 'Sit on the stool, it's your berth from now on. We've no cells on the ship but in here you'll be under observation twenty-four hours a day.' He hooked the padlock to a ring on the end of the chain and then locked it to a rung on the ladder. 'If the ship is in peril, you will be freed and get equal opportunity to reach safety.'

The chain from the manacle to the rung was less than six inches long so, when I stood upright, it pulled down on my arm. When I sat on the stool, however, it held my left arm aloft. Whatever I did I would be uncomfortable and eating off a plate would be well nigh impossible.

The control room had not been designed to accommodate a large man sitting on a stool behind the ladder. Not all of the crew took advantage of this by trampling on my feet or kicking my legs but most refused to speak to me. That very first night someone tried to kill me.

I had been given a bowl of potato soup for supper. Only because I was ravenous, did I not reject the tasteless mush. Unable to sup it with a spoon, I poured the liquid directly from the bowl into my mouth. I removed what I first thought to be a particle of grit from my tongue but which, when I examined it more closely, turned out to be a tiny, needle-sharp sliver of glass. The sludge remaining at the bottom of the bowl held scores of these razor-edged particles, some of which I must surely have swallowed had I used a spoon. Not only did someone want me dead, they wanted me to die in the agony of a lacerated stomach haemorrhaging.

When I displayed my find to the officer on watch, he simply laughed. 'Always thought the food on this ship was lethal!'

My life was not worth a dime of their concern! It took little imagination for me to see that my death could be accomplished in a score of horrific ways. Sleep would leave me defenceless. I was not so much afraid as overwhelmed by a feeling of lonely isolation.

A strange light-headedness affected me. Almost from the moment of my birth I had been thrust like a gaming cock into the pit to fight for my existence. I was no stranger to terror. I knew, too, the weird effects of being mentally deranged by alcohol. Never before, however, had my faculties seemed so to detach themselves from my body. It was as if I now looked down from above on the sordid wretch huddled on the stool - the foul carcase which was me.

Why did I bait and torment that pitiable creature so mercilessly? Yes, I could accuse no one of being so unrelentingly cruel to me as I was myself. I was my own sadistic torturer. Where was my clemency when, time and time again, I stupified myself to a disgusting, mumbling abomination or rolled sodden and sick in a gutter?

No, I could not blame my cruel father, jealous circus artistes, the greedy rat in the brown coat, nor even the old spy in London for my predicament. If my life were to go on like this, would it not be an act of clemency to let the Germans end it now and dump my poor afflicted corpse into the ocean?

My thoughts unfolded sluggishly. For some reason, I had never chosen the easy or obvious path. Always I had sought to contend ... to win ... to attain something which forever stayed beyond my grasp. Even when I had won fame, fame had not – and never would – keep me sober. It had not – and never would – fill that void, that insistent longing which I had striven to assuage since infancy.

Only once in my life had I glimpsed what it was that my soul hungered for. In those few moments after I had unwrapped Rosalind's present I had enjoyed a serene contentment - no, not contentment, a sense of worth. I had felt that Sergei Melnikov was more than just a name to one other person on this earth.

I could not now return to London and carry off my princess but, if my future life was to have meaning, I must do so one day. I would find Rosalind, rescue her and devote my life to making the dreams

I had created for her come true. In return, my princess would shield me from the curse of drink. I had once vowed to justify her love and trust with success and fame. I would do so, but first I had to show the world that I was neither hypocrite, coward nor traitor.

The experience through which I went in those few minutes while, as it were, my body and soul were parted seemed to have scoured my being. I felt like a new man - a man re-born. Never had I known such a clear and powerful sense of purpose. In that strange interlude of objective clarity, I recognised not only that I might well fail to regain fame but also that fame meant little to Rosalind. What really mattered now was that the name Melnikov would not be reviled as that of a drunken scumbag. My little princess deserved better than that.

I looked back on how, in that lonely little house on the shores of Loch Dorch, I had defied temptation. For the first time in ten years I had dragged myself clear of the spiralling pull of an alcoholic vortex. I had been within an ace of freeing myself not only from the clutches of the old masterspy, but of my lifelong curse. Another day and I would have been a new man starting life afresh. At the very least I owed myself a second chance. I must not let that German rabble or any German court deny me my first chance of true happiness.

My happiness? I would let nothing stop me from rescuing my damsel and leading her into the kingdom of sunshine and comfort I had promised! That end, and not fame, was the star which would now guide my life.

My eye lighting on the lethal bowl of soup, reunited my spirit and body. In reality, the courses open to me were few indeed. My disadvantages were many and plain.

For another hour I pondered my plight. I reasoned that the only way I could leave the U-boat alive and before it returned to base was to force it to surrender to a target ship. Could I make that happen without myself being killed?

I realised immediately that I would have no choice in the nationality of my rescue ship. Indeed, the most likely vessel to be in the vicinity of the U-boat was a British cargo ship. In that I must take my chance. The trick was to sabotage the submarine in such a way that it was forced to surface just minutes or seconds before it released its torpedoes. And then what? Then I must trust in Providence. Ladies and gentlemen! The Great Melnikov is about to perform the most dangerous trick of his career! He will catapult himself from the core of a U-boat twenty feet underwater onto the deck of an American luxury liner – and without a safety net!

The last part was mere capricious thinking but it never-the-less lifted my spirits. I was chained to an iron ladder, shunned by everyone and I knew almost nothing about U-boats. Still, the very madness of the idea appealed to me. The odds on saving my life if I did nothing at all were no better, so why should my last act not be one of glorious daring?

Whatever my chance of success, my mind was fully occupied. The crew of the U-boat were now clearly my enemy. As such, I must discover where they were most vulnerable. In probing for information I would camouflage my real interest behind a facade of guileless ignorance.

'Is life in a U-boat ever dangerous, Petty Officer?' I asked one of the men sitting on stools on the other side of the control room.

'For you Russian, very dangerous.'

'Oh sure, for me. But for the crew is it not simply a safe and cosy place in which to hide throughout the war? Even a hurricane cannot harm a submarine when it is deep underwater.'

'God forbid you ever find out just how dangerous it can be!'

'Huh, like what?'

He yawned. 'You won't find it cosy if a hurricane does hit us, or a mine, or a torpedo, or a depth bomb. Submarines have been run down, rolled over or split open by other vessels when they're coming to the surface. The crew can be gassed if seawater gets to the batteries. And that's without listing a possible thousand varieties of mechanical failure.'

Many of the dangers he listed were of no use to me. However, in the thousand varieties of mechanical failure there might just be one which suited my purpose. 'Mechanical failure? Huh!' I said dismissively, 'You'd just loaf about on the surface like this until it was repaired.'

'Sure, sure, if it could be repaired and if we could get to the surface, and if there wasn't an enemy warship waiting for us when we did.' He tapped the wheel in front of him. 'This operates the hydroplanes - the large fins which stick out from the side of the ship at the bow and at the stern. They control the pitch of the ship when she's diving. If the hydroplane controls were to fail when we're diving, the U-boat would go headlong, deeper and deeper and deeper. When she got below the red sector on that depth gauge up there, the ocean pressure would be so great it would crush her like an egg in a vice. Ever fancied being the meat in a corned beef can?' He laughed and half-glanced over his shoulder. 'Still not afraid, Russian? You should be!'

I sat silent. Only as a last resort must I sink the U-boat and destroy myself.

Thinking he had alarmed me into silence, the petty officer grunted, 'Stop worrying about the dangers of mechanical failure. You, Ruskie, have more to fear from the crew and, right now, from the first officer catching you smoking below decks.'

I nipped the glowing tip of the cigarette I had absentmindedly put in my mouth. As I watched the last wisp of smoke spiral up into the conning tower, I thought of a way to make the U-boat surface just when I wanted: a well-timed fire on board!

Chapter Twenty-Two

When I looked around the control room, I concluded that the one risk the commander need not fear was fire. Except for papers on the chart table, everything in the submarine appeared to be made of steel or brass. Then a fuel gauge caught my eye. Not everything! A fuel pipe fractured at the right moment and its spilling contents set ablaze would surely force the U-boat to the surface.

Pipes of every size and description abounded. It was not, however, discovering which one contained fuel or even devising a means to fracture it that troubled me. Any game involving fire held life and death perils. A minor spillage would too easily be dealt with by the crew, whereas an uncontrolled blazing flood might roast us all before the U-boat got to the surface.

Almost certainly I would be chained to the ladder when the U-boat went into action so whatever I did to start a fire would have to be done from where I sat. I looked around. Only one half-inch copper pipe lay within my reach. Not only was it within reach but it had a coupling joint which I could surely find a way to slacken and tighten and thus control the flow of spilling liquid. The question was: did it contain fuel oil?

Whatever else, I must give no inkling of what I planned. Best I just go on playing the simpleton and learn what I wanted obliquely. Luckily the watch had changed while I had been pondering and another pair of seamen sat at the hydroplane controls.

Pointing to the tangled mat of rubber-insulated electric cables which spread across the roof of the control room I asked, 'Those air pipes for the saddle tanks?'

'No, you stupid Cossack, they're electric cables,' the sailor replied.

'Electric cables! Oh sure. I guess air pipes would be larger. More like this.' I laid my hand on the half-inch copper pipe which ran along the wall at my back.

'Water for the galley.' Plainly bored, he stretched his arms above his head and yawned. 'Tell me, Ruskie, is it true that you lived in a cave in the hills with no soap or water?'

A water pipe was of little use to me.

Having put my faith in a well-timed fire, I could think of nothing else. It was, I think, while I watched wood shavings fall from the knife of a seaman whittling the shape of a submarine out of a wooden log that a rather obvious thought came to me. If there was nothing combustible within reach of my hand, I must gather together materials which were.

I now began to steal and hoard anything which would burn. When exercised - exercise consisted of an escorted walk the full length of the ship and back - I almost always found something. An old newspaper left on a bunk, wood shavings which the carver had swept up and put in a paper bag for dumping, an empty candy box, were all deftly slipped into or under my old black overcoat. Once, as I passed a stoker cleaning a part of the engines, I stooped to tie my shoe lace and somehow his bottle of white spirit found its way into my sock.

Very soon it became inconvenient to carry on my person all the materials I had acquired. One evening at the end of a walk but before my wrist was locked to the ladder, I took off my old overcoat and hung it from a bolt-tail on the roof behind where I sat. There, its pockets, sleeves and lining became my secret storehouse. The skirt of the coat I draped round my shoulders to screen me while I stuffed the lining or flattened what I had plundered the better to conceal it.

Oh yes, from time to time voices were raised and accusations made about things lost. But no one looked with suspicion at me. My lean body, clad only in jacket, shirt and trousers, plainly harboured none of the missing articles.

Preoccupied with my plot, I became less concerned with being murdered and I had little use for sleep. I watched with fresh interest what each member of the crew did in order to learn the routine of the ship. The most trivial detail might, at some stage, be vital to success.

The flammable secrets of my overcoat were constantly at risk. Because the control room was always brightly lit, there was for me neither night nor day. My preparations had to be carried out furtively for I knew I would not long outlive discovery of my intention. My nerves became taut as frayed violin strings. A crewman had only to glance at my overcoat for my stomach muscles to clutch into a knot.

Except for bodily functions, I refused to take exercise - claiming that my life was in danger from members of the crew. I insisted on preparing my own food, not only to protect myself from being poisoned but because the galley was a useful source of materials. I stole syrup and sugar because they would burn readily; I filled an old envelope with lard because, once alight, I hoped it would make a stinking smoke. I even scooped a handful of dried peas into my pocket for no reason I could think of. Although tempted, I did not steal a knife or anything of value because I had no wish to prompt a search of my belongings.

I removed my celluloid collar and tore it into thin strips. I then wove the strips into a ball like a bird's nest and poured a mixture of syrup and engine grease into the spaces between strands. This I wedged into the space behind a steel beam where it was both concealed and protected. Burning, it would emit a dense, choking smoke. Time and again I checked the distance between where I stood behind the ladder and where the first officer would be standing to fire the torpedoes when the ship went into action.

I became steadily weaker with fatigue and more excitable and suspicious with lack of sleep. The most innocent question produced in me a sort of hysteria. Anyone making to come behind the ladder was confronted with a hissing, snarling, spitting creature very much like a trapped wild animal. The crew thought I was going mad, and in a way I was.

My imagined fears became confused with real alarms. On one occasion the diving alarm roused me out of a twitchy doze. Hatches were clanging shut and men scrambling down the ladder. Unsure of what was happening and panic-prone, I took the box of matches from my pocket and crouched ready to strike a match when I overheard the navigating officer tell the hydroplane operators that a lookout had spotted a fishing boat and we were going underwater lest its crew saw the U-boat and reported its position.

As I struggled to recover composure after the incident, the engineroom petty officer said curtly as he passed through the control room, 'Take your coat down from there, Russian. I'm going to inspect and clean the pressure valve behind it in half an hour.'

My frayed temper flared and I almost screamed defiant curses at the man. I was now too tired to think of any way by which I might conceal my preparations or delay his inspection going ahead.

Believing my whole future depended on the incendiaries I had so intricately constructed, I could not bring myself to dismantle them. Indeed, even had I been able to strip and hide the materials without someone seeing me and guessing what I had in mind - which they could scarcely fail to do - I was convinced that I would never again find the vitality or the courage to reconstruct them.

I put off starting demolition for five minutes, gambling on the petty officer finding something which needed his attention more urgently or on the U-boat finding a target ship. The odds against anything of the sort happening were colossal, and I lost. I gambled another five minutes – five unbelievably short minutes - and lost again. Although I recognised in myself the contemptible weakness I had seen in desperate gamblers when I dealt them hopeless cards in Mistress Pettyleg's back room, I wagered precious minutes again and again – and lost.

My half-hour was up and the U-boat was back on the surface. I still had done nothing to hide the evidence of my plot. My brain was inflamed with fatigue to a drunken recklessness. I staked my life on yet another five minutes and on the petty officer forgetting altogether about his assignment with the valve. I fumed at the commander for not finding a target. Had days not gone by without the U-boat coming across anything larger than a fishing boat? It seemed incredible that the sea should be so empty. The coward, I began to suspect, was evading action.

An hour at least must have passed since I had been warned to remove my coat. The engineroom petty officer pushed through the bulkhead door. His gaze was fixed purposefully on my coat. Blood throbbed in my ears. Tears flooded my eyes. Feebly, I held up my free hand as if to fend him off.

Someone shouted something from the conning tower. The petty officer turned aside and propped himself against the chart table. The engines of the U-boat rumbled on. My breathing was as laboured as if I were climbing Dunmallach Hill. The clangour of the diving bell filled the control room. 'A big one on the horizon,' the first man down from the conning tower said. The engineroom petty officer pushed himself off the table and went back the way he had come.

I was now committed beyond any going back. My heart pounding in my chest almost choked me. Terror numbed my body. I knew from my days of stardom that without the relaxing warmth of a shot of vodka, I could do nothing. I could neither think nor act. Then, inside my head - softly at first - I heard again the roll of drums heralding my circus act. Their tempo and volume increased to a crescendo. Schnorr cracked his whip. I was on!

I came alive. Tense beyond words and impatient to show off my matchless talent, I felt wiser, more dextrous, more ingenious than any man had ever been!

Seamen tumbled down the ladder and dispersed to their stations. The commander descended in an almost leisurely manner. He stood to my left with his hands deep in his pockets. 'Something worth waiting for, Hugo,' he said to the first officer, 'but she's zigzagging to make things difficult for us. I'd prefer a surface attack when she got within range but they'll have a masthead lookout and we might be spotted too soon. Better we wait. Her main course looks about right for bringing her on to us.'

Pleased no doubt with having found a target for his U-boat, the commander strutted round the control room tapping the dials of all the instruments. To the chief engineer he said, 'Ship balanced and ready, eh? Keep us at periscope depth. I'll be disappointed if this one gets away.' He placed a hand on a rung of the ladder. Catching sight of my unshaven, sweat-oiled face staring at him, he laughed, 'You look fevered, Yetstone. Seasick or battlesick?' And with a laugh he climbed up to the conning tower.

Although the crew knew nothing of it, this time I had my part to play in the engagement. Crouching behind the ladder like a black crab in a rock crevice, I observed everything and listened for my cue to act. To the Germans I was little more than a silent, hunchback shadow as they waited for their prize to come within striking distance.

'Make bow tubes ready!'
'Bow tubes ready!'
'Starboard ten!'
'Starboard ten!'
'Slow ahead!'
'Slow ahead!'
'Lower the periscope!'
'Periscope down!'
'Up periscope!'
'Periscope up!'
The commander, his face pressed to the periscope, relayed

what only he could see of the world above the waves. 'Eight thousand tons ... Canadian flag ... range, one thousand metres ... stand by to fire number one ...'

Without haste, not to attract attention, I reached my unshackled hand into my overcoat pocket and, keeping the rest of my body motionless, pulled the cork from the bottle of white spirit and turned it upside down. A dark stain spread down as the spirit soaked through the fabric. I caught a whiff of the vapour, too.

Knowing that the whine of the electric motors and the stream of commands and acknowledgements would cover the sound, I scraped a match. Carefully cupping it in my free hand to shroud its light, I held the little flame below a ribbon of paper inside my coat then swiftly moved it to the ball of syrup-coated celluloid strips.

'Fire one!'

The success of my plan required that the torpedoes miss their target. I gripped the ladder and pushed my backside in the direction of the first officer until the manacle cut into my wrist, then I lashed out twice with my foot. My heel smashed into the back of the first officer's knees as I hoped it would. His legs buckled and he staggered backwards towards me. His thumb missed the red button. Recovering his balance, he stabbed it with his forefinger on a second attempt. 'Number one away!' Snarling, he turned on me.

I saw the flames at my back reflected on his moist face. His eyes opened wide with horror and his lips moved wordlessly.

'Fire two!' The commander was not yet aware that his control room was turning into a furnace.

Thick, grey smoke was now gushing from the ball of celluloid fibres and blending with the yellow flames and black choking smoke from my overcoat.

As if in a trance, the first officer stood blinking. Then, gathering his wits, he spun round and jabbed his thumb on the second red button. 'Number two away!'

I now picked up the stool and crouched behind the ladder, ready to protect the conflagration. Heat scorched the back of my neck and head.

Though smoke now hid the roof and a choking fog filled the control room, the chief engineer's voice went steadily on issuing orders. His priority was to keep the U-boat safely on an even keel.

The first officer threw himself at me, trying to reach the burning coat. I drew my right knee up to my chest and let him come on until his stomach hit the sole of my shoe then, as I had done with the sailor on the train, I flung him back so violently he crashed on his back taking another sailor with him.

With one hand manacled, I was forced to twist my trunk awkwardly to shield the flames from attack on my other side. Two seamen, striving to reach and beat out the fire with their caps became wedged between the ladder and the periscope well. I smashed the stool down on one man's head and brought my knee up into the other's groin. They tumbled in a tangled heap and obstructed others from getting to my coat.

The acrid smell of burning rubber insulation from cables on the roof mixed with the sour reek of smouldering wool from my overcoat. The heat was intolerable. I knew the back of my jacket was on fire. Papers which had fallen to the floor from the chart table were curling and turning brown. I could no longer see the chief engineer's head just two feet beyond the ladder. The petty officer on the hydroplane wheel was protesting that he could not see the gauges.

I was now crouched as low as the short chain on my wrist permitted. Through streaming eyes I watched the flames, now starved of oxygen, begin to dwindle. Then the forward bulkhead door was thrown open and the flames leaped again as fresh air reached them.

Two men unrolling a hose came in. As they approached I threw handfuls of dried peas at their faces but it did nothing to deter them.

The heat was now beyond human endurance and I was on the point of passing out. It took all of my strength to raise the stool and deflect a jet of water from the hose upwards and away from my coat. The deflected jet swept splashing and hissing across the glowing charred cables covering the roof. Like Chinese crackers, blue sparks crackled among the cables. The lights everywhere went out. Curses and bawled orders echoed through the darkness.

Someone on the floor clutched my legs and struggled to drag me out from behind the ladder. All I could do then was to pull the stool over my head to protect my skull from the raining blows of hammers and spanners. A second before a boot struck my chin I heard the screaming whistle of compressed air entering the saddle tanks. The U-boat was surfacing.

Chapter Twenty-Three

LIKE A NAUSEOUS TIDE, consciousness drifted in and out, each time depositing me higher on a scorching shore. A star floated in the blackness which bound me like a straitjacket. Even as I tried to fix the star it resolved itself into a gold signet ring reflecting light. The ring was on a hand unlocking the chain from my wrist to the ladder. Words, fluffy and indistinct, fell on my ears. 'Don't think he's quite dead, sir. Shall I fetch a gun and finish him off?'

'And waste more time? Let the sea finish him off! Just get on with it! Pitch him over the side. Do anything you bloody well like but get him out of here! I've no time to discuss the matter!' I recognised the chief engineer's voice.

I felt my ankles being gripped and then my body was dragged across the control room floor. Two men, grunting and cursing, began to haul me feet first up through the conning tower hatches. Blood flowing down to my brain helped clear my faintness but I went on feigning unconsciousness. It was fortunate my jacket and shirt had fallen over my head and concealed my face, because I found it almost impossible not to cry out as my poor battered body was scraped and bumped against the iron ladders and hatches.

Never having learned how to swim, I knew I had to seize any opportunity which presented itself to break free before I was dumped in the sea. That opportunity came when they dropped my body on to the deck at the base of the conning tower.

I sprang to my feet. Though barely conscious, I lashed out with the short chain – still attached to my wrist - at anyone who got in my way. Half-reeling, I stumbled towards the stern of the U-boat and staggered to a halt only when the deck narrowed to less than three feet wide and I could reach and grip the jump wires which stretched from above the conning tower down to a shackle on the tail of the boat.

I braced myself, ready to take the crew on one at a time.

No one had pursued me. I stood alone and unheeded. Round the conningtower seamen posed like statues; most of them open-mouthed, gaping over the sea to starboard.

I followed their gaze and saw why my escape had gone unhindered. Less than two hundred yards away, the bow of an enormous ship, like the sharp end of an axe, sliced through the sea directly for the middle of the U-boat.

I dropped back a step and clutched the jump wires with both hands.

Although the U-boat's propellers churned the sea, it seemed scarcely to move. The huge steamship hurtled down on us. Foot by sluggish foot the submarine crawled forward. Then the bows of the steamship were towering above me. I heard the hiss and ripple of its stem splitting the brine. Letting go of the jump wires, I crouched on my knees and gripped the deck grating as if to wrench the U-boat from the sea.

Even as the shadow of the steamer's bow fell on me, the U-boat turned sharply to starboard, swinging her stern away but not quite clear of the charging vessel. With a mighty clang and shuddering impact the steel forepart of the steamer struck the projecting stern hydroplane of the U-boat. For a fleeting moment I could have placed my hand on the hull plating of the vessel as it rushed past.

The submarine rolled half over under the blow then, with what seemed a great effort, she heaved herself upright and bobbing like a porpoise, passed alongside the ship.

The steamship's crew looked down on us from her rails. I waved my manacled hand to show I needed assistance but not until twenty feet separated the vessels did they understand and throw a lifebelt. It landed in the sea just four feet from the stern of the U-boat but instantly that four feet became ten then twenty. Then the lifebelt was lost in the white turbulence of the mingling wash of both ships. The stern of the S.S. Homestar went away from the submarine as swiftly as her bow had borne down on it.

Although the U-boat had escaped disaster by no more than a fraction of a second, many of the crew were dancing and laughing and shouting as if they had performed a clever and hilarious exploit. One shouted to the commander who was looking over the conning tower screens, 'Give them a fish from our stern tubes, sir!'

Most of the U-boat's crew continued to follow the course of the Homestar, but not all. Three men moved out and began walking towards the stern. Schiller led them.

I rose to my feet, and again holding on to the jump wires to steady myself, endeavoured to fathom what they intended.

At about twenty paces from me the three stopped because the deck was too narrow for them to walk abreast. Schiller laughed unpleasantly, 'Time to feed the fishes, Russian!'

Relieved to see they were unarmed, I called back, 'Well sure, Schiller, but we feed them together.'

They came a yard closer. One of his gang had a pocketful of iron bolts which he began to throw at me but they all missed their mark.

Schiller pushed himself forward from between the other two. 'No, Ivan, you take this bath alone.'

I eased back towards the stern where the deck was less than two feet wide. Schiller would have to tackle me without help from his friends and, I guessed, Schiller did not possess that sort of courage. Renewing my grip on the jump wire so that I would not easily be dislodged, I spoke with more confidence than I possessed. 'You knew I was the better man when you faced me in the bow of the U-boat, didn't you?'

Schiller faltered and then stopped when he was still more than ten feet away. He seemed to have no idea what to do next. The other two fell back.

To further confuse his thinking, I jeered, 'Why not try a rush with a punch to my face?' for I saw that was what he planned, 'Then as you flounder in the sea and before you drown you can work out what went wrong.'

He glowered, fidgeted and finally called over his shoulder, 'Bring me a gun, Ulrich, and I'll shoot the pig!'

His mates had lost interest in me and were now making their way back to the conning tower.

I saw his weakness and, waving the chain on my wrist, took a couple of steps in his direction. 'Be brave just for once and do something on your own.'

The fists with which he had threatened me were now limp hands hanging at his sides.

'A big mouth and no guts, eh, Schiller?'

He backed off, snarling, 'We'll get you yet, Russian!'

A coward is the most dangerous enemy a man can have.

The creamy wake of the Homestar was taking the shape of a crescent as she came round to have another go at running down the U-boat. This time she would not fail to ram it. I searched for something to keep me afloat when she did.

Forward of the conning tower I saw the barrel of the U-boat's four-inch gun swing out. But the Homestar had made her turn and now, bow-on, presented a small target. With the U-boat bobbing and rolling it was well nigh impossible to lay the gun and fire it before the cargo ship was upon us.

The gun swung in again and a signal lamp flashed from the conning tower. Our speed fell away.

The commander leaned over the conningtower screens with a hailer. 'Prepare to abandon ship! We cannot dive because the stern hydroplanes are out of action and, crippled, we cannot escape being run down. If it were nightfall I would try making a run for it on the surface, but there are eight hours of daylight ahead and if you look at the Canadian ship's masthead, you'll see that she has a radio. No doubt we'll have a British destroyer to contend with soon. You may collect personal belongings, but hurry!'

Reluctantly, men moved towards the conning tower.

The Homestar's bow slanted away from a collision course and her speed fell away. As she drew alongside the submarine, her propellers churned astern briefly to stop forward movement. Gently, she drifted close to the U-boat.

Within minutes, a side ladder was lowered from the ship's rail and the crew of the U-boat began shuffling towards it.

I too, moved towards the conning tower, but I kept my distance from the crew. I was happy to wait until they had all been taken off. While I waited, I took the gunmetal watch from my pocket. The old masterspy in London was certainly astute but not even he could have foreseen the outcome of giving it to me. For me the watch had been a symbol of enslavement. Laughing more with relief than with amusement, I tossed it over the side and watched it sink.

The commander looked down along the length of the ship. His face was a mask of distress. One of the crew – a boy not yet eighteen – seeing me laugh and mistaking the reason, came aft with tears in his eyes and his fists trembling with passion.

'You thankless rat! The commander was the only man on the U-boat who wanted you to live and now you're laughing at him!'

He would have thrown himself at me but an older man came up behind and drew him back. 'The Russian's been taken care of, he's going down with the U-boat.' To me he growled, 'If you believe in God, say your last prayer.'

They had opened the U-boat's seacocks and she was already settling in the water. The deck plates at the stern were awash.

The Germans, as they were transferred to the Homestar, gathered round the top of the ladder. I could see they meant to raise it as soon as the last member of the U-boat's crew had been taken off. I waved and shouted to the crew of the ship to move them away. I guessed that, even if I did get on to the ladder, they would overturn it and throw me off before I reached the ship's rail. Every time I called up, the crew of the U-boat drowned my words with chanting and shouting in chorus.

The last German sailor was taken off. Frantic now, I screamed my pleas to the crew of the Canadian ship. Only when a gap of four feet had opened between the ships did they seem to realise my plight. Some then tried to drive the Germans back. Others shouted, 'Jump, you fool! Jump! The U-boat's being scuttled!' But a mob of Germans had broken through and got to the ladder again.

I could not swim and I feared that if I missed the ladder, I would fall into the sea and drown.

The U-boat's stern was now completely underwater and I was forced to climb her slanting decks. The ships had drifted ten feet apart. I no longer looked up at the ship's rail but watched with helpless fascination as the sea crawled up the deck after me like a voracious monster.

Even as the bow of the U-boat reared prior to sliding stern first to the bottom of the ocean, a rope fell on my shoulders. With the haste of desperation, I wound it round my chest and knotted the end.

The submarine dropped from under my feet but now suspended from the line, I swung thirty feet through the air and crashed body and skull against the steel of the ship's hull.

* * *

I came to between white sheets in a spacious, airy cabin. The manacle had been removed and my arms and shoulders bandaged where the flesh had been torn or burned. My head throbbed and I felt sick. I lapsed again into unconsciousness.

When next I opened my eyes, I felt a little better. A plump, black face grinned down at me. 'Yo' lookin' at me, suh? Yo' like I git y' somethin' maybe?'

'Please, a drink.'

'Sure! Whisky, wine, beer or milk, suh? Yo' can have jus' what yo' fancy.'

'Water.'

'Jus' plain water, suh?'

'Water. I've sworn off alcohol for the rest of my life, buddy.'

'Then water it is. Yes suh!'

I saw that he locked the cabin door when he went out and also when he returned with a glass on a tray.

'Not lockin' yo' in. Jus' the Gerries keep breaking out an' they ain't lookin' to wish you a Merry Christmas.'

He handed me the glass of water then deftly spun a chair and sat leaning over its back. 'Nearly lost yo' – know that? Saw the chain on yo' arm but we thought yo' was jus' a misbehavin' Gerry. Yo' bin fighting a one-man war they say. That right, suh? Cap'n says he gonna see yo' git the biggest medal there is fo' savin' his ship. Want somethin' else, suh?'

'I've a thumping headache.'

He swung himself off the chair and went to the door. Before he unlocked it, he turned and asked, 'Yo' ain't swore off aspirin?'

Epilogue

To: Captain J.L. Jannet, D.S.C., R.N.

24th November 1916

PERSONAL AND CONFIDENTIAL

Dear Captain Jannet,

I have made enquiries regarding the matter of which we spoke yesterday.

The rumour circulating in your Division to the effect that the sentence passed on the spy, Melnikov, has been commuted to deportation emanates from information published in certain Canadian newspapers. I can, however, confirm that the information is indeed based on fact.

You will recall that at the time of his trial, the Canadian press attempted to make Melnikov into something of a hero (despite Melnikov himself confessing his actions in saving the Canadian ship were inspired solely by self-interest).

I fancy the change of sentence has come about through diplomatic pressure rather than from production of fresh evidence but no official explanation or announcement has been made. I know that having the original sentence set aside will do little for the morale of officers in your Division who have the difficult task of bringing these things to light and securing a verdict. Nevertheless, in the circumstances I strongly advise that you neither confirm nor deny the rumour. More momentous events will soon displace interest in the affair.

Yours sincerely,
James Hutcheon
Captain R.N.

END

Some other books published by **LUATH** PRESS

FICTION

The Bannockburn Years

William Scott

ISBN 0 946487 34 0 PBK £7.95

A present day Edinburgh solicitor stumbles across reference to a document of value to the Nation State of Scotland. He tracks down the document on the Isle of Bute, a document which probes the real 'quaestiones' about nationhood and national identity. The document ends up being published, but is it authentic and does it matter? Almost 700 years on, these 'quaestiones' are still worth asking.

Written with pace and passion, William Scott has devised an intriguing vehicle to open up new ways of looking at the future of Scotland and its people. He presents an alternative interpretation of how the Battle of Bannockburn was fought, and through the Bannatyne manuscript he draws the reader into the minds of those involved.

Winner of the 1997 Constable Trophy, the premier award in Scotland for an unpublished novel, this book offers new insights to both the academic and the general reader which are sure to provoke further discussion and debate.

'*A brilliant storyteller. I shall expect to see your name writ large hereafter.*'
NIGEL TRANTER, October 1997.

'*... a compulsive read.*' PH Scott, THE SCOTS-MASN

FOLKLORE

Tall Tales from an Island

Peter Macnab

ISBN 0 946487 07 3 PBK £8.99

Peter Macnab was born and reared on Mull. He heard many of these tales as a lad, and others he has listened to in later years. Although collected on Mull, they could have come from any one of the Hebridean islands. Timeless and universal, these tales are still told round the fireside when the visitors have all gone home.

There are humorous tales, grim tales, witty tales, tales of witchcraft, tales of love, tales of heroism, tales of treachery, historical tales and tales of yesteryear. There are unforgettable characters like Do'l Gorm, the philosophical roadman, and Calum nan Croig, the Gaelic storyteller whose highly developed art of convincing exaggeration mesmerised his listeners. There is a headless horseman, and a whole coven of witches. Heroes, fools, lairds, herdsmen, lovers and liars, dead men and live cats all have a place in this entrancing collection. This is a superb collection indeed, told by a master storyteller with all the rhythms remembered from the firesides of his childhood.

A popular lecturer, broadcaster and writer, Peter Macnab is the author of a number of books and articles about Mull, the island he knows so intimately and loves so much. As he himself puts it in his introduction to this book 'I am of the unswerving opinion that nowhere else in the world will you find a better way of life, nor a finer people with whom to share it.'

'*All islands, it seems, have a rich store of characters whose stories represent a kind of sub-culture without which island life would be that much poorer. Macnab has succeeded in giving the retelling of the stories a special Mull flavour, so much so that one can visualise the storytellers sitting on a bench outside the house with a few cronies, puffing on their pipes and listening with nodding approval.'* WEST HIGHLAND FREE PRESS

The Supernatural Highlands

Francis Thompson
ISBN 0 946487 31 6 PBK £8.99

An authoritative exploration of the otherworld of the Highlander, happenings and beings hitherto thought to be outwith the ordinary forces of nature. A simple introduction to the way of life of rural Highland and Island communities, this new edition weaves a path through second sight, the evil eye, witchcraft, ghosts, fairies and other supernatural beings, offering new sight-lines on areas of belief once dismissed as folklore and superstition.

LUATH GUIDES TO SCOTLAND

These guides are not your traditional where-to-stay and what-to-eat books. They are companions in the rucksack or car seat, providing the discerning traveller with a blend of fiery opinion and moving description. Here you will find *'that curious pastiche of myths and legend and history that the Scots use to describe their heritage... what battle happened in which glen between which clans; where the Picts sacrificed bulls as recently as the 17th century... A lively counterpoint to the more standard, detached guidebook... Intriguing.'* THE WASHINGTON POST

These are perfect guides for the discerning visitor or resident to keep close by for reading again and again, written by authors who invite you to share their intimate knowledge and love of the areas covered.

Highways and Byways in Mull and Iona

Peter Macnab
ISBN 0 946487 16 2 PBK £4.25

'The Isle of Mull is of Isles the fairest, Of ocean's gems 'tis the first and rarest.'
So a local poet described it a hundred years ago, and this recently revised guide to Mull and sacred Iona, the most accessible islands of the Inner Hebrides, takes the reader on a delightful tour of these rare ocean gems, travelling with a native whose unparalleled knowledge and deep feeling for the area unlock the byways of the islands in all their natural beauty.

South West Scotland

Tom Atkinson
ISBN 0 946487 04 9 PBK £4.95

This descriptive guide to the magical country of Robert Burns covers Kyle, Carrick, Galloway, Dumfries-shire, Kirkcudbrightshire and Wigtownshire. Hills, unknown moors and unspoiled beaches grace a land steeped in history and legend and portrayed with affection and deep delight. An essential book for the visitor who yearns to feel at home in this land of peace and grandeur.

The Lonely Lands

Tom Atkinson

ISBN 0 946487 10 3 PBK £4.95

A guide to Inveraray, Glencoe, Loch Awe, Loch Lomond, Cowal, the Kyles of Bute and all of central Argyll written with insight, sympathy and loving detail. Once Atkinson has taken you there, these lands can never feel lonely. 'I have sought to make the complex simple, the beautiful accessible and the strange familiar,' he writes, and indeed he brings to the land a knowledge and affection only accessible to someone with intimate knowledge of the area.

A must for travellers and natives who want to delve beneath the surface.

'Highly personal and somewhat quirky... steeped in the lore of Scotland.'
THE WASHINGTON POST

The Empty Lands

Tom Atkinson

ISBN 0 946487 13 8 PBK £4.95

The Highlands of Scotland from Ullapool to Bettyhill and Bonar Bridge to John O'Groats are landscapes of myth and legend, 'empty of people, but of nothing else that brings delight to any tired soul,' writes Atkinson. This highly personal guide describes Highland history and landscape with love, compassion and above all sheer magic.

Essential reading for anyone who has dreamed of the Highlands.

Roads to the Isles

Tom Atkinson

ISBN 0 946487 01 4 PBK £4.95

Ardnamurchan, Morvern, Morar, Moidart and the west coast to Ullapool are included in this guide to the Far West and Far North of Scotland. An unspoiled land of mountains, lochs and silver sands is brought to the walker's toe-tips (and to the reader's fingertips) in this stark, serene and evocative account of town, country and legend.

For any visitor to this Highland wonderland, Queen Victoria's favourite place on earth.

NATURAL SCOTLAND

Rum: Nature's Island

Magnus Magnusson

ISBN 0 946487 32 4 £7.95 PBK

Rum: Nature's Island is the fascinating story of a Hebridean island from the earliest times through to the Clearances and its period as the sporting playground of a Lancashire industrial magnate, and on to its rebirth as a National Nature Reserve, a model for the active ecological management of Scotland's wild places.

Thoroughly researched and written in a lively accessible style, the book includes comprehensive coverage of the island's geology, animals and plants, and people, with a special chapter on the Edwardian extravaganza of Kinloch Castle. There is practical information for visitors to what was once known as 'the Forbidden Isle'; the book provides details of bothy and other accommodation, walks and nature trails. It closes with a positive vision for the island's future: biologically diverse, economically dynamic and ecologically sustainable.

Rum: Nature's Island is published in co-operation with Scottish Natural Heritage (of which Magnus Magnusson is Chairman) to mark the 40th anniversary of the acquisition of Rum by its predecessor, The Nature Conservancy.

Wild Scotland: The essential guide to finding the best of natural Scotland

James McCarthy

Photography by Laurie Campbell

ISBN 0 946487 37 5 PBK £7.50

With a foreword by Magnus Magnus-son and striking colour photographs by Laurie Campbell, this is the essential up-to-date guide to viewing wildlife in Scotland for the visitor and resident alike. It provides a fascinating overview of the country's plants, animals, bird and marine life against the background of their typical natural settings, as an introduction to the vivid descriptions of the most accessible localities, linked to clear regional maps. A unique feature is the focus on 'green tourism' and sustainable visitor use of the countryside, contributed by Duncan Bryden, manager of the Scottish Tourist Board's Tourism and the Environment Task Force. Important practical information on access and the best times of year for viewing sites makes this an indispensable and user-friendly travelling companion to anyone interested in exploring Scotland's remarkable natural heritage.

James McCarthy is former Deputy Director for Scotland of the Nature Conservancy Council, and now a Board Member of Scottish Natural Heritage and Chairman of the Environmental Youth Work National Development Project Scotland.

An Inhabited Solitude: Scotland – Land and People

James McCarthy

ISBN 0 946487 30 8 PBK £6.99

'Scotland is the country above all others that I have seen, in which a man of imagination may carve out his own pleasures; there are so many inhabited solitudes.'

DOROTHY WORDSWORTH, in her journal of August 1803

An informed and thought-provoking profile of Scotland's unique landscapes and the impact of humans on what we see now and in the future. James McCarthy leads us through the many aspects of the land and the people who inhabit it: natural Scotland; the rocks beneath; land ownership; the use of resources; people and place; conserving Scotland's heritage and much more.

Written in a highly readable style, this concise volume offers an understanding of the land as a whole. Emphasising the uniqueness of the Scottish environment, the author explores the links between this and other aspects of our culture as a key element in rediscovering a modern sense of the Scottish identity and perception of nationhood.

'This book provides an engaging introduction to the mysteries of Scotland's people and landscapes. Difficult concepts are described in simple terms, providing the interested Scot or tourist with an invaluable overview of the country... It fills an important niche which, to my knowledge, is filled by no other publications.'

BETSY KING, Chief Executive, Scottish Environmental Education Council.

LUATH PRESS LIMITED

The Highland Geology Trail

John L Roberts

ISBN 0946487 36 7   PBK £4.99

Where can you find the oldest rocks in Europe? Where can you see ancient hills around 800 million years old? How do you tell whether a valley was carved out by a glacier, not a river? What are the Fucoid Beds?

Where do you find rocks folded like putty? How did great masses of rock pile up like snow in front of a snow-plough? When did volcanoes spew lava and ash to form Skye, Mull and Rum? Where can you find fossils on Skye?

'...a lucid introduction to the geological record in general, a jargon-free exposition of the regional background, and a series of descriptions of specific localities of geological interest on a "trail" around the highlands.

Having checked out the local references on the ground, I can vouch for their accuracy and look forward to investigating farther afield, informed by this guide.

Great care has been taken to explain specific terms as they occur and, in so doing, John Roberts has created a resource of great value which is eminently usable by anyone with an interest in the outdoors...the best bargain you are likely to get as a geology book in the fore-seeable future.'

Jim Johnston, PRESS AND JOURNAL

WALK WITH LUATH

Mountain Days & Bothy Nights

Dave Brown and Ian Mitchell

ISBN 0 946487 15 4 PBK £7.50

Acknowledged as a classic of mountain writing still in demand ten years after its first publication, this book takes you into the bothies, howffs and dosses on the Scottish hills. Fishgut Mac, Desperate Dan and Stumpy the Big Yin stalk hill and public house, evading gamekeepers and Royalty with a camaraderie which was the trademark of Scots hillwalking in the early days.

'The fun element comes through... how innocent the social polemic seems in our nastier world of today... the book for the rucksack this year.'

Hamish Brown, SCOTTISH MOUNTAINEERING CLUB JOURNAL

'The doings, sayings, incongruities and idiosyncrasies of the denizens of the bothy underworld... described in an easy philosophical style... an authentic word picture of this part of the climbing scene in latter-day Scotland, which, like any good picture, will increase in charm over the years.'

Iain Smart, SCOTTISH MOUNTAINEERING CLUB JOURNAL

'The ideal book for nostalgic hillwalkers of the 60s, even just the armchair and public house variety... humorous, entertaining, informative, written by two men with obvious expertise, knowledge and love of their subject.'
SCOTS INDEPENDENT

'Fifty years have made no difference. Your crowd is the one I used to know... [This] must be the only complete dossers' guide ever put together.'

Alistair Borthwick, author of the immortal Always a Little Further.

The Joy of Hillwalking

Ralph Storer

ISBN 0 946487 28 6 PBK £7.50

Apart, perhaps, from the joy of sex, the joy of hill-walking brings more pleasure to more people than any other form of human activity.

'Alps, America, Scandinavia, you name it – Storer's been there, so why the hell shouldn't he bring all these various and varied places into his observations... [He] even admits to losing his virginity after a day on the Aggy Ridge... Well worth its place alongside Storer's earlier works.'
TAC

Scotland's Mountains before the Mountaineers

Ian Mitchell

ISBN 0 946487 39 1 PBK £9.99

How many Munros did Bonnie Prince Charlie bag?

Which clergyman climbed all the Cairngorm 4,000-ers nearly two centuries ago?

Which bandit and sheep rustler hid in the mountains while his wife saw off the sheriff officers with a shotgun?

According to Gaelic tradition, how did an outlier of the rugged Corbett Beinn Aridh Charr come to be called Spidean Moirich, 'Martha's Peak'?

Who was the murderous clansman who gave his name to Beinn Fhionnlaidh?

In this ground-breaking book, Ian Mitchell tells the story of explorations and ascents in the Scottish Highlands in the days before mountaineering became a popular sport - when bandits, Jacobites, poachers and illicit distillers traditionally used the mountains as sanctuary. The book also gives a detailed account of the map makers, road builders, geologists, astronomers and naturalists, many of whom ascended hitherto untrodden summits while working in the Scottish Highlands.

Scotland's Mountains before Mountaineers is divided into four Highland regions, with a map of each region showing key summits. While not designed primarily as a guide, it will be a useful handbook for walkers and climbers. Based on a wealth of new research, this book offers a fresh perspective that will fascinate climbers and mountaineers and everyone interested in the history of mountaineering, cartography, the evolution of landscape and the social history of the Scottish Highlands.

LUATH WALKING GUIDES

The highly respected and continually updated guides to the Cairngorms.

'Particularly good on local wildlife and how to see it'
THE COUNTRYMAN

Walks in the Cairngorms

Ernest Cross

ISBN 0 946487 09 X PBK £3.95

This selection of walks celebrates the rare birds, animals, plants and geological wonders of a region often believed difficult to penetrate on foot. Nothing is difficult with this guide in your pocket, as Cross gives a choice for every walker, and includes valuable tips on

mountain safety and weather advice.
Ideal for walkers of all ages and skiers
waiting for snowier skies.

Short Walks in the Cairngorms

Ernest Cross

ISBN 0 946487 23 5 PBK £3.95

Cross wrote this volume after overhearing a walker remark that there were no short walks for lazy ramblers in the Cairngorm region. Here is the answer: rambles through scenic woods with a welcoming pub at the end, birdwatching hints, glacier holes, or for the fit and ambitious, scrambles up hills to admire vistas of glorious scenery. Wildlife in the Cairngorms is unequalled elsewhere in Britain, and here it is brought to the binoculars of any walker who treads quietly and with respect.

SPORT

Over the Top with the Tartan Army (Active Service 1992-97)

Andrew McArthur

ISBN 0 946487 45 6 PBK £7.99

Scotland has witnessed the growth of a new and curious military phenomenon - grown men bedecked in tartan yomping across the globe, hell-bent on benevolence and ritualistic bevvying. What noble cause does this famous army serve? Why, football of course!

Taking us on an erratic world tour, McArthur gives a frighteningly funny insider's eye view of active service with the Tartan Army - the madcap antics of Scotland's travelling support in the '90s, written from the inside, covering campaigns and skirmishes from Euro '92 up to the qualifying drama for France '98 in places as diverse as Russia, the Faroes, Belarus, Sweden, Monte Carlo, Estonia, Latvia, USA and Finland.

This book is a must for any football fan who likes a good laugh.

'I commend this book to all football supporters'. Graham Spiers, SCOTLAND ON SUNDAY

'In wishing Andy McArthur all the best with this publication, I do hope he will be in a position to produce a sequel after our participation in the World Cup in France.

CRAIG BROWN, Scotland Team Coach

All royalties on sales of the book are going to Scottish charities, principally Children's Hospice Association Scotland, the only Scotland-wide charity of its kind, providing special love and care to children with terminal illnesses at its hospice, Rachel House, in Kinross.

Ski & Snowboard Scotland

Hilary Parke

ISBN 0 946487 35 9 PBK £6.99

How can you cut down the queue time and boost the snow time?

Who can show you how to cannonball the quarterpipe?

Where are the bumps that give most airtime?

Where can you watch international rugby in-between runs on the slopes?

Which mountain restaurant serves magical Mexican meals?

Which resort has the steepest on-piste run in Scotland?

Where can you get a free ski guiding service to show you the best runs?

If you don't know the answers to all these questions - plus a hundred or so more then this book is for you!

Snow sports in Scotland are still a secret treasure. There's no need to go abroad when there's such an exciting variety of terrain right here on your doorstep. You just need to know what to look for. Ski & Snowboard Scotland is aimed at maximising the time you have available so that the hours you spend on the snow are memorable for all the right reasons. This fun and informative book guides you over the slopes of Scotland, giving you the inside track on all the major ski centres. There are chapters ranging from how to get there to the impact of snowsports on the environment.

'Reading the book brought back many happy memories of my early training days at the dry slope in Edinburgh and of many brilliant weekends in the Cairngorms.'

EMMA CARRICK-ANDERSON, from her foreword, written in the US, during a break in training for her first World Cup as a member of the British Alpine Ski Team.

SOCIAL HISTORY

The Crofting Years

Francis Thompson

ISBN 0 946487 06 5 PBK £6.95

Crofting is much more than a way of life. It is a storehouse of cultural, linguistic and moral values which holds together a scattered and struggling rural population. This book fills a blank in the written history of crofting over the last two centuries.

Bloody conflicts and gunboat diplomacy, treachery, compassion, music and story: all figure in this mine of information on crofting in the Highlands and Islands of Scotland.

'I would recommend this book to all who are interested in the past, but even more so to those who are interested in the future survival of our way of life and culture'
STORNOWAY GAZETTE

'A cleverly planned book... the story told in simple words which compel attention... [by] a Gaelic speaking Lewisman with specialised knowledge of the crofting community.'
BOOKS IN SCOTLAND

'The book is a mine of information on many aspects of the past, among them the homes, the food, the music and the medicine of our crofting forebears.'
John M Macmillan, erstwhile CROFTERS COMMISSIONER FOR LEWIS AND HARRIS

'This fascinating book is recommended to anyone who has the interests of our language and culture at heart.'
Donnie Maclean, DIRECTOR OF AN COMUNN GAIDHEALACH, WESTERN ISLES

'Unlike many books on the subject, Crofting Years combines a radical political approach to Scottish crofting experience with a ruthless realism which while recognising the full tragedy and difficulty of his subject never descends to sentimentality or nostalgia'
CHAPMAN

MUSIC AND DANCE

Highland Balls and Village Halls

GW Lockhart

ISBN 0 946487 12 X PBK £6.95

Acknowledged as a classic in Scottish dancing circles throughout the world. Anecdotes, Scottish history, dress and dance steps are all included in this *'delightful little book, full of interest...*

both a personal account and an understanding look at the making of traditions.'
NEW ZEALAND SCOTTISH COUNTRY DANCES MAGAZINE

'A delightful survey of Scottish dancing and custom. Informative, concise and opinionated, it guides the reader across the history and geography of country dance and ends by detailing the 12 dances every Scot should know – the most famous being the Eightsome Reel, "the greatest longest, rowdiest, most diabolically executed of all the Scottish country dances".'
THE HERALD

'A pot-pourri of every facet of Scottish country dancing. It will bring back memories of petronella turns and poussettes and make you eager to take part in a Broun's reel or a dashing white sergeant!'
DUNDEE COURIER AND ADVERTISER

'An excellent an very readable insight into the traditions and customs of Scottish country dancing. The author takes us on a tour from his own early days jigging in the village hall to the characters and traditions that have made our own brand of dance popular throughout the world.'
SUNDAY POST

Fiddles & Folk: A celebration of the re-emergence of Scotland's musical heritage

GW Lockhart

ISBN 0 946487 38 3 PBK £7.95

In *Fiddles & Folk*, his companion volume to *Highland Balls and Village Halls*, now an acknowledged classic on Scottish dancing, Wallace Lock-hart meets up with many of the people who have created the renaissance of Scotland's music at home and overseas.

From Dougie MacLean, Hamish Henderson, the Battlefield Band, the Whistlebinkies, the Scottish Fiddle Orchestra, the McCalmans and many more come the stories that break down the musical barriers between Scotland's past and present, and between the diverse musical forms which have woven together to create the dynamism of the music today.

'I have tried to avoid a formal approach to Scottish music as it affects those of us with our musical heritage coursing through our veins. The picture I have sought is one of many brush strokes, looking at how some individuals have come to the fore, examining their music, lives, thoughts, even philosophies...' WALLACE LOCKHART

' "I never had a narrow, woolly-jumper, fingers stuck in the ear approach to music.
We have a musical heritage here that is the envy of the rest of the world. Most countries just can't compete," he [Ian Green, Greentrax] says. And as young Scots tire of Oasis and Blur, they will realise that there is a wealth of young Scottish music on their doorstep just waiting to be discovered.' THE SCOTSMAN, March 1998

For anyone whose heart lifts at the sound

of fiddle or pipes, this book takes you on a delightful journey, full of humour and respect, in the company of some of the performers who have taken Scotland's music around the world and come back enriched.

of them were actually victims of the later Clearances. It was history at first hand, and there was no romance about it'. But Peter Macnab sees little creative point in crying over ancient injustices. For him the task is to help Mull in this century and beyond.'

SCOTS MAGAZINE, May 1998

BIOGRAPHY

Tobermory Teuchter: A first-hand account of life on Mull in the early years of the 20th century

Peter Macnab

ISBN 0 946487 41 3 PBK £7.99

Peter Macnab was reared on Mull, as was his father, and his grandfather before him. In this book he provides a revealing account of life on Mull during the first quarter of the 20th century, focusing especially on the years of World War I. This enthralling social history of the island is set against Peter Macnab's early years as son of the governor of the Mull Poorhouse, one of the last in the Hebrides, and is illustrated throughout by photographs from his exceptional collection. Peter Macnab's 'fisherman's yarns' and other personal reminiscences are told delightfully by a born storyteller. This latest work from the author of a range of books about the island, including the standard study of Mull and Iona, reveals his unparalleled knowledge of and deep feeling for Mull and its people. After his long career with the Clydesdale Bank, first in Tobermory and later on the mainland, Peter, now 94, remains a teuchter at heart, proud of his island heritage.

'Peter Macnab is a man of words who doesnit mince his words - not where his beloved Mull is concerned. 'I will never forget some of the inmates of the poorhouse,' says Peter. 'Some

Bare Feet and Tackety Boots

Archie Cameron

ISBN 0 946487 17 0 PBK £7.95

The island of Rum before the First World War was the playground of its rich absentee landowner. A survivor of life a century gone tells his story. Factors and schoolmasters, midges and poaching, deer, ducks and MacBrayne's steamers: here social history and personal anecdote create a record of a way of life gone not long ago but already almost forgotten. This is the story the gentry couldn't tell.

'This book is an important piece of social history, for it gives an insight into how the other half lived in an era the likes of which will never be seen again'
FORTHRIGHT MAGAZINE

'The authentic breath of the pawky, country-wise estate employee.'
THE OBSERVER

'Well observed and detailed account of island life in the early years of this century'
THE SCOTS MAGAZINE

'A very good read with the capacity to make the reader chuckle. A very talented writer.'
STORNOWAY GAZETTE

On the Trail of Robert Service

GW Lockhart

ISBN 0 946487 24 3 PBK £7.99

Robert Service is famed world-wide for his eye-witness verse-pictures of the Klondike gold-drush. As a war poet, his work outsold Owen and Sassoon, and he went on to become the world's first million selling poet. In search of adventure and new experiences, he emigrated from Scotland to Canada in 1890 where he was caught up in the aftermath of the raging gold fever. His vivid dramatic verse bring to life the wild, larger than life characters of the gold rush Yukon, their bar-room brawls, their lust for gold, their trigger-happy gambles with life and love. 'The Shooting of Dan McGrew' is perhaps his most famous poem:

A bunch of the boys were whooping it up in the Malamute saloon;

The kid that handles the music box was hitting a ragtime tune;

Back of the bar in a solo game, sat Dangerous Dan McGrew,

And watching his luck was his light o'love, the lady that's known as Lou.

His storytelling powers have brought Robert Service enduring fame, particularly in North America and Scotland where he is something of a cult figure.

Starting in Scotland, On the Trail of Robert Service follows Service as he wanders through British Columbia, Oregon, California, Mexico, Cuba, Tahiti, Russia, Turkey and the Balkans, finally 'settling' in France.

This revised edition includes an expanded selection of illustrations of scenes from the Klondike as well as several photographs from the family of Robert Service on his travels around the world.

Wallace Lockhart, an expert on Scottish traditional folk music and dance, is the author of Highland Balls & Village Halls and Fiddles & Folk. His relish for a well-told tale in popular vernacular led him to fall in love with the verse of Robert Service and write his biography.

'A fitting tribute to a remarkable man - a bank clerk who wanted to become a cowboy. It is hard to imagine a bank clerk writing such lines as:

A bunch of boys were whooping it up...
The income from his writing actually exceeded his bank salary by a factor of five and he resigned to pursue a full time writing career.'
Charles Munn,

THE SCOTTISH BANKER

'Robert Service claimed he wrote for those who wouldnit be seen dead reading poetry. His was an almost unbelievably mobile life... Lockhart hangs on breathlessly, enthusiastically unearthing clues to the poet's life.' Ruth Thomas, SCOTTISH BOOK COLLECTOR

'This enthralling biography will delight Service lovers in both the Old World and the New.'
Marilyn Wright,
SCOTS INDEPENDENT

Come Dungeons Dark

John Taylor Caldwell

ISBN 0 946487 19 7 PBK £6.95

Glasgow anarchist Guy Aldred died with 10p in his pocket in 1963 claiming there was better company in Barlinnie Prison than in the Corridors of Power. 'The Red Scourge' is remembered here by one who worked with him and spent 27 years as part of his turbulent household, sparring with Lenin, Sylvia Pankhurst and others as he struggled for freedom for his beloved fellow-man.

'The welcome and long-awaited biography of... one of this country's most prolific radical propagandists... Crank or visionary?... whatever the verdict, the Glasgow anarchist has finally been given a fitting memorial.'
THE SCOTSMAN

POETRY

Blind Harry's Wallace

William Hamilton of Gilbertfield
ISBN 0 946487 43 X HBK £15.00
ISBN 0 946487 33 2 PBK £7.50

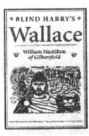

The original story of the real braveheart, Sir William Wallace. Racy, blood on every page, violently anglophobic, grossly embellished, vulgar and disgusting, clumsy and stilted, a literary failure, a great epic.

Whatever the verdict on BLIND HARRY, this is the book which has done more than any other to frame the notion of Scotland's national identity. Despite its numerous 'historical inaccuracies', it remains the principal source for what we now know about the life of Wallace.

The novel and film *Braveheart* were based on the 1722 Hamilton edition of this epic poem. Burns, Wordsworth, Byron and others were greatly influenced by this version 'wherein the old obsolete words are rendered more intelligible', which is said to be the book, next to the Bible, most commonly found in Scottish households in the eighteenth century. Burns even admits to having 'borrowed... a couplet worthy of Homer' directly from Hamilton's version of BLIND HARRY to include in 'Scots wha hae'.

Elspeth King, in her introduction to this,

the first accessible edition of BLIND HARRY in verse form since 1859, draws parallels between the situation in Scotland at the time of Wallace and that in Bosnia and Chechnya in the 1990s. Seven hundred years to the day after the Battle of Stirling Bridge, the 'Settled Will of the Scottish People' was expressed in the devolution referendum of 11 September 1997. She describes this as a landmark opportunity for mature reflection on how the nation has been shaped, and sees BLIND HARRY'S WALLACE as an essential and compelling text for this purpose.

'Builder of the literary foundations of a national hero-cult in a free and powerful country'.

ALEXANDER STODDART, sculptor

'A true bard of the people'

TOM SCOTT, THE PENGUIN BOOK OF SCOTTISH VERSE, on Blind Harry.

'A more inventive writer than Shakespeare'

RANDALL WALLACE

'The story of Wallace poured a Scottish prejudice in my veins which will boil along until the floodgates of life shut in eternal rest'

ROBERT BURNS

'Hamilton's couplets are not the best poetry you will ever read, but they rattle along at a fair pace. In re-issuing this work, the publishers have re-opened the spring from which most of our conceptions of the Wallace legend come'.

SCOTLAND ON SUNDAY

'The return of Blind Harry's Wallace, a man who makes Mel look like a wimp'.

THE SCOTSMAN

Poems to be read aloud

Collected and with an introduction by Tom Atkinson

ISBN 0 946487 00 6 PBK £5.00

This personal collection of doggerel and verse ranging from the tear-jerking *Green Eye of the Yellow God* to the rarely printed, bawdy *Eskimo Nell* has a lively cult following. Much borrowed and rarely returned, this is a book for reading aloud in very good company, preferably after a dram or twa. You are guaranteed a warm welcome if you arrive at a gathering with this little volume in your pocket.

Luath Press Limited
committed to publishing well written books worth reading

LUATH PRESS takes its name from Robert Burns, whose little collie Luath (*Gael.*, swift or nimble) tripped up Jean Armour at a wedding and gave him the chance to speak to the woman who was to be his wife and the abiding love of his life. Burns called one of *The Twa Dogs* Luath after Cuchullin's hunting dog in *Ossian's Fingal*. Luath Press grew up in the heart of Burns country, and now resides a few steps up the road from Burns' first lodgings in Edinburgh's Royal Mile.

Luath offers you distinctive writing with a hint of unexpected pleasures.

Most UK bookshops either carry our books in stock or can order them for you. To order direct from us, please send a £sterling cheque, postal order, international money order or your credit card details (number, address of cardholder and expiry date) to us at the address below. Please add post and packing as follows: UK – £1.00 per delivery address; overseas surface mail – £2.50 per delivery address; overseas air-mail – £3.50 for the first book to each delivery address, plus £1.00 for each addition-al book by airmail to the same address. If your order is a gift, we will happily enclose your card or message at no extra charge.

Luath Press Limited
543/2 Castlehill
The Royal Mile
Edinburgh EH1 2ND
Telephone: 0131 225 4326 (24 hours)
Fax: 0131 225 4324
email: gavin.macdougall@luath.co.uk
Website: www.luath.co.uk